CRACK THE KAIMIRA CODE

www.kaimiracode.com

KAIMIRA : BOOK ONE

THE SKY VILLAGE

MONK ASHLAND & NIGEL ASHLAND

illustrated by Jeff Nentrup

WALKER
BOOKS

This is a work of fiction. Names, characters, places and incidents are either products of the authors' imagination or, if real, are used fictitiously.

First published 2008 by Walker Books Ltd
87 Vauxhall Walk, London SE11 5HJ

2 4 6 8 10 9 7 5 3 1

Text and illustrations © 2008 Star Farm Productions, LLC

Based on the Kaimira world, characters and story verse created by
Chris Rettstatt

This book has been typeset in Manticore

Printed and bound by Clays Ltd, St Ives plc

British Library Cataloguing in Publication Data:
a catalogue record for this book is available from the British Library

ISBN: 978-1-4063-1586-8

www.walkerbooks.co.uk

To the amazing kids who read early versions of *The Sky Village*
and gave us your honest and insightful feedback. You know
who you are. It's a better story because of you.

To everyone who will read this story and find inside it shapes
and meanings of your own creation. You bring to the story
its most important ingredient: your imagination.

And to Cary Erickson and Joan Powers, who made
The Sky Village happen. You are the hook rope.

1
Sky Village

Hundreds of hot-air balloons bobbed in the wind, their baskets tied together with long stretches of rope. From the ground, the Sky Village looked like a giant net, poised to capture the clouds as it drifted far above. Mei strained her eyes to make out the figures painted on the two closest balloons – a dragon and a phoenix, both symbols of power.

Mei had glimpsed the Sky Village only a few times in her life as it passed high over Luo Ye Village, like a parade of upside-down teardrops gliding across the sunrise. Now it was making a rare descent, on her account. But Mei did not want this special honour. She wished a sudden great gust of wind would blow the whole village high into the sky, far away from her and the home she wasn't ready to leave.

She and her father stood on the peak of the highest mountain in the region, the lowest point to which the sky villagers were willing to descend. Mei's father squeezed her hand as he glanced nervously at the trees just beyond the clearing. Mei hadn't seen the meks chasing them, but she'd heard them clanking through the trees. She and her father had lost them by scrambling up a pass that was too steep for their metallic bodies.

Mei could see the woven bamboo of the baskets, and laundry hung on lengths of rope, flapping in the wind. The few sky villagers who were awake this early in the morning waved greetings to Mei as they walked across ropes from one basket to the next. They seemed completely unconcerned about the dangers on the ground.

A small balloon near the front suddenly dropped below the rest. A woman wearing a feathered vest unhooked the ropes connecting her balloon to the others and let go of all but one. She appeared to be in her early twenties, with four beauty marks under her left eye in the shape of an animal footprint. She adjusted the flame until the balloon hovered just above the ground. She smiled and nodded at Mei and her father. Mei summoned the cold frown she had been practising for this moment as her father greeted the woman.

"You've grown up, Ai-ling," he said.

"And you've grown old, Kai." She laughed, then turned serious. "You promised you'd look after Pei-shan."

"I'll find her," Mei's father said. "But there's no time to talk now. The meks are right behind us."

"Don't worry," Ai-ling said. "We never touch ground for long. Say your goodbyes."

How could her father be so polite at a time like this? Yes, he had asked the Sky Village to take Mei away for safekeeping, but he was losing valuable time. Every moment he spent in conversation with these people, the further away the mek army took her mother. Besides, Mei didn't need safekeeping; she needed to help find her mother! Since that morning, when Mei's father braided her hair into a neat rope, there had been near silence between them. Now, as he kissed her on the forehead and rested his hands on her shoulders, Mei tried to fight off tears. It was no use. She wanted to hug her father just as much as she wanted to pound on his chest for making her go. She wiped her eyes with her sleeve.

Mei's father's hands were strong and warm, and they made her feel safe. Maybe she could still convince him! But she knew her father never changed his mind.

"Mei, you'll be safer in the Sky Village. You were born here. These are your mother's people."

"I was only a baby when we left," Mei said, looking into his eyes. "They won't even remember me."

Her father turned away, shaking his head.

"Father, I should come with you," Mei said. "I can help you track those machines."

"You're going to fight meks? I've made too many sacrifices to keep you safe. You're my little dragonfly."

"But I'm not little any more," Mei insisted. "Mother needs me. You need me."

Ai-ling turned away while they argued. At least she was decent enough to mind her own business, Mei thought. Perhaps she could see what Father couldn't – that sending Mei away was a terrible mistake.

"Dragonfly," her father said, "you can help me from the safety of the sky. The sky villagers are information traders. Learn from them, and help me find your mother."

"But how? Why can't I just go with you?"

He looked at her a moment, with an intensity she'd never seen in his eyes. He pulled a small book out of his pocket and held it out to her.

"The Tree Book," Mei said. It was the book of faraway stories her mother had read to her every night as far back as she could remember. She'd never allowed Mei to touch it or look inside its pages. Mei reached for it, but Kai pulled it away.

"Pay attention. There's a reason we could never let you touch this book. Now, there's no other choice. You have to guard it. But, Dragonfly, you must not open it. You aren't ready yet."

"It's just a book. I won't break it."

"It's not just a book. Guarding what's inside this book is the most important thing you will ever do." He looked straight at her, and she knew he was serious. He handed her the book.

"Mei," he continued, "you must understand that I cannot be the guardian of this book. I don't have the power. And I can no longer protect you while I search for your mother. It looks like the meks and beasts may be going to war again. If your mother found out I took you on a mek hunt, she'd kill me." He tried to laugh. "Then she'd use her science to revive me and kill me again, just to make sure she'd made her point."

Mei stared at the Tree Book. She ran her fingers over the large tree etched into the cover. *What if you can't find her? Or what if you're too late?* she thought, but it was too terrible to say. Ai-ling had begun to fidget, glancing nervously at the rocks around the landing.

Mei felt like pulling away and running back home, back to her ruined and empty village, but she knew she could not. Her father would follow, and her mother would be taken further away. And what if she ran into meks?

Maybe Father was right. It was true that the Sky Village travelled wide and far. She might be able to find out where the mek army had taken her mother and the others. Mei stuffed the Tree Book into her bag, next to a few brittle old books and other items she'd gathered quickly before the morning's journey.

"And take this." Her father slipped his yak-bone knife into Mei's pocket. He turned her around so that she faced Ai-ling.

Hovering above was a sea of balloons painted every colour Mei had ever seen and some she'd never imagined. Small children hung from ropes with one hand, staring at Mei and her father, while older children sneaked curious glances.

"It's beautiful, isn't it?" Mei's father said.

Mei nodded before she could catch herself. She'd always loved watching the Sky Village pass over her town – she'd stare straight up, imagining what life must be like for her mother's people, many of whom had never set foot on the ground. Sometimes she'd catch her mother watching the sky when there was nothing there, and Mei knew she must have been looking into the past, at her old life among the balloons. Mei always wondered why her mother had chosen to give up the Sky Village to marry a soldier. When Mei asked for stories about life in the clouds, her mother always responded, "Circling the fires of the past, however warm, will only singe the wings of the future."

"I liked it better from a distance," Mei said quickly.

"Go on, now," her father said. "I'll send word when your mother is safe. Keep the Tree Book hidden, and don't open it."

He stooped over so Mei could kiss him on the cheek. She didn't want to let him go. She felt so safe when he was near. He gave her a gentle push, and she took a few reluctant steps towards the basket. It was bigger than her bedroom at home, made entirely of bamboo, with furnishings of bamboo and balsa wood. There was a sturdy rug on the floor, and a series of boxes hanging like a ladder from the lip of the basket.

"Safe travels, Kai," Ai-ling said. Mei noticed that the woman's smile was cold. Then she turned to Mei and bowed, her face full of warmth. "Welcome to the Sky Village, Mei. Give me your hands."

Ai-ling's arms were thin but muscular, and she pulled Mei over the edge of the basket easily. She dropped Mei gently on the padded floor and then adjusted a lever to increase the flame. The balloon rose until it was level with the bottom layer of the Sky Village. People in neighbouring balloons threw ropes with carved wooden hooks, which Ai-ling connected to the edges of the basket, securing it once again to the group.

Mei held tightly to a handle on the basket and leant over. As the village rose, she saw four metallic forms emerge into the clearing below.

"We have to go back," Mei said. "Those are meks."

Ai-ling put her hand on Mei's shoulder. "Your father has much experience fighting meks. He can take care of himself." Mei watched as her father armed his bow. She knew he had once been a soldier in the Trinary Wars, but during her lifetime she'd never seen him fight anything more dangerous than garden weeds.

He let the arrow fly. It struck a mek in the neck and exploded. The head toppled off and rolled towards Mei's father.

With a powerful kick, he sent it hurtling towards the nearest mek's legs. That one fell forward as an arrow pierced its shoulder and exploded. It crawled towards Mei's father, but four exploding arrows later, it was still.

The other two closed in, swords fused to their oversized arms. One mek began to rotate, its torso twirling like a deadly top, as it continued to move forward. Mei's father shot an arrow, but the spinning blades deflected it.

The other mek shot a length of rope from its arm compartment. Kai grabbed the rope and yanked the mek towards him, then lassoed his other attacker. The rope caught on the spinning torso, and Mei's father rolled clear as the two collided. Metal pieces flew across the clearing.

Kai looked up and waved. Mei waved back, speechless, barely breathing. She'd never seen her father fight; he made it look so easy.

"He looks like a child's toy down there, doesn't he?" Ai-ling said as they both eyed Kai, now little more than a speck far below. "Land walkers all look like that. Tiny toy soldiers, waving or fighting, rooted like plants to the ground."

Mei had never been higher than the mountain, and she had been so busy worrying about her father that she had forgotten her fear of falling. Now the fear rushed back. She moved away from the side, suddenly dizzy. Then she staggered again to the edge and called out to him, unable to stop the tears.

It was no use. He was too far away to hear. Mei felt as though the ground had just been ripped out from under her. It was as if something inside her was tethered to her village, to her parents, and the further away she got, the more it squeezed her.

He'll be OK, she thought. *He'll find Mother, and then he'll come back for me.*

She thought of her village as she'd seen it last, broken and burned. She imagined meks dragging her mother away. She felt rage building up inside her. She struggled to find words to fit the surge of hatred. *I'll tear those meks apart and use their bodies to rebuild my village.* The brutality of the thought surprised her. More surprising was the realization that she really meant it.

2

THE TREE BOOK

As she gazed across the net of balloons stretching as far as she could see, Mei thought about everything that had happened. Had it been just two days since she and her father had gone to the next village to trade arrows for vegetables? Weapons were not permitted in their village. They lived close enough to the mek border that any show of armament might seem threatening, but the arrows Mei's father made were highly prized. They'd returned late and knew something was wrong even before they saw their home.

Most of the buildings were nothing but smoking piles of charred wood. There was no sign of life, and no bodies. Mei had known it couldn't have been beasts, because they would leave bones, and anyway the nearest beast settlement was days away. It had to be meks. They often used fire and were known to take prisoners. What they did with the prisoners was a mystery to Mei, but the thought had frightened her.

Mei had searched for her mother's secret pet, Feifei, a tiny creature neither mek nor beast, which sometimes accompanied Mei on her adventures. Mei knew that if her mother's pet was alive, her mother would be as well, because the two were linked in some mysterious way. But there was no sign of Feifei.

Now, in the Sky Village, Mei assumed the worst. What could her father do against a mek army? And what reason would those cruel machines have not to kill her friends, and her teachers, and the others in her village they had taken?

But if the meks were going to kill them, why hadn't they just done it in the village? That question gave Mei hope. That was all she had now.

As Ai-ling manoeuvred the small balloon into place among the rest of the village, Mei could see baskets barely large enough for a few people to stand, while others hung from multiple balloons and looked more like bamboo mansions. Most had damp clothes hanging on lines of rope, drying in the morning sun. She half listened as Ai-ling pointed out the parts of the village they passed. A dumpling shop functioned as a teahouse and mah-jongg room; a classroom was lined with maps and full of small bamboo chairs; young women in a hair salon gave early-morning shampoos to older women;

and families were beginning their morning routines in baskets of all shapes and sizes.

The basket jerked, nearly knocking Mei off her feet, and the ropes groaned and stretched as the entire Sky Village changed direction. Mei looked wide-eyed at Ai-ling.

Ai-ling smiled. "There's nothing to be afraid of. We don't bite unless we're really, really hungry. The only thing you have to worry about is falling."

"I'm not afraid," Mei said sharply, tucking a strand of hair behind her ear. "I was born here."

Ai-ling stepped closer to Mei, looking at her uncertainly. "All right then. I suppose civility is an old-fashioned concept among land walkers. I just know that our worlds are very different. Speaking of which, I've been wanting to ask: is it true land-walker women rub charcoal over their eyes before weddings to make their eyebrows look fuller?"

Mei snorted in response. This was the woman's pressing question? She'd never heard of such a thing, and it sounded unaccountably silly.

"What?" asked Ai-ling. "Is it true or not?"

Mei shrugged. "Is it true sky villagers travel so close to the sun that they get their eyebrows burned off?"

Now it was Ai-ling's turn to snort. It was a good-natured one that became a laugh. "Ah, you are your mother's daughter after all."

"You know my mother?"

"Of course. She was my aunt, which makes us cousins. I was nine when she left. I knew her better than almost anyone."

Well, she is my mother, Mei thought, *so I think I know her best.* "Why are you talking about her in the past tense?" Mei demanded, suddenly jealous of her mother's relationship with this stranger.

"When someone leaves the Sky Village, they become part of the past. Pei-shan made her choice. She loved your father more than she loved us." Her voice wavered. She cleared her throat. "Anyway, there's plenty of time for questions. Do you want some breakfast?"

Mei's stomach rumbled in response, but she shook her head. She was more exhausted than anything from the long journey to the mountain top.

"Hey, Morning Man!" bellowed Ai-ling with the gusto of a Yangtze fishmonger. "Some breakfast for our new land-walker friend."

An old Korean man in a nearby balloon scowled down at them. His head was shaved down to white fuzz, and the scars on his leathery face marked him as a former warrior. A girl about Mei's age stood next to him shading her eyes with her hand. She had wooden chopsticks in her bushy hair, and her wide cheeks and unusually large eyes made her look like she was in a constant state of surprise. She cast repeated glances in Mei's direction, then abruptly returned to her work.

"Morning Man was a land walker," Ai-ling whispered to Mei. "Just like you. But he doesn't like to talk about it."

Morning Man's balloon was painted with a giant forest oriole against a sunrise and floated a little higher than those around it. Using the flame that heated the air in his balloon, the old man fried noodles and cabbage in a massive rounded pan, tossing and catching the food every few seconds. Mei detected the scent of Szechuan pepper, one of her favourite spices; freshly crushed in a stone bowl, it smelled like lavender flowers, and cooked, it numbed the mouth. The wide-eyed girl held a bowl while Morning Man filled it, then she took it over to a rope connected to Mei's balloon. The girl's expression suddenly turned mischievous.

"Catch, land walker!" she yelled, giving the bowl a furious push so that it hurtled down the rope towards Mei.

"Sumi!" roared the old man.

Mei reached out to catch the bowl, but it came so fast that the contents nearly spilled on her thin knitted jacket. Two rounded weights hanging from the grooved bottom kept it balanced, but barely.

Above, Morning Man scolded Sumi, who mumbled an apology even as her eyes smiled at Mei.

"That little beast," Ai-ling said, laughing.

Beast is right, Mei thought, imagining a hideous boar. She ate slowly, savouring the effect of the pepper, soothing the burn with sips of warm soya milk. At least they know how to cook up here, she thought. She watched Sumi and Morning Man repeat the routine a dozen times. The balloons moved like wheels within wheels as neighbouring villagers circled for breakfast, shouting greetings and barking requests as Morning Man filled their bowls. Sumi caused as much chaos as possible when her grandfather's back was turned.

Then, with unspoken rhythm, everyone threw ropes back and forth, and the Sky Village readjusted in a symphony of slow creaks and near crashes, so that a new group of balloons encircled the cooks for breakfast. Morning Man's was one of several breakfast balloons, Mei learned, each servicing a section of the village.

By the time Mei's balloon reached the edge, the Sky Village was bustling. Small children swung on ropes like acrobats, giggling and shouting as they whooshed through the cold morning wind. Mei looked at the long drop down to the ground, and had to grab the side of the basket to steady herself. She had imagined it would be easy to learn their tricks, but watching them now, she couldn't imagine herself taking such chances. These children had grown up in the sky, playing on ropes thousands of metres in the air since the time they'd learnt to walk.

A ladder seemed to drop out of nowhere and landed between Mei and Ai-ling, nearly hitting Mei's nose. A white-haired couple climbed down from the balloon above and stood between them.

The woman smiled at Mei. "Pretty little one, just like her mother. But she looks like she might bite. And what's this she's wearing? She'll catch a sneeze." The old woman shuffled through a pile of clothes and forced a heavy shawl over Mei's shoulders.

The man sighed. "No time for land walkers today. We're late to an emergency Council meeting. Ai-ling, put this one to work," he added.

"Yes, Father," Ai-ling replied, her voice less bold.

The couple muttered to each other as they hurried back up the ladder.

Ai-ling rolled her eyes. "They're always late for some important meeting. Usually, it's just an excuse to gossip with the other elders."

Ai-ling lifted a tarp hanging across a corner of the basket. Behind it was a feather bedroll covered by a patchwork quilt, stitched with crude figures.

"That quilt tells the history of the Sky Village. This is where I've slept my whole life, but now it's yours. Make yourself comfortable. It's like sleeping on a cloud. You'll have sky dreams, Dragonfly."

She can't call me that, Mei thought. But something about Ai-ling's voice felt soothing. Mei realized with a shock that it was her accent, the way she turned the tones slightly and drew them out as if she had all the time in the world. This was the accent of the Sky Village. It was the way her mother spoke.

Mei sat down and studied the quilt. Carefully crafted pictures depicted a variety of dramatic scenes: human hands reaching into the sky as hot-air balloons passed overhead, leaving them behind; battles between fearsome machines and beasts; the Sky Village entering a dark cloud full of lightning; birds and flying meks swirling through the air around the balloons, locked in combat. Each square on the quilt was a reminder of how much the Sky Village had survived to become what it was.

In the centre, a square depicted a tall figure with long hair and robe flowing in a strong wind that was made up of strange symbols. Mei recognized it as the myth of West Wind. It was the story the elders told young children when they asked why science was forbidden, or how the Trinary Wars among humans, beasts and machines had started. According to the myth, West Wind was a scientist who tried to use science to save the world and instead nearly destroyed it. It was nothing more than a cautionary tale, but Mei had always admired how proud West Wind looked in the drawings.

Mei spread the contents of her bag across the quilt. She had grabbed a few of her favourite books, yellow and brittle with age, before her father rushed her out the door. One ancient book titled *Szechuan Wildlife Park* had illustrations of beasts and descriptions of how they lived and what they ate. "If you know your enemy as you know your friend," her mother had said when she gave Mei the book, "then there is hope your enemy will become your friend."

The most amazing thing about the book was that some pictures showed humans moving among the beasts in rolling metal machines called cars. In one photo, a girl Mei's age reached through a window and actually *touched* a yak! As repulsive as they were, Mei had practised drawing these various beasts in all of their gruesome detail, wondering how they smelled and what their skin felt like.

Some of the Luo Ye village elders, when they had too much to drink, told stories about their battles against the beasts. The village children pelted them with questions. How did they smell? How big were their teeth and horns? Mei knew they were every bit as dangerous as the meks, but it was hard to think of them as enemies, because they lived so far away. But when she looked at the beasts in this book, she knew the elders' stories must be true.

Another book showed a history of weapons, from simple swords to mek warriors. The book's title was *Weapons of Order and Chaos,* by Hiro Miyazaki. Her father had not wanted Mei to see this book. "It will put adventurous thoughts in her head," he had said.

Her mother had won the argument with a single question: "You would keep knowledge from our child?"

Mei loved looking at the swords and lances, so beautiful and simple. She rarely turned to the later parts, the pages of meks looking cold and cruel in their gleaming metal skin.

Then there was the Tree Book, her mother's collection of stories her father had given her to guard. Here were the stories about Breaker, Lizard Girl and others, who had such interesting lives compared to Mei's. Mei knew this book had to be as old as the rest, but it had no worn corners, no fading colours. It looked new.

Mei had seen the cover so often it seemed etched into her mind, but she never thought she would have the chance to look inside. She ran her hand over the cover and felt the intricately carved images – birds, flowers and a giant tree with a massive trunk and an explosion of branches and leaves.

Mei knew the characters inside this book so well, she thought of them as friends. Breaker, who lived in a city controlled by beasts, tried so hard to protect his little sister. He had a tendency to break things when he got angry, but also a talent for fixing them. Then there was Lizard Girl, a member of a travelling circus who sometimes seemed so wise, but other times was frightfully naive. And the others, each with a story that seemed so unimaginable and yet so real.

They were just characters in stories, but Mei felt she'd grown up with them. She remembered listening as her mother read and struggling to stay awake for one more chapter. Mei must have heard thousands of those stories. The characters aged along with her, and Mei always looked forward to hearing of their adventures.

The book was warm and humming faintly. Was her mother's science responsible for preserving it? Mei had once seen her mother writing in the book. Had she used it to record her thoughts, or details from her experiments and expeditions into mek territory or even further afield into the lands controlled by the beasts? Mei had long wanted to look inside, but her parents had made it clear that she was never to do this.

But the Tree Book was the only thing she had of her mother's. She understood why her parents kept secrets from the villagers of Luo Ye. Their laboratory, their secret experiments with meks, their expeditions to the mek border – they'd be banished if any of that was discovered. But why keep secrets from their own daughter?

Mei pulled the tarp closed, worried that someone would see her. She sat on a tiny mahogany stool and put the book on her lap. She ran her palm over the tree carved into the cover, then took a deep breath and opened the book. There was a flash of blinding light, and the book grew hot in her hands. Mei shrieked and dropped it.

This wasn't a book at all! It was a piece of science in disguise. Something forbidden, and most likely dangerous. Before the Trinary Wars, she knew from the old stories, humans had all sorts of mechanical tools to help them. But the meks had quickly learnt how to turn those tools against their masters, and since then such objects were considered dangerous.

Could this really be the same book that had introduced her to new worlds and had carried her to sleep so many nights? After a moment, Mei touched the cover gently to see if the book had cooled, and it had. She took a deep breath. Everything was different now. How dangerous could it really be? She picked it up again and turned to the first page.

The paper was thick and coarse. In a corner of the page, strange symbols swirled. They reminded Mei of the symbols she often saw in drawings of the myth of West Wind. Lettering appeared across the page, and she could hear the words on the page spoken inside her head by an inhuman voice like the distant rumble of thunder.

Who are you?

Mei looked around to make sure the voice wasn't coming from someone playing a trick on her. Had the meks taken control of the Tree Book? Something inside her told her this was not the voice of a mek. It was something else entirely, something both familiar and profoundly strange.

Dangerous or not, it was the only thing she had of her mother's.

"I'm Mei."

No, who are you?

"I don't understand. I'm Mei Long, daughter of Pei-shan and Kai."

Mei is a name. A name is "what". Who are you?

"My mother calls me Dragonfly."

Why?

"I don't know."

Incorrect. Why?

This was getting annoying. But Mei wasn't ready to give up yet. She paused to think. She'd never thought about why her parents called her Dragonfly. She was so used to it. But now that she'd experienced the Sky Village, something occurred to her.

"Maybe it's because she misses the Sky Village, and whenever she looks at me, she thinks about what she gave up."

Mei felt the spine of the book warm up, and the word _Dragonfly_ appeared. The swirling symbols grew brighter and swirled faster.

She felt that she should stop. As far back as she could remember, her teachers had talked about the dangers of science and technology. She knew that in the old days, the mind of a machine could be in almost anything, from a cooking stove to a child's toy. Still, it might be her only chance to get some real answers.

She began by asking, "Are you real or are you a machine?"

I am Animus. I am machine, animal and human. The Guardians are machine, animal and human.

Animus? What did that mean? She decided to move on. "Do you know where my mother is?"

My power can help you.

The images in the Tree Book began to swirl once more. The symbols formed in the corner and a black line bisected the page. On one side, Mei saw herself, staring at the book. She was in a basket. When she moved her hand, the hand in the picture moved.

On the other side of the line, she saw a drawing of a boy. His black curls were in tangles as he raced across the sand, pursued by several large beasts. Who was it? Mei reached out to touch the picture, but the image disappeared.

"How is that supposed to help me? Who was that?" she asked.

My knowledge can help you. Free me.

"If you have knowledge, then why don't you answer any of my questions?" Mei asked. "How can I free you?"

Only the Guardians of the Kaimira Code can free me. I am machine, animal and human. The Guardians are machine, animal and human.

"I don't understand what you're asking me to do," Mei said.

The Tree Book was silent. Then it said, *Free me,* its voice a low rumble, filling Mei's head. *The book is the door to my prison. Free me. Knowledge. Power. Help your mother.*

"Where is she?" Mei shouted. "Where did they take my mother? What are they going to do to her?"

The Tree Book went blank, then grey swirls formed on the page. At first, it looked as if the page had been burnt, but slowly the shapes formed a moving picture. Smoke billowed from a blazing cornfield, and Mei could just make out the shapes of meks marching through it, burning everything in their path. They were massive figures, much larger than the ones her father had fought.

The book was showing her the mek army! But was this an event from the past, or was this happening right now? She studied the image for clues, but the smoke obscured the details.

"Where are they?" she shouted, trying to rip the page out of the book before it went blank again. She could not dislodge it, and the wrinkled page smoothed itself out. "Show me my mother!" Mei knew she had already gone too far, toying with this device. Her father had looked so sombre when he reminded her not to open it. It was the last thing he'd said to her.

The image zoomed in through the smoke and fire to a row of cages on wheels. The image panned past them – and Mei caught a glimpse of a frail figure lying still on the floor of one cage. Mei gasped. "Mother?" But she couldn't be certain.

The humming stopped, and the Tree Book went blank again. Mei quickly flipped through the book, but every page was now empty. She threw the book down, tears forming in her eyes. It had to have been her mother. But where was she? Where were the meks taking her? Was she even alive?

Mei's heart raced as she considered the possibilities. Why would her mother's book torture her with only shreds of information?

Mei collected the Tree Book and brushed off a few grains of seed. If Mei wanted to see her parents again, she was going to have to stop acting like a child and figure out a way to help. The Sky Village was another world, the views around it breathtaking, most of the people kind and friendly. But they lived with their heads in the clouds, removed from the problems on land. The meks were on the move, and they were too terrible for words. She couldn't spend her time walking across ropes. Her mother needed her. Tomorrow she would figure out how the sky villagers got their information, and she'd use it to find her mother.

At that moment, Mei saw brightly coloured butterfly wings flying towards her. The wings were attached to a tiny lemur with bright orange eyes. It was Feifei, her mother's secret pet. Her mother was alive!

Feifei settled on Mei's wrist. Her feet tickled Mei's skin and soothed her. Her mother had often let her take Feifei on adventures, but Mei had to promise never to show anyone.

Feifei flew in a few tight circles around Mei's head. How could anyone be afraid of such a small and beautiful creature?

"Hello, little one." Mei held out her finger, and Feifei landed on her knuckle. The wings flittered, then shifted up and down slowly. "I wish I had wings like yours. Then I'd fly right away from this place and find Mother myself." She studied the wings, their deep scarlet flecked with patterns like electrical circuits. Mei held the creature up to her face and tried to read her expression – the tiny snout wrinkled and the bright orange eyes almost glowed. "You're so cute," Mei whispered, gently rubbing its fuzzy belly. The butterfly-lemur hugged her finger.

"I wish I knew where Mother found you," she said. "Or did she make you?" Meks and beasts were forbidden in the human world, and Feifei had features of both as far as Mei could tell. All her mother would ever say was that Feifei was a secret.

Feifei fluttered her wings in response. Mei felt for a moment that the creature understood, even though she knew that was impossible. She was glad she had a pet to talk to – something other than the strange book that raised more questions than it answered.

"I'll tell you a secret," Mei whispered. The cold wind whistled above her, the sound growing to a roar as a forceful gust shook the balloon. "This morning I was so angry at my father, I wished the meks had taken him instead of my mother."

Feifei made a series of tiny, frantic squeaking noises.

"It's terrible, isn't it? Sometimes I can't help thinking things like that."

Feifei waved her wings quickly, and Mei could feel the barest breeze across her hand. "Oh, all right. I don't really mean that. The truth is, I'd give anything to be with him now."

Feifei shifted so that the sunlight through her wings created a small rainbow across the basket. It cheered Mei up. She didn't know whether Feifei was a mek or a beast or something else entirely, but she knew the tiny creature was her friend and ally and, right now, the only one she had. Mei would have to hide Feifei here just as she had back home. Human hatred for meks and beasts ran deep, and Mei had no reason to believe it was any different in the Sky Village. After decades of war followed by only a few years of uneasy peace, humans had learned to stick with their own kind.

Mei wrapped her arms around the book, exhaustion finally catching up with her as the wind gently rocked her basket from side to side.

3

HOGGING

Got one!" Ai-ling shouted from beyond the tarp, startling Mei out of her sleep. The sun was on the other side of the sky.

Mei hurried into the open. Ai-ling was standing at the edge of the basket holding a bamboo pole attached to a thick coil of twine as big as a bucket.

"What are you doing?" Mei asked.

"Hogging!" Ai-ling responded with a grin. "Like fishing, but without the fish. Or the water."

Mei made no effort to hide her disgust as she peered over the edge of the basket and saw a wild pig suspended from the rope. Far below, she saw a group of beasts in a clearing. More hogs, she assumed. They looked as tiny as beetles. Nearby, an elephant and a rhinoceros sparred, kicking up clouds of dust, while a pride of lions watched from the shade.

Mei's hands trembled on the edge of the basket. This was her first time in beast territory, and if the Sky Village landed here, she knew, the villagers would all be eaten, probably while they were still alive.

She remembered a story she often heard from the village Water Master, who managed the wells and irrigation ditches. As a young man during the second Trinary War, he had volunteered to fight on the front lines in a nearby province. The beasts had just wiped out the meks in the area, and many were injured. Rather than wait for the beasts to lick their wounds, the human army attacked. They learnt quickly that there's nothing as deadly as a wounded animal. Only a few human soldiers made it out alive.

Ai-ling grunted as she reeled in the pig. She looked back at Mei and winked. "I see you're skilled in the art of nap taking." She did a little dance as she continued to pull the rope. "Look, it's a big one. For a land walker, you're a regular good-luck charm."

"That's so disgusting. How can you eat an animal?" Mei asked, scrunching her nose. In her village, eating beasts, or interacting with them in any way, was forbidden. They were considered dirty and dangerous.

Ai-ling smiled without looking up. "It's one of our ways that hasn't changed much since we took to the sky a century ago. Before the Trinary Wars, many humans ate beasts. They also kept them as pets and used them for labour, the same way they used meks."

Ai-ling struggled with her catch. Mei got behind her and helped pull, coiling the thick twine in circles on the floor of the basket. The pig was dead by the time it reached them. Ai-ling gutted the pig while it hung from the side of the basket, letting the entrails and blood drop to the ground below.

Mei stared at the beast in awe. It had hair as bristly as a wire brush and tusks that curled over its snout. It smelled dreadful and was the ugliest thing she'd ever seen, but its eyes looked intelligent, as if the light inside had not yet been completely extinguished.

"This pig will be our breakfast tomorrow. It'll bring us just the luck we need." Using a rope suspended from the balloon above, she swung the drying pig across the sky to Morning Man's balloon. Morning Man caught the pig and hauled it inside. He grunted loudly.

"It's a bit scrawny," he shouted. "I don't know what you expect me to do with it." As he said it, he sharpened a butcher knife and eyed the beast.

"Wild-boar dumplings," Ai-ling shouted back. "I told you already."

Morning Man mumbled under his breath and continued sharpening his knife.

Ai-ling turned to Mei. "Are you feeling a bit more settled in?"

Mei took a quick look below. She saw an abandoned factory surrounded by rice fields. In the distance, she could just see the outline of a ruined city, the tall buildings like long fingers reaching into the sky.

"Does anyone ever fall?"

Ai-ling paused a moment, then answered softly. "Not often."

Mei didn't find that answer reassuring. "Isn't it awful?"

"It's the way things go, Mei. We are celestial people and belong to the sky. When someone falls over land, it means the earth is pulling them home, snapping them back to its bosom. Others are summoned home by the sea."

Mei's face was still grave. "Do you search for the people who fall? Do they ever survive?"

"Once things are done, they can't be undone. When someone leaves the Sky Village, we never look back. Touching the ground in unfriendly lands puts us all at risk." Ai-ling added hot water to Mei's cup. "And these days, most lands are unfriendly. Only once in my life have we gone back for someone. When I was a little girl. We landed in the Himalayas, in a city of rogue scientists and technology pirates, where the humans are more vicious than the beasts and meks. We lost a lot of lives."

"That's why you talk about my mother as if she's dead. Because as far as you people are concerned, she is."

"I miss her, too, Mei. I've missed her a lot longer than you have, and it doesn't get any easier. But in time, you'll learn to love your new life."

Mei forced a smile. "It doesn't really matter. I won't be here long."

Ai-ling looked at her as if she were speaking a foreign tongue. "Oh no, didn't your father tell you? Joining the Sky Village is no small matter. It is a contract with the birds and clouds that you cannot break. You will never leave."

Mei was still angry when she returned to her sleeping area. Was she a prisoner? Had Father known, when he asked the Sky Village to accept her, that she wouldn't be permitted to leave, and that he might never see her again?

There was no way the sky villagers could keep her here for ever. Father would send for her, once Mother was safe.

She heard a hum and saw a soft glow coming from under her pillow. Mei pulled out the Tree Book and ran her palm across the cover. She was afraid to open it, afraid of the images she might see inside, and of the terrible, inhuman voice that rumbled inside her head. But she was on her own now, and helping Mother was more important than following rules.

Mei opened the book. In the corner, instead of the

swirling symbols, she saw a simple line drawing of the boy she had seen the last time. He was in some kind of dark room leaning over a book on the ground, staring wide-eyed at its pages. Once again, the image was moving.

"Hello? Anyone home?" she asked.

She waited nervously for the inhuman voice, the one that called itself Animus, to come back. Instead, Mei heard a different voice. At first it spoke a foreign tongue, and the written words, too, were in a strange language. But before her eyes, the words rearranged into recognizable characters, and the voice began speaking her village's dialect.

What am I doing?

Mei stared at the words. Was it possible that the boy was answering her? She wanted to drop the book and back away, but then she saw the boy's tangled hair. He looked as lonely and exhausted as Mei felt. Who was he? What had happened to him? She touched the page gently and was surprised to see a stroke of black where her finger had been. She traced a character with her finger, and it appeared on the page.

It was exciting and scary to be in the presence of such advanced science. Mei had always wondered how so many thousands of stories could fit into such a small book, and she'd long suspected her mother was inventing most of them. If the book could create stories and show her pictures of mek armies, how was she supposed to know what was real? And what else could it do?

Now Mei knew she could communicate with the Tree Book by speaking or by drawing with her fingers. She chose to speak in a whisper.

"How am I supposed to know what you're doing?" Mei said. There was a pause. The boy raised his eyebrows.

They've taken her. Hybrid demons made of liquid metal. And I've agreed to fight.

"Who are you?"

Rom. Code name Breaker.

Mei stared in disbelief. Could this really be Breaker, whose story her mother had read so often? She wasn't ready to accept that a story character was talking to her. "What's your sister's name?"

Riley. The face in the picture tensed up.

Mei couldn't believe it was him, and she was talking to him. Had her mother ever talked with the characters in the Tree Book?

"My mother used to read made-up stories about a boy named Breaker. He lived in beast territory with his little sister. In a skyscraper."

I'm not made-up, and neither is Riley. Who are you, anyway?

"My parents call me Dragonfly."

Breaker leant in closer to the book, so that only his face showed in the picture. He looked confused. *Why are you sitting in a box?*

"It's a basket. You can see me?"

Why are you sitting in a basket?

"It's attached to a hot-air balloon."

My father used to read to me about a girl in China named Dragonfly. Sometimes she'd sneak off on missions to the mek border when she wasn't busy reading old books or dancing around in the garden. She had a weird little pet, Feefo—?

"Feifei," said Mei. "She's my mother's pet."

Right. It was Riley's favourite story when she was little. She always told me she wished she had a pet like Feefo—

"Feifei."

Right. But my favourite story was always—

They said "Lizard Girl" at the same time.

Breaker opened his mouth. *Hey, can you do something?* The illustration reached towards her, and a life-size fingerprint appeared. *Try it.*

Mei stared at the dark fingerprint, with circles of colour rippling out from it. Was he touching the book somehow? Was it possible that Breaker was real, and the Tree Book was translating his words? Or was this a trick of the book, pretending to have a conversation with her? And how would the book know anything about her life in the village? She saw more words forming on the page.

Are you still there?

Mei's heart raced. If this was Breaker, and he was real, she wouldn't be alone. She had known him for as long as she could remember. Mei reached out and touched the fingerprint.

The book pulsed and glowed. For a split second, Mei sensed Breaker as if he were sitting right across from her, pressing his finger against hers.

She wasn't alone.

"I can't believe this," she said, her finger still tingling. Somehow, all this time, the Tree Book had been sharing stories about real kids. But why? And would she be able to talk to the others?

You're really her, Breaker said. *You're Dragonfly.*

Mei was speechless. Finally, she asked, "Where's Riley? Is Riley OK?"

After a moment of silence, Breaker responded. *She will be soon.*

4

BREAKER

Maple syrup was the final thing Rom needed for Riley's birthday breakfast. His little sister, eight as of midnight, would be awake in an hour or so. It had been an insane idea to begin with – trying to make johnnycakes like their grandmother's – and Rom had made matters worse by waiting until the last minute to find the ingredients. Still, it looked as if he might pull it off. Rom had traded seeds he found in a long-abandoned university genetics lab to travelling merchants in exchange for cornmeal and corn oil, and he had found salt in one of the uninhabited neighbourhoods off the strip where all the houses were the same colour. All he needed was the syrup.

The meeting had been set up by Rom's friend Mr Ramirez, an old scientist who took Rom's scavenged tech parts, fixed them, and traded them to tribes outside the city for food. Ramirez was cranky and possibly a little crazy, but he was fair, and he'd taught Rom a lot about fixing remtech so that it worked like new. Ever since Rom and Riley's father disappeared two years ago, Ramirez had made a point to check on them. If the person he was meeting was a friend of Ramirez's, there was nothing to worry about. Rom had four power cells in his bag, three of them fully charged. He figured the syrup was worth three cells, and he would try to get it for two.

Rom had been saving up for years – power cells, copper bars, anything that looked valuable – hoping that the story of the Demon Caves was true, and that he could buy entrance for himself and Riley. It was the only way he could give his little sister a normal life away from the beasts. Rom had known other tech scavengers, or buzzers, who had gone in search of the caves and hadn't returned. Rumour had it that the entrance was guarded by demons, and if you didn't have enough goods to trade for admittance, they'd tear you apart. Foolish superstition, Rom thought, but superstition was often rooted in fact, and if there were people living underground, it would be a lot safer than the streets of Las Vegas. Rom's goal was to get himself and his sister in there. He felt a little guilty about using up power cells for something as trivial as breakfast, but he wanted Riley to have something special on her birthday.

The tribesperson removed a ragged hood when Rom came close, revealing a girl of thirteen or so, the same age as Rom. Her black hair was long and tangled with twigs and leaves. She smelled faintly of wild berries. She looked at him with enormous black eyes.

"Ramirez says you have syrup. I'm Rom, but you can call me Breaker."

The girl smiled, and Rom noticed that her two front teeth were missing. A lot of people were missing teeth, but there was something funny about the girl: the gap was perfect, and all of her other teeth were white and straight. "I'm Myra," she said, sounding more than a little nervous.

Rom saw her shyness as a chance to get a deal. He was certain Myra would trade the syrup for less than it was worth — perhaps just one power cell. Rom knew exactly how he would play this one. It was going to be so easy he almost felt bad.

"OK," Rom said. "Let's see it."

While Myra dug through her bag, Rom scanned the horizon for beasts. It was a habit so ingrained that he hardly noticed he was doing it. The beasts patrolled the city in packs of mixed species. It was their city now. The few humans who lived within the city limits like Rom, Riley and Ramirez, did so in a constant state of alert. Most humans, like Myra, lived out in the desert in dirty, makeshift camps, clinging together for survival, growing what food they could, and trading for the rest. Their lives seemed boring and miserable, they always

41

looked like they bathed in sand, and Rom had vowed never to join their numbers.

Myra opened a dirty cloth and revealed a cracked glass jar filled with thick brown liquid. It looked exactly like their grandmother's maple syrup. "Oooh," he said, shaking his head in fake disgust. "I was hoping for something better. It's my little sister's birthday, and I really wanted to give her a special treat."

"It's the best we can do," said Myra, frowning. "Maple syrup is so hard to find."

"It looks like muddy water," said Rom. "I want to surprise my sister, not make her throw up."

Myra looked genuinely upset. "You don't want it? I came all the way here."

Rom bent down close and looked. "I don't know," he said. "I need it, but I was hoping for something I would actually, you know, want to eat. I guess this was a mistake." Rom kept his mask of disgust and added a little sigh of disappointment for effect.

Myra wrapped the jar in the cloth and returned it to her bag. She pulled her hood up and slung the bag over her shoulder. "I'm sorry to have wasted your time," she said. She turned and walked away.

Rom let her get about ten steps before he called out, "Hold on a minute."

Myra turned and started shuffling back.

It was time to go for the kill. "I hate to have you come all the way out here for nothing. How about I give you one power cell, fully charged, and I'll do my best to use that mud puddle you're trying to pass off as syrup."

"It's very tempting, but I was thinking something more like four power cells," Myra said.

Rom knew at once that her innocence had been a front. Instead of feeling bad for her, now he almost admired her. It was time for the real bargaining to start.

"Four power cells?" said Rom. "Are you serious? Have you ever traded before?"

"I'd hate to have you come all the way here and go home empty-handed. It is your sister's birthday and everything."

Rom regretted mentioning the occasion – now Myra knew he had to have the syrup. "I'd rather go home empty-handed than get robbed," said Rom. "Ramirez said you were OK."

"He said the same about you," Myra snapped back.

Rom knew he was no longer in a position to get a deal. "How about two cells. Fully charged. That's what it's worth."

"Four cells or I walk," said Myra. Her mouth was set, but her eyes were smiling. She was clearly enjoying herself. "Take it or leave it."

"You're a thief," said Rom.

Myra only shrugged.

Rom tried to think fast. "I'll give you three power cells.

Three's all I got. Three power cells for a jar of watered-down syrup? How can you say no?"

"I'll show you how," said Myra. "Nooo." She drew out the word, pushing it through the gap where her front teeth should have been. "You wouldn't have come here with only three cells."

Rom groaned and threw four power cells on the ground. Myra handed over the syrup. Rom was about to tell her that he would never trade with her again when he spotted something on the horizon. The sun had made its way over the mountains by now, and he could see shadowy black shapes looming in the distance.

"Beasts," Rom said, pointing. He knew they had better get moving.

"Enjoy your breakfast." Myra didn't look scared. She winked at Rom and took off at an easy run.

"Yeah, yeah," grumbled Rom before heading in the opposite direction.

The beasts were galloping now. Rom glanced behind him as he ran, hoping they'd target Myra and she'd be the one who would have to lose them, but it soon became clear that he was the prey. He ran full speed towards a crumbling building, hoping to climb the fire escape to safety.

Wolves, coyotes and mountain lions charged in a pack. If they caught him, they would tear him to shreds and leave whatever they couldn't chew for the buzzards.

Rom knew he wasn't fast enough to outrun the beasts. He

could hear their paws slapping the sand. They were gaining on him. The hot air burnt his lungs as he pushed his legs to go faster. Dropping the breakfast supplies would distract the beasts and buy him some time, but he could not bring himself to do it. One of the mountain lions shrieked. It was an awful sound, like a girl screaming.

Rom took two final huge strides and sprang for the fire escape. For a moment, he thought he had miscalculated and missed, but his hands grasped the first rung of the rusty ladder. In the seconds it took Rom to secure his grip, one of the coyotes clamped on to his ankle. Rom twisted and kicked, but the coyote's jaws were strong. Its sharp teeth punctured his skin, and he cried out. The other beasts circled below, salivating.

With a bellow, he swung and kicked both legs with all his force, hurtling the coyote against the wall. It fell to the ground, stunned. Rom pulled himself onto the first platform of the fire escape, out of the beasts' range. They howled and hissed below. "Nice try," he shouted.

A mountain lion leaped, scraping the platform with its outstretched paw. Rom scurried up the fire escape to the top of the building, trying to ignore the pain in his leg. From there he made his way from rooftop to rooftop, following a series of creaking, makeshift walkways. His ankle was starting to throb with pain, and he stopped to catch his breath. He hadn't been bitten in over two years, which gave him bragging rights over most of the buzzers his age. There was no way he'd be able to hide this wound from them.

He looked around. On the next roof he saw a vulture's nest built around the rafters. It was as large as Riley's bed, for vultures the size of hang gliders. Rom scrambled towards it, fuming. The beasts were evil, all of them. He wished he could wipe them all out. His father used to say that the beasts were just doing what came naturally to them. "We're more like them than you think," he'd say.

"I'm nothing like them," Rom said as he pulled at the nest with all his strength. It came free of the rafters, and he hurled it off the roof. It shattered on the cracked cement below.

As Rom raced home, he wondered about the syrup girl. Who was she? Why would her people send her to do the dangerous work of trading? Maybe she was fiercer than she looked. She certainly knew how to get the best of a deal. Though he regretted the loss of all four of his batteries, Rom smiled, imagining the look on Riley's face when she saw her birthday breakfast. He hoped she would still be asleep when he reached home.

THE BEAST

Rom arrived on the thirtieth floor of the abandoned sky-scraper where he and Riley lived. He knew he should bandage his leg. This wasn't the first time a beast had attacked him, and he knew infection would set in if he waited too long, but first he wanted to check on his sister.

He moved quietly to her room. She was sleeping soundly, curled into a ball and half covered by a tattered blanket, sur-rounded by marionette puppets she had made from clay, wood and tech scraps. Rom knelt beside her and pulled the blanket to her chin. Next to her lay a puppet representing their mother, finished except for the hair. Rom was amazed at how accurate the puppet was, from the small nose to the high cheekbones, considering the fact that Riley had never seen her mother and relied on Rom's descriptions. Riley had even stained the fingernails red with berries.

Riley always begged Rom to help when they performed puppet shows for the other buzzers. He teased her, but he always relented because he felt that it was somehow important to spread these stories. Surrounded as they were by beasts, it made them feel more human. And it kept Riley occupied. The next show was in a couple of days, and Riley was determined to finish the puppet in time, which meant they'd have to go buzzing later.

Rom closed her door tightly. As he imagined the smell of hot johnnycakes with real maple syrup, he heard something thump in the kitchen. He edged down the hall. The sound came again, followed by the sound of footsteps, grunts and long, low growls. Something was there – something large, hungry and, Rom hoped, alone. Beasts had never been able to gain access to the top floors of the skyscrapers. But they were getting smarter every day.

Rom grabbed a rusty pipe and edged towards the kitchen. He could hear the sound of footsteps. The only way to fight a beast, Rom had learned, was to strike fast and hard enough to make the beast believe you were a threat. It would certainly flee rather than fight – so long as it was alone.

Rom took a deep breath and stormed into the kitchen, shouting. Then he stopped short.

He recognized his father at once, even though the thing

standing in front of him barely resembled the man who had disappeared two years ago. Rom dropped the pipe and stared: he had assumed his father was dead.

His father bared his teeth like a threatened gorilla. He clutched a half-eaten loaf of bread. As Rom tried to approach, his father backed into the corner of the kitchen, holding the bread tightly in his filthy hands.

Rom stopped. Whatever his father had become didn't want to be hugged. He looked more like he might attack. Rom put up his hands. "I don't want to hurt you, Dad."

His father snarled and advanced. Rom looked into his eyes. There was a faint glimmer of recognition, but mostly Rom saw wariness—the eyes of a beast.

Rom took a step back, wishing he had held on to the pipe. "Calm down," he mumbled. "It's just me. Rom."

His father advanced another step. Rom was scared, but he had been in many dangerous situations, and he acted without hesitation. He grabbed the jar of syrup and tossed it on the floor so that it split open. His father fell upon it at once and began licking the thick, sticky liquid from the floor.

Rom picked up the pipe.

His father grunted as he slurped the syrup. When he finally stopped, he gasped, "Water."

The voice was the same one Rom remembered. He wondered what could have transformed his father into this pitiful, terrifying figure.

"Water!" his father shouted. "Seventeen!"

"What?" asked Rom.

"Water," said his father.

Rom pulled a bucket from the cupboard. There was a funnel on the roof, with a pipe running down to the bucket. It didn't rain much, but when it did, Rom and Riley collected what they could. Rom handed the bucket to his father, who drank greedily.

"What do you want?" Rom asked. He thought of Riley. He had to get their father, or whatever it was their father had become, out of the house before his little sister woke.

"I need something," Rom's father said.

Rom gripped the pipe.

His father's eyes shifted around the room. "There's something I need you to get. Can you get it?"

"If you need it so bad, why don't you get it?"

His father grunted. "I can't get it."

Rom longed for the days when his father never got around to the point and seemed to talk for ever. "What is it you want me to get?"

"Thirty-four."

"Thirty-four what?" It was the second time his father had mentioned a number.

"A book."

Rom had never known his father to read anything but bedtime stories. But that was another life, when they'd been safe and happy with their mother's nomadic tribe. Their father had read to them every night from the Tree Book as they lay bundled under a pile of furs in their small tent. When the story got scary, Riley would secretly squeeze Rom's hand rather than betray her fear to their father.

Though they never felt truly scared with him around. He had a way of dealing with beasts. Rom remembered once, when an enormous snake had slipped into their tent, their father had simply stared at it, the vein in his temple twitching, and it had slithered away.

But this was not the same man.

"My book. Your book," Rom's father said. "Don't open it. Valuable book. Very valuable."

The man had been gone for so long, and all he cared about was an old book? Rom scowled. It seemed unlikely that it was worth anything. Tech was valuable; books weren't. And what did he mean by *my book, your book*? "Why can't you get it?"

"They want me to do terrible things. I don't want to be captured."

Neither do I, thought Rom. He heard Riley moving in the other room. Rom pulled one of the empty water buckets up to the rusty, overturned refrigerator they used as a table. "Where is it?"

His father grunted and pulled up a seat of his own. "Safe place. Secret. I put my things there. Very safe." He picked up the water bucket and took another gulp.

"Where is it?" Rom asked again, eyeing the door, half expecting to see Riley standing there. He had no interest in an old book, but if this was his father's "safe place", there might be something valuable there that could help them buy their way into the Demon Caves.

Water sloshed onto his father's scraggly beard and dripped to the floor. He was busy drinking in this manner when Riley walked into the kitchen rubbing the sleep from her eyes.

Riley screamed when she saw him. Their father jumped up and growled, lurching for her.

Rom swung the pipe as hard as he could, but his father ducked. The pipe hit the wall with a thunderous crack. His father jolted up and growled. Riley screamed again. Rom readied the pipe and shouted, "Everyone calm down!"

No one was calm.

"Daddy?" asked Riley. "What's the matter with you?" A tear trickled down her cheek.

The voice seemed to trigger a glimmer of something in the man's eyes. He looked from Rom to Riley in confusion.

"What happened to him?" Riley asked, her voice trembling as she turned to Rom.

"He's acting just like a beast," said Rom, who saw no point in withholding the truth. "His mind is gone. He's eating our entire food supply."

"Is he ... does he know who we are?"

"He knew enough to come here," said Rom. He had to

stay calm, for Riley's sake, but seeing his father like this made him want to slam his fist through the wall. The rage boiled inside him, but he pushed it down. He swallowed and tried to focus. "So why do you want this book?"

"Fifty-six!" shouted his father.

"Fifty-six what?" asked Riley.

"I don't know," said Rom. "He keeps shouting numbers." Rom was losing his patience, and he wanted to throw the pipe through what was left of the kitchen window.

"Daddy, do you remember our names?" asked Riley.

"Where is it?" asked Rom.

"Alamino Casino," said their father. "More food?"

"You just ate it all," said Rom.

"Food," said their father. "More food."

Rom considered his options. He could not very well leave Riley here with their father. It would also be dangerous in the Alamino Casino, which was located in a section of the city known as the Triangle, where there were no walkways connecting the rooftops and consequently few escape routes. The Triangle was also rumoured to be the location of a secret entrance to the Demon Caves, which was another reason to steer clear. You didn't want to be anywhere near the caves if you couldn't buy your way in. Buzzers disappeared that way. But Rom saw little choice – he would have to take Riley with him. "Where in the Alamino Casino?" he asked.

His father slammed his hand on the overturned refrigerator. "Seven," he said.

"The seventh floor?" asked Riley. "Are there even seven floors?"

"Where in the casino?" Rom demanded.

"Basement vault!" Rom's father shouted. "Alamino Casino! Eighteen!"

Their father rummaged through the rest of the birthday-breakfast ingredients. He found the corn oil and guzzled it like water.

Rom sighed and turned to his sister, who was wearing her pack already. She still looked upset, but determined, too.

"Can we 'chute down, Rom?" Riley asked.

"You patch your 'chute?" Rom asked.

"What do you think?" she said, a hand on her hip. "I want to die on my birthday?"

Rom washed his ankle and wrapped it in a clean cloth. He got up and grabbed his gear. They backed away from their father, who was rummaging through the kitchen, no longer paying them any attention. Rom couldn't very well kick him out, though the thought of having to find new food made his head hurt worse than his ankle.

A steel pole ran from the thirtieth floor to the ground through what was once the elevator shaft. Rom put on leather gloves to protect his hands, then made sure his sister did the same.

"Riley," Rom said, pausing at the shaft and turning to face his sister.

She looked up at him. "What?"

He wanted to tell her how sorry he was about her birthday breakfast and about the hard life she'd had to live. He tried his best to be a father and mother to her, but every year it grew more difficult. Most of all, he was sorry that he lost patience with her so often, and that his plans to make it up to her didn't always pan out.

But he couldn't say any of these things to Riley. She would just roll her eyes and give him that look. Maybe later, if he managed to find her another birthday present, they could talk. For now he said, "Happy birthday, little sister."

She rolled her eyes.

Rom grabbed the pole and twirled down, followed closely by Riley. It was thrilling no matter how many times he did it, and for a moment it took his mind off his father. The air whooshed past his ears as he descended, faster and faster, towards the ground. They pulled the strings on their parachutes when they passed the fifth floor and floated the rest of the way. They always raced to see who could fold the chute into the backpack faster. Rom let Riley get close, but he never let her win.

6

ALAMINO CASINO

Sand filled the dusty cracks of the street outside the sky-scraper, and Rom and Riley, still breathing hard, walked quickly past the shells of burnt-out cars. Their rough-hewn, oat-coloured pants and shirts flapped in the morning breeze that kept the day a few degrees from unbearable.

Riley ran ahead. Rom moved more cautiously. He had outrun hundreds of beasts; he knew the streets better than anyone.

Still, he felt shaken by the morning's events. He scanned the horizon, but saw nothing unusual as he and Riley set off towards the Triangle. They passed shattered glass, broken cars, scrap metal, and windows patched with misshapen slabs of corrugated iron to keep out the sun and heat – all remnants from the time when humans still controlled Las Vegas.

Most of what Rom knew about those times he'd heard from Ramirez. Before the Trinary Wars had ruined everything, the Triangle had bustled day and night with people from all over the world. It was filled with high-tech hotels, staffed by meks designed to do everything from walking guests' pets to dealing cards. Rom wished he'd been around then, when tech was everywhere and new innovations came out every day. The Triangle casinos even had vaults that, according to Ramirez, could survive nuclear bombs and nanoparticle infestations.

After the humans were driven into hiding, the meks controlled the area until their energy supplies ran out. That's when the beasts arrived – wild dogs, gila monsters, hummingbirds, elk, deer, bobcats and the more exotic occupants of local zoos. The battle lasted several weeks, during which time many buildings were destroyed. The fight ended with the arrival of the giant black bears from northern Arizona. They were as big as cars. They tore the meks to pieces, and the city of Las Vegas fell under the beasts' reign.

As Riley bobbed ahead of her brother, kicking at scraps, hoping to uncover something valuable, Rom tried not to think about his father. A skeletal monkey with mangy fur loped across the street ahead of them, and Rom pulled Riley into an alley. The monkey scampered off. It did not seem to be looking for anything other than scraps of food. As soon as it was out of sight, they moved back into the street.

Rom was worried about Riley. He and his sister were accustomed to hardships and disappointments, but their father's transformation had been shocking. Following their mother's death giving birth to Riley, their father had become gradually more frenzied, aggressive and fearful. He'd disappear for weeks, sometimes months. Then, two years ago, he had disappeared for good. Or so they thought.

But what they'd just witnessed was something more. Rom wondered what could have caused it. Before Riley could get out of his sight, he called to her. "Are you OK?"

Riley did not look up from the ground. "What do you think happened to him?"

Rom scanned the dusty streets for signs of beasts. "I have no idea, but there must be some way to fix him."

Riley scrunched up her face. "It was like he barely even recognized us," she said.

Riley planted a foot on the rusty bumper of an old, wedge-shaped car, vaulted herself onto the hood, jumped forward, and landed on the street again. She was the only person Rom knew who was better at acrobatics while deep in thought. The rusted wheels collapsed and the car's frame crashed to the ground behind her, sending up a cloud of dust. Riley danced away from the tumult. "It was easier thinking he was gone."

Rom knew exactly what she meant. "Why is our whole family so weird?"

Riley smiled. "Speak for yourself." Her smile faded. "Do you think maybe it's genetic?"

"No way," Rom said, though he was uncertain. Their father's side of the family had more than its fair share of eccentric characters.

"What do you think he's got in the casino?" Riley asked. "Other than some old book?"

"Who knows?" Rom said. "But there's got to be something we can trade."

Riley shrugged. "If there's anything valuable in there, someone's probably guarding it."

Rom had been thinking the same thing. "I guess we'll find out," he said.

"That's reassuring," said Riley.

They moved down the abandoned street together.

"Just for once, be careful when we get to the Triangle," said Rom. "Something just feels funny out here today." Rom flinched at his choice of words. He sounded like Ramirez, who was always going on about how the air "felt funny", or how vibrations in the ground warned that the meks were coming to take Las Vegas from the beasts.

"Maybe there are demons at the Alamino, waiting to snatch us," said Riley.

"You shouldn't make jokes like that," said Rom.

"Oh, please," said Riley. "Not you, too."

"I just asked you to be careful," Rom snapped. Now he really sounded like Ramirez, but there was no helping it. He looked ahead as they neared the place where they would turn right and enter the Triangle. Vultures circled near the great pyramid in the distance. Something must have died. He thought of Myra but dismissed the thought. Bandits like her never got caught.

The once-grand, circular lobby of the Alamino Casino was filled with trash. Riley leant down and picked up a silvery triangle.

"Hey, Rom, this thing looks live."

"Let me see that," said Rom, grabbing it from her. He loved that about buzzing. There was always a chance you'd find something you had never even imagined before, some bit of tech wizardry the meks had left behind, or even before that, when humans had mastered technology and dominated the world.

They hunched over to study it.

"I've never seen anything like it," Riley whispered reverently.

Neither had Rom, and it spooked him a little. Though the triangle was solid, the metal covering swirled like liquid, and underneath a blue light pulsed through a network of tiny, vessel-like tubes. As he held it, the pulse grew stronger. This was the work of scientists; it was way too shiny to be an artifact of the old times.

"Throw it in the bag," he said, figuring it would probably turn out to be just another fancy-looking piece of garbage. He would examine the object later. They crept through the deserted casino to the back stairs that led to the vault room, where he pulled a torch out of his backpack and lit it with his tinderbox. Riley held the torch a step behind him as he started down the stairs.

Rom had been in the vault room before. The smaller safes that lined the walls had been busted open years ago, but explosives had had no effect on the main vault. Charred circles spotted the walls around it, evidence of years of attempts to blow it open.

Rom had tried countless times to crack the lock, hoping to find a secret entrance into the caves, or at least a few musty old stacks of paper money – good kindling for fires on cold desert nights. He pulled out a taped-together keypad with a large battery strapped to the bottom and tack-hacked it to the lock. As he typed, he tried programs he'd used to open other vaults, and the big dial spun back and forth with soft clicks. None of the combinations worked.

He was interrupted by a loud yawn from Riley. "I don't know why you keep pretending," she said. "You don't have magical power over technology."

"Sometimes it works," Rom said. "Just be quiet."

"What about those numbers he was shouting?" Riley said. "Fifty-six and seven."

"How could he possibly remember anything?" Rom asked.

"You got a better idea?"

Rom keyed in the numbers. Seventeen, thirty-four, fifty-six, seven and eighteen.

Nothing happened.

"I told you," Rom said.

"Did you try pushing on the door?"

"The lock didn't click," Rom said.

Riley pushed her hands against the vault, and the heavy door opened.

"Some buzzer you are," Riley said. Rom rushed into the vault and waved his torch around, trying to see what was inside.

The vault looked like the lair of a beast. There was a large hole in the floor, and around it were piles of random objects, from bones to painted rocks. As they rifled through the mess, they noticed objects that had belonged to them and to their mother and father. A pair of dolls Rom's father had made out of cornhusks. A wooden boat. A drawing of a mek Riley had made years ago for her father. There were enough tech scraps here to trade for food for a week, but not enough to get them into the Demon Caves.

How had his father got the combination? And how had he remembered it in his current state?

"I guess we know where Dad's been hiding out," Riley said, holding the drawing. She'd never seen a mek, so the image was based on the marionette puppets Rom made to represent mek forces in Riley's puppet shows.

All this time, Rom thought, and their father had been so close – and alive, if alarmingly transformed. He hadn't made any attempt to see them until he needed help. Maybe it was for the best, considering what he'd become.

"There aren't any books in here," Rom said. "Maybe it's in there." He approached the hole slowly and looked down. It was a little more than a foot wide, but Rom couldn't see the bottom. He thought about the Demon Caves, rumoured to be flooded in gold and jewels and packed with food, and about the demons that were rumoured to guard the entrance. His parents had even used the myth of the Demon Caves in the ridiculous story they liked to tell about how they first met. Could any part of that fantastic story have been true?

If his father was right about there being an important book in the vault, it could only be down that hole. Rom bent down and listened. He didn't hear anything. Cautiously, he tried to lower himself through the opening, but his shoulders jammed against the rough sides. He was stuck. Riley clutched her sides as she laughed.

He tried to squirm through, but it was no use, and Riley only laughed harder.

"C'mon, help me out!" he finally yelled.

Riley rolled her eyes and offered him a hand. "My turn," she said when he had manoeuvred himself out. Rom grabbed the torch and lowered it down into the hole, revealing a cave floor not far below.

"No way," said Rom. "We have no idea what's down there."

"Rom, we came all the way here. Someone has to go down."

Rom studied the hole. "I don't know, Riley."

She peered in. "Even if Dad is completely crazy, aren't you curious?"

"Of course I'm curious. But you're not going down there by yourself."

Riley nodded. "C'mon."

While tempting, it was a bad idea and Rom knew it. He tried to think of some other solution, but if there was anything valuable down there, Rom wasn't going to leave without it. Their father owed them that much.

Rom supposed that the beasts would have no way of getting into the vault or the hole. And as for demons – well, they were only superstition, and if they did exist, they probably had better things to do than patrol some old abandoned tunnel.

Riley did not push for his permission. She shimmied through the gap.

"Hey," Rom shouted, but Riley was already inside the cave. Rom lowered the torch to her.

"I'm just going to look for the book and come right out," she said.

Rom shoved his head into the hole, but it was too dark to see much.

"Rom, have people been here before?"

"How should I know? What do you see?"

"There are bottles all over the place." Her voice and footsteps grew fainter. "Here's some wire. Different colours. Hey, I can use this black wire for Mom's hair."

"What about the book?" shouted Rom.

"This is perfect. I'm going to give her such long hair. Wait. Rom, I think I see it!"

"The book?"

"Yeah, I see a book!"

"All right, Riley, grab it and come up."

"It's heavy," Riley said. "Hey, it's the Tree Book!"

"Grab it and get out of there," said Rom.

"It's making a weird noise," said Riley. "Let me open it."

"Just throw it up here!" yelled Rom.

The book flew through the hole and landed with a thud. "Got it," Rom shouted.

"I'm going to look around some more," Riley called. "There's a ton of stuff down here."

"Leave it. We'll come back." Rom took a closer look at the book. Riley was right. It was the Tree Book. Rom's father had never let him touch it, but now he ran his hand over the cover. Intricate images of birds and flowers had been hand tooled around the edges. In the centre a large tree exploded into a thick plume of foliage. How long had his father been hiding it here?

"There's way more down here than I can carry," Riley shouted. Rom heard a crash and the sound of scraping metal.

"Be careful," he mumbled. He knew it was time to get bossy and hurry her up, but it was her birthday, and he still felt bad about the breakfast. He thought about the stories in the book. He had been disappointed when his father never got around to finishing the tale of Lizard Girl. Riley had wanted to hear more about Dragonfly.

Another crash came from below. "Riley," Rom said, getting annoyed, "take what you like the best and give me your hands."

"There's too much," said Riley. "I need help."

"Leave it," mumbled Rom. Tentatively, he pulled open the cover of the book.

There was a flash of light. On the page, Rom saw a painting of himself in the vault looking into the book. He leant closer. The image disappeared, and the pages went blank.

The pages moved. Images formed and spread over the paper. On the left a black circle widened slowly, like a puddle of spilled ink.

"Riley," he shouted, "come and see this!"

The Tree Book tingled in Rom's hands, and the feeling spread across his entire body. The images on the page disappeared, lost in a swirl of colours that formed a picture of his father before he had changed, reading from the book as four-year-old Rom leant against him. His father looked just as Rom liked to remember him, with combed hair, a bright white smile, and crinkles that formed around his eyes when he laughed. Rom reached out to touch the picture, remembering the way his father altered the pitch of his voice for each character, but the image swirled again.

Rom hoped to see his mother, but a different image took shape. Rom saw a dark place lit only by torches. He peered closer. In the flicker of torchlight, he saw his father as he looked now, leaning back in a stone chair, a metal helmet on his head. His face was twitching, contorting with pain. He was shaking his head back and forth like a dog trying to escape its leash.

The colours swirled and here was another dark place, though the torchlight was brighter. Rom felt as if he were there. He heard the roar of a crowd and smelled the smoke from the torches. Two creatures were at the centre of a great circle of dirt, locked in combat. They were covered in metal armour, and their eyes flashed intense red. They looked like some kind of beast-mek combination. The crowd shrieked and stamped their feet. The creatures staggered, clearly exhausted. One rammed the other and flashed its metal fangs.

The image returned to Rom's father, unconscious. People were gathered around him.

Is he out?

Was it a meltdown?

He won. That's all that matters.

The images faded and in the corner appeared a small whirlwind of strange symbols. Words formed on the page, accompanied by a voice that sounded like a distant rumble of thunder. The voice was more advanced than any newtech voice simulation Rom had ever heard.

Who are you?

"Rom. Who wants to know?"

Rom is a name. Who are you?

"What do you mean? I'm Rom Saint-Pierre."

A name is a "what". Who are you?

"My dad used to call me Breaker."

Yes. Why?

"I don't know why."

Incorrect. Why?

"I don't know. It's from some old language used by transporters. My dad was a transporter."

Yes. Why?

"Calm down. Maybe it's because Dad and I both like old technology. People used breakers to stop surges of power. To protect their tech."

Incorrect. Why?

"Well, maybe it's because I used to like to break things."

Like, liked, have liked, used to like, did like, would like, still like.

"OK, fine. I still like to break things."

The book pulsed, and the word *Breaker* appeared. Rom ran his finger over the spine.

I am Animus. I have power. You need power. Free me.

"Why don't you show me my father again? I want to know what happened to him."

I am Animus. I am machine, animal and human. The Guardians are machine, animal and human. Only the Guardians of the Kaimira Code can free me.

"Show me my father!" Rom shouted.

The symbols in the corner of the page began to swirl, and Rom saw the outline of a human form just coming into focus. A loud crash sounded from below, and Rom slammed the book shut. "Riley, now!" he yelled.

What had he just seen? Were they visions of the Demon Caves? Could the voice tell him what had happened to his father?

"My bag's too heavy now," Riley groaned.

"I told you to leave it!" shouted Rom. She was silent for a moment, and Rom felt bad about losing his temper. "I'm sorry, Riley, but we've got to go now."

"Rom, I just heard something." Her voice quavered.

Rom shoved the book into his pack, walked over to the hole, and reached his hand down as far as it would go. He heard a tapping sound.

"Riley, just get out of there. I'm not kidding!" Rom shouted.

"Rom, what was that?"

"Reach up!"

"Pull me!" Riley said, the panic rising in her voice.

Rom grabbed his sister's hand. A sharp, regular tapping echoed through the tunnel. Rom smelled burning rubber.

"Rom, it's getting closer!"

Rom grabbed Riley's other hand and pulled her to the top of the hole. Suddenly, she slipped. "Rom!" she shouted, dropping the torch.

"Jump," yelled Rom. "I'll grab you."

"Something's coming."

"Just jump!"

The jagged metal side scraped his arm as he reached as far as he could. Finally, he caught her hand. It was slippery with sweat, but he held his grip and pulled her out. She was breathing hard. Rom had never seen such a look of terror on her face.

"What was it?" he asked.

"I saw them. They were some kind of giant things," said Riley. "I don't think they're friendly."

Riley jumped up, about to bolt for the door, but Rom held her. He saw shadows dancing against the side of the hole. The tapping sound grew louder. Then there was silence.

"Let's get out of here, Rom," Riley whispered, squeezing his hand.

"Wait a minute," he whispered. "Maybe they're gone." He'd learnt that hiding was often a better bet than running.

All was quiet for a few seconds, and Rom started to relax. Then a sudden rush of air pushed through the room. The floor shook and what appeared to be the skull of a large metal beast bit into the side of the hole, violently warping the floor. Rom and Riley ran for the door.

The sounds of rending metal, scuffling and tapping followed them as they dashed through the casino and out of the revolving door.

They were blinded for a moment by the bright daylight. "Are you OK?" asked Rom, still panting.

Riley didn't move. She was looking back at the casino. The entire wall around the revolving door crumbled as if it were made of rotten wood. Through the falling debris emerged several creatures the size of lions, half obscured by the building's shadow. Their spiderlike limbs spread out in all directions. Were they beasts or meks, Rom wondered, as curious as he was terrified. Then he realized. They were demons from the caves. The creatures stood like statues, as if waiting for a command, their eyes fixed on Rom and Riley.

Rom grabbed his sister's arm, and they sprinted across the street. In a single leap, one of the creatures landed next to Riley and grabbed her ponytail in a silvery tentacle, ripping her away from Rom. Riley shouted Rom's name as she struggled to get loose.

The demon's canine head shone like silver, set with beetle-shell eyes. Liquid muscle rippled and pulsated across its body,

as if it were an animal turned inside out. Four metallic limbs
sprouted from the creature's back, more like spider's legs than
tentacles. Rom heard the rhythmic pulse as some mechanism
churned beneath a metal shield on its chest. It did not breathe
or growl or snarl.

Rom had seen pieces of meks, and he knew these creatures were not meks. And they were certainly not beasts.
They were unnatural, mixtures of mek and beast, some kind
of hybrid maybe. The most improbable explanation was the
only possible one: the Demon Caves were real.

Riley shrieked as the creature extended another tentacle
around her and dragged her towards the casino. "Get it off
me, Rom!" she shouted.

Two other creatures advanced on Rom, their silvery legs
raised, ready to attack.

"Riley!" he shouted. He felt like he was moving under
water. His entire body trembled, and a sharp ache shot up
his spine and into his eyes, which felt like they might burst.
He'd never known such fear before, even when facing off
against packs of desert cats. But there was another feeling,
too – a surge of power.

As if by instinct, he charged straight at the demon, driv-
ing his head into it with all his strength.

Rom heard a crash as the pain ricocheted through his
body. His legs gave way, and he reeled to the pavement. He
tried to shout his sister's name, but his mouth wouldn't

respond. He shook his head, desperate to clear the fog from his vision, trying to make sense of the blurry shapes and scuffling noises around him.

Rom struggled to push himself up but fell again. He could not catch his breath. As his vision cleared, all he could do was watch as the creature pulled Riley through the doors. Her legs flailed, kicking up dust. The other demons, half hidden in the shadows, followed. One of them lay in pieces on the nearby kerb. As Rom stared, the pieces dissolved, scattering like smoke into the air.

Rom lay on the ground, calling Riley's name with what little breath he could summon. He struggled to his feet. His head pounded as he steadied himself. He staggered, slowly at first, and then at a mad gallop, into the casino as Riley's shouts grew dimmer. He reached the hole in the vault, but somehow it had been welded shut. A clump of black wire lay on the floor. Rom shoved it into his pocket, then stomped on the spot with his boot and kicked until his foot throbbed, refusing to believe his sister was gone, and that he could do nothing to save her.

Rom dropped to the floor, exhausted. His mind raced as fast as his heart.

It was his fault. All of it.

He tried to sort his thoughts, but all he felt was anger, fear. Lost.

He ran back outside, with no thought of where to go, and

nearly ran into a grazing rhino. The beast looked up and snorted. Rom knew it could smell him, but its poor eyesight worked in his favour. He ducked behind an elephant skull and caught his breath. He was out of the Triangle. He had to get help.

He knew just the person to ask.

7

Mr Ramirez

They took her," Rom said, breathless from the two-mile run to Mr Ramirez's shack, which was built on top of a fortified old bank. "They came out of the ground and took Riley."

Ramirez glanced up from his chair and grunted. "Knocking before entering is what separates humans from beasts," he said. His scraggly grey hair was clumpy and uneven – flat in some places, sticking straight up in others. There were deep creases in his forehead, and the puffy bags beneath his eyes quivered as he scanned his book.

"I need help," Rom said.

Ramirez stood up. He looked neither surprised nor worried. "Let's go inside," he said.

Rom clambered around the water-collection devices – many of them elaborate contraptions that had never worked – and made his way down the ladder to the main floor of the bank.

The building smelled of sweat and smoke. The bank's secure doors and impenetrable vault made it an ideal place for Ramirez's makeshift laboratory. The vault reeked of chemicals. Piles of books, lab equipment and scrap parts covered the floor. There were two lamps wired to an ancient generator, which Ramirez clicked on for light. The only clear space was a large round table in the middle of the room, with one chair in front of it.

"It won't do us any good to panic, Rom," said Ramirez. "I want you to calm down. Let's have some tea, and you can tell me everything that happened."

Rom almost shouted no, but he restrained himself. To be rude to Ramirez would only result in more grumbling and time wasting.

"No tea," Rom said, trying to stay calm. He twisted his pack around. He thought of showing Ramirez the Tree Book, but something told him to keep it a secret for now. Instead, he pulled out the silver triangle Riley had found in the casino and slapped it on the table.

Ramirez searched his pocket for his glasses. The glasses were made from scrap parts, and one lens was twice as large as the other. One stem was broken, and Ramirez had to hold them up to his face.

"An unexpected turn of events," said Ramirez, peering at the object. "What were you doing in the Triangle? And how did you escape?"

Rom slammed his hands on the table. "I don't know what happened exactly. I head-butted one of them, and then everything went fuzzy. I ran after them, but they took her down below. I think they went to the Demon Caves. How do I get there?"

Ramirez bent down to retrieve his glasses, nearly stepping on them. "Calm, now. Stay calm. Tell me exactly what happened."

"There's no time for that," Rom said angrily. "They've got my sister." Ramirez knew a lot, but he was no man of action, holed up here in his vault. "You didn't see those monsters."

Ramirez took another wary look at the triangle. He picked it up and rolled it in his fingers. "I've seen them," he said quietly. "This takes me back. It's called a triggit. It's used to summon a demon. It creates the link that allows a human to control the demon. And sometimes for the demon to control the human, when things go badly." He held up the triangle under the light. "You shouldn't have gone into their territory."

Triggits? Demons? Rom wondered why Ramirez hadn't told him any of this before. Humans controlling those terrifying creatures? He was always asking about the caves, and

Ramirez was always saying that most of what Rom heard was "buzzer nonsense".

"I don't have time for a lecture," said Rom. "I need to know how to get down there, and where they took her."

"Why were you there?"

"My father sent us."

Ramirez scowled. Rom wondered why the old man didn't look more surprised. After all, he had never had a kind word to say about Rom's father and seemed relieved when he had disappeared for good. "Sending a child on a man's errand," he muttered. "Why didn't you come to me first?"

"Are you going to help me or not?"

"I don't think you know what you'd be getting into down there, Rom."

"It's nothing I can't handle," Rom said, wishing he could sound more confident. "I have to get Riley back!"

Ramirez sighed. "I suppose they might be open to some sort of trade. But I wouldn't count on it, Rom. It's a bad idea. Terrible idea." Ramirez shook his head. "Pure foolishness to venture down there."

Rom stared into the old man's eyes, fully aware of how guilty he was making him feel. He knew Ramirez had a soft spot for Riley.

"Humph," said Ramirez. "Don't think you can pull that trick on me. Of course I feel terrible, Rom. Riley doesn't deserve to be involved with the people in the caves, if you can call them people. They're no better than the beasts. Worse, in some ways."

Rom said nothing.

"But there's not really anything to be done..."

Rom held his gaze and waited.

"I just – you don't understand..." Ramirez let out a long breath. "Oh, fine," he finally said, his sour expression returning. "I'll take you, but we're both going to regret it."

Rom wanted to hug him but settled for slapping the old man on the back. Ramirez hacked dramatically and handed him the triggit. "Well, don't kill me before the cave dwellers get a chance to!"

Rom smiled and shoved the triggit in his pocket.

Once Ramirez made his decision, Rom helped him gather food, torches, warm clothes and blankets. Rom had no idea how long or involved such a journey to the underground would be, but Ramirez seemed to be anticipating at least a few nights. The prospect of an adventure did nothing to dim the memory of Riley's screams. *If those demons did anything to her...*

While Ramirez searched for his travelling glasses, Rom fidgeted, sweating. He grabbed a bottle of muddy liquid from a shelf and tossed it into the air, catching it carelessly. If Ramirez didn't hurry, there was no telling what those creatures would do to Riley. Rom felt like hurling the bottle against the wall, but Ramirez grabbed it and placed it back on the shelf.

Rom tried to push the destructive thoughts from his head. Riley had to be alive. They could have killed her on the spot if they'd wanted to. So what did they want?

Ramirez complained a great deal about what a terrible mistake they were making by going into the caves, but continued procuring supplies. Then he shoved the gear into two dirty canvas backpacks.

"When do we go?" asked Rom.

Ramirez pushed an old cabinet aside and pulled open a creaky metal door. "Right now."

8

PEACHES

Your own private entrance to the caves?" Rom asked as Ramirez pulled the door shut behind them and lit a torch. "Is that why you moved to the bank?"

"It wasn't because of the view," Ramirez said, grabbing a handful of mud. He and Rom painstakingly spread mud over the door until it looked like part of the cave wall.

The tunnel had a rounded ceiling and the markings of a well-trodden path, and the two were able to travel quickly. The straps of the heavy pack cut into Rom's shoulders, his legs buckled slightly under the weight, and his ankle throbbed from the coyote bite, but he ignored the pain. He was surprised that Ramirez didn't mention his arthritis, his heart, his hip, the ringing in his ears, the chalky taste in his mouth, his sore arches, his corns, his warts, his blurred vision, or any of the other ailments he usually catalogued in all their unpleasant detail. Now that they were in the tunnel, Ramirez seemed driven. The old man moved so quickly that Rom had a difficult time keeping up.

After hours of hard hiking, the tunnel suddenly spilled into a massive cavern filled with the sound of rushing water, and Ramirez came to an abrupt stop.

Rom turned and stared. "What are you doing?" he asked.

Ramirez threw off his pack and sat with a groan. "Food," he said.

Rom was not hungry. He did not remove his pack. "Have you lost it completely? Riley could be food herself by now."

Ramirez did not get up. "If she is, there's nothing we can do. If she isn't, you're going to need your strength if you want to help her. It's lunchtime. Eating on schedule is what separates us from the beasts."

Rom sat. The sound of rushing water was soothing, and a slight current of air blew through the cavern, cooling him at once.

Ramirez foraged in his pack. "I know I put it in here somewhere," he grumbled, finally pulling out a can. Rom leant forward. The label had worn off. It had been a while since he had seen one of these cans. They were a big deal, especially if they contained fruit.

"Lima beans, most likely," said Ramirez. "I have two cans left. I don't know what's in them, but I've been saving them for a special occasion. We'll eat one now and another to celebrate making it out of the caves alive."

Fantastic, thought Rom. He did not want to seem ungrateful, but canned beans were one of the few things he would not eat.

Ramirez chuckled as he used a can opener to peel off the lid. Rom grew concerned, fearing that all of the physical exertion was taking its toll on the old man's mind. Rom had seldom seen Ramirez smile, let alone laugh. "What?" asked Rom.

Ramirez steadied himself with a hand, then fished something orange out of the can. He shoved it into his mouth. "These lima beans taste almost exactly like peaches," he said.

Rom had only had peaches once – an occasion he had never forgotten – and these tasted even better, the sweetness melting in his mouth. It saddened Rom to remember the experience.

More than once his father had gambled their entire food supply, but this time he had won big. He came home with bags and boxes full of food, and a shallow knife wound in his shoulder from an unhappy opponent. That night they played a game. If Rom or Riley could guess what was inside a can, they got to eat the whole thing. Riley had won the single can of peaches, but had shared.

Rom and Riley had gorged until their stomachs ached, and afterwards, in the dwindling light, they put on a puppet show for their father. It was their interpretation of a story he used to read to them from the Tree Book, about a girl called Dragonfly, whose mother had lived in a village made of hot-air balloons. Their father had given them a standing ovation.

Rom settled back against a wall of the tunnel and chewed with his eyes closed, trying to forget the memory and focus on the peaches.

"There's something I should tell you before we go too much further," Ramirez said. "It's probably going to upset you a little."

Rom opened his eyes. "What?"

"Or maybe it will upset you a lot," said Ramirez, grabbing back the can of peaches. "But remember – I had my reasons for keeping you in the dark about a few things."

"Like what?" Rom asked.

"I've known a lot more about your father than I've let on."

Rom stood up. All those times he had asked Ramirez about his father, about what could have happened – Ramirez had always said he had no idea. Rom looked Ramirez in the eye. "All this time, and you never said anything?"

"Please calm down. As I said, I had my reasons, and I'll share them with you if you let me talk. The people in the caves also knew him."

Rom could only wish that he were surprised. "He stole

from them, didn't he?" Rom had come across people his father had double-crossed, and they were all too happy to exact their revenge on Rom.

Ramirez shook his head. "It's a little more complicated. Every year in the caves they have fights between creatures like the ones who took Riley. The cave dwellers call them demons, for good reason, but in reality they are an advanced form of beast-mek hybrid. People come here from tribes all over the continent hoping to win supplies by gambling on the fights. You've seen them, desperate people with nothing left to lose, willing to trade everything they own for a chance to be safe."

Rom nodded. This time of year there were always more humans in the area, pulling wheeled crates stuffed with goods, easy prey for beasts and buzzers alike as they searched for an entrance to the Demon Caves. "How do you know so much about the Demon Caves?"

"I helped create them," he said. "Years ago, I was part of a group that discovered a powerful science. It allowed humans to conjure these demons out of thin air, and eventually to control them. Controlling them requires a great deal of talent. The ones who have it are called demonsmiths."

"What does any of that have to do with my father?"

"He was the best demonsmith there ever was. No one could beat him. But the thing was, he didn't need the technology to summon the demon and control it. He had the technology *inside him* somehow. Studying his link with the creatures, we were able to make such advances in our understanding of how—"

"You saw him do it?" Rom interrupted, remembering the images of his father in the Tree Book.

Ramirez nodded. "There was a time when I was the only friend he had down here."

A jumble of questions flooded Rom's mind, but he only had time enough to stammer, "What happened to him?" before a crashing sound echoed down the tunnel, then stopped abruptly.

Ramirez held his finger to his lips.

There was a terrible silence.

Then Rom heard the tapping sound.

"Whatever you do," Ramirez whispered, "don't move."

Don't move? Rom strained to see down the corridor, but there was only the sound. Rom did not intend to stick around to hear more. He wanted to run. He took a step back, but Ramirez tightened his grip. "They're faster than us, and their jaws are powerful enough to break you in two with one bite. And they already know we're here. The best thing to do is stay still and try to think of something pleasant."

Rom was incredulous. "Like what?"

Ramirez shrugged. "Peaches?"

Then Rom saw the demons, a flash of gleaming metal in the darkness, barely illuminated by the torchlight. They were running towards them.

"Stay still," whispered Ramirez.

Rom did not have much choice. Within seconds of seeing the silver flash in the dark, the hybrid demons were directly before them. The silence and swiftness of their movements was almost supernatural. They were at once beast, machine and phantom.

He tried not to react to the demons, tried to resist the urge to run as they moved centimetres from his face, seeming to wait for orders. There was something darkly beautiful about these horrors – the metallic sheen of their skin, the rippling of their liquid muscles, the six powerful limbs, each ending in a three-fingered hand. Who had created these terrifying, magnificent creatures? And who was controlling them?

Rom was fascinated and utterly terrified. Now the demon was looking directly into his eyes. Rom froze completely. He held the hybrid's blank and bottomless gaze, and sensed intelligence there, but not a kindred spark of life. He felt his insides grow cold as he faced down the unfeeling cruelty of this incredible entity.

And then Rom blinked.

The creature hunched low and pounced, its nimble limbs moving all at once, raising Rom onto its back and holding him down. Rom's fascination melted into terror as he found himself bound on the back of the hybrid, his torch left in the dirt. He tried to look ahead, but he couldn't budge. He called out for Ramirez, but there was no response. The demon wheeled around and picked up speed until Rom became so dizzy he had to close his eyes. It glided along silently at a steady gallop, its cargo secure, its mission accomplished. And there was nothing Rom could do. He thought of Riley, strapped to one of these creatures, having no idea where it was taking her. Rom would have to stay strong for both of their sakes. He'd let the beast take him deep into its lair. And then he'd find his sister.

9

DIAMOND TEETH

When the hybrid demon slowed to a stop and released its grip, Rom fell to the ground. He was surprised to find the floor was covered in soft, silky fabric.

Rom heard Ramirez yelp and then felt a thud as the old man landed next to him.

Laughter emerged from the darkness. "Same old Ramirez," said the voice, a sinister edge of mockery lurking beneath the jovial tone. "Always the clumsy fool."

The lights flashed on. Rom blinked to shield his eyes from the sudden brightness. Everywhere he saw red. The walls had been painted a deep shade of crimson – the same shade as the carpet brushing against his face. Stacks of gold, silver and copper bars lined the walls, along with chests stuffed with jewels, power cells and food packages. Rom turned on his back and looked up. Every inch of the dome-shaped ceiling was covered with jewels.

"Stand up," the voice commanded. Rom stood silently. Ramirez followed, grumbling.

A man with muscular shoulders, a barrel chest and a protruding belly barely covered by a red velvet jacket came into view from behind a massive wooden desk. Lacy, white, bell-shaped cuffs protruded from the sleeves, reminding Rom of a ridiculous pirate. The man's head was bald on top, but he combed the hair above his ears forward, almost to his eyes. He had a bulbous nose and a cruel frown, but his large, intelligent eyes gave him an aura of supreme authority. On either side of him sat the metallic demons, sitting perfectly still except for their pulsing black eyes.

There was another presence in the room as well, half obscured by shadow. Rom could not make it out at first, but as his eyes adjusted to light, he realized it was a boy, dressed completely in black, with dark skin and a shaved head. He was sitting cross-legged in the corner, staring straight ahead, as if he couldn't be bothered to look at anyone else in the room.

Rom glanced over at Ramirez, who was clutching his hip and grimacing in a fashion that was reassuringly familiar. "Hello, Diamond Teeth," Ramirez said. There was no warmth in the greeting. He scanned the room. "You've done well for yourself."

The big man smiled, revealing the source of the nickname: his teeth were made entirely of diamonds. The jewels glittered grotesquely in the soft light of the chandelier. He continued to smile while he spoke. "If you ever call me that again, Ramirez, I'll put you in a room full of starving rats. I have one, you know. I call it my Thousand Teeth Suite, and its last occupant has recently checked out." The threat was made without sarcasm. Diamond Teeth turned to Rom. "My name is Julius, young man, and you must be Rom. Please forgive your ageing friend. He seems to have forgotten that, despite our underground circumstances, we do our best in the caves to maintain a degree of civility. It's what separates us from the beasts."

"Where's my sister?" Rom demanded. "And what did you do to my dad?"

Diamond Teeth sighed. "Another feisty one, I see. Please refrain from shouting while I remind you two why you're still alive." He walked slowly across the floor and patted one of the demons on the head. "I sometimes think that the majority of my life is spent in the business of reminding. I have to remind the battle demons that I can turn them back into atoms and molecules any time I please. I have to remind the demon-smiths that I control *them*. I have to remind all these other parasites that it's my blood they are sucking; it's my blood that gives them nourishment. The reminding business, Rom, is a tedious one, but one for which I possess a certain flair. Do you know why?"

Rom shook his head, slightly confused. He looked at the boy in the corner, who was still staring off into space.

Diamond Teeth pointed his thumb at himself. "Because what's good for Julius, my friend, is good for everyone."

Ramirez coughed.

"Would you disagree with that proposition, Mr Ramirez?"

Ramirez shook his head. "I wouldn't dream of it."

Diamond Teeth gestured to the wall behind him. "Rom, your friend Mr Ramirez created a place for people to hide like frightened children after the beasts took over the city, but I was the one who turned it into somewhere you'd actually want to live."

"You forgot to remind us why we're alive, Julius," Ramirez interrupted. "Let's get to the point. Rom didn't come for a history lesson."

"He came with the wrong guide then, didn't he? You're always so full of lessons. To be completely honest, I would have liked to avoid the entire situation. Dirty, shameful business, all of this. It's always worse when it involves children, isn't it, Ramirez?"

"My sister has nothing to do with any of this," said Rom. He glared at the motionless demons. "Take me and leave her alone."

Diamond Teeth smiled. "I wish I could do that, Rom," he said. "But two of anything is always better than one."

The more he smiled, the more uncomfortable Rom became. The smile had a poisonous insincerity. "Let me see her," he said.

Diamond Teeth put up his hands in mock surrender. "She's safe. You'll be with her soon enough. You have my word on that. Unfortunately, I can't just give her to you, no matter how much it would please me to do so."

"My sister didn't do a thing," Rom said, the anger in his voice rising.

"You couldn't be more right, Rom. She's an innocent victim. And innocent victims are the worst sort, are they not? I wish I could do something. I really do. The fact is, I'm confronted with something of a problem. Your father, believe it or not, is a man of certain talents, and those talents are extraordinarily valuable to me. But your father left the caves, and since he refuses to come back, I need to remind him of his priorities. Unless..."

"Just come out with it," said Ramirez.

"Unless, Ramirez, you are offering this boy up as a fighter."

Ramirez started to speak, but Rom interrupted. "I'll do anything it takes."

Diamond Teeth flashed his grin at Ramirez. "See, Ramirez, the boy is reasonable. A little pushy, but he understands the score. Nothing like his father."

Ramirez frowned. "Speaking of which, we don't know if he has his father's gift."

My father's gift, Rom thought. His father's gifts were usually more trouble than they were worth.

Diamond Teeth frowned. The look went from jovial to ruthless in the space of a blink. "My gut tells me that he does, and my gut has never let me down." His smile returned, and he slapped his velvet-swaddled belly with both hands. "Whenever my gut starts talking to me, I know it's time to gamble big."

Ramirez's face turned grey. "He gets a fair chance, doesn't he? A couple of months to learn, at the very least. There are protocols, Julius."

Diamond Teeth slammed down his fist. "The only protocol that matters here is that I don't kill demonsmiths and their sponsors during fight season, even if they are old enemies who stabbed me in the back." He stood up and straightened his vest. "We're short on fighters this year, and if this kid is anything like his father, he should prove entertaining for the gamblers even if he hasn't practised." He turned to Rom. "If you want your sister back, you better learn how to fight."

"Even if he has the gift," said Ramirez, "it doesn't mean he'll be able to control it. Look what happened to his father."

"I'll do it." Rom looked from Ramirez to Diamond Teeth to the boy in the corner, whose mouth now betrayed the slightest sign of a smile. "I'm not my father," he said with confidence. But he wasn't at all sure. Everyone in the room seemed to know more about his family than he did himself.

"That's what I like to hear," said Diamond Teeth. "You didn't happen to find a little silver triangle, did you, kid? Your father neglected to return it before he took his leave."

Ramirez interrupted before Rom could answer. "What do you propose, Julius? You can't just throw him into the ring."

"I have a triggit," Rom said.

Diamond Teeth clapped. "He found his father's triggit! Marvellous! The prince inherits the crown! I hope you find this as moving as I do, Ramirez."

"He needs time," said Ramirez.

Diamond Teeth grunted. "The tournament starts in a week, and this is the blood son of Jack Saint-Pierre. What if the kid is as good as his father? A real beast! Ready for the kill."

"Enough," Ramirez interrupted through gritted teeth. "Give me some time to explain it to him. That's all I ask, Julius. You have what you want, don't you?"

The glittering smile came at once. Rom now understood that like a flash of lightning, that smile was a sign of bad things to come.

10

THE DEMON CAVES

Rom was given his own quarters with a giant chandelier, running water and a large wooden bed covered with silk blankets so soft he was tempted to rub them against his cheek. Everywhere, jewels glittered in the walls. Rom had spent his life in abandoned places, in rooms covered by dust that billowed through broken windows. The cleanliness made him a little uneasy. He never would have guessed that such a place could exist.

Somewhere outside, Rom could hear the murmur of a crowd. He looked around the room. Gold walls and silky blankets while everyone on the surface starved? It didn't make sense. He had imagined the caves so often. Now here he was, and all he wanted to do was be aboveground with Riley, in the warmth of the sun.

Rom wanted to be alone for a while with the Tree Book – to find out if it could tell him anything about Riley – but Ramirez had followed him in. The old man sneered at the surroundings and slung his dirty backpack down to the floor with no regard for the luxurious carpet.

"What are you so angry about?" Rom asked.

"You haven't studied enough to know it," said Ramirez, "but this was how it was in the old world. People were obsessed with luxuries, with *things*. They were so preoccupied with them that they were willing to kill for them. That's the sort of world Diamond Teeth would bring back."

Beyond the thick cave walls, Rom could hear the soft thump of drums. Ramirez was still for a moment, listening. "It's the sound of the arena," he finally said. "It'll grow louder, up to the final fight, until it gets so loud you'll feel like it's inside your head." He sighed and slumped down into a chair.

"Who plays the music?" Rom asked.

"The gamblers. And I wouldn't call it music. It's more like a feral racket. People beating on rocks and pans and each other's heads. The fights make them crazy, and that's exactly how Diamond Teeth wants them."

Rom was confused. If that was the case, why did everyone want to get into the caves? "What was it like before?"

"We founded this society on rituals, Rom. We founded it on noble aspirations. We believed that a group of scientists working towards a common goal could take the city back from the beasts, because we would be better than the beasts. It all started with technology found by people not unlike yourself and your friends. The first buzzers, you might say."

"You found triggits," Rom guessed.

"That's right. We knew they were powerful, part of a science far beyond anything we'd ever read about. It was our chance to take back the city."

"If the technology was supposed to help you fight the beasts, why did you fight each other instead?"

"At first, the fights helped us. They gave people a goal – and a way to master the science before we sent the hybrids into battle on the surface. It wasn't like it is now. The fights were honourable. It wasn't about gambling. It wasn't even about winning. It was about improving the science so we could fight our real enemies. Then Diamond Teeth found out what we were doing. He was helpful enough at first – he had tremendous resources – but he had ideas of his own."

Rom was suddenly overwhelmed. The artificial light made him queasy, and the idea of being trapped half a mile underground didn't help.

"Are you OK?" Ramirez asked.

Rom put his hand to his forehead and felt that he was sweating. "Is this all really necessary? I just want to get Riley and get out of here."

"Trust me, this is the only way to save your sister." Ramirez avoided Rom's gaze and cleared his throat. "And it won't hurt to see if you really do have the gift. I think you can go all the way with this. I'm betting my life on it."

Rom didn't want to think about what was at stake. "What was my father like? When you two were down here, I mean?"

"He was a lot like you," Ramirez said, chuckling, "but with even less common sense, if you can imagine that."

Rom frowned at the comparison. "How did he turn into ... what he is now?"

Ramirez stood up. "He was careless. There are rules down here, or at least there used to be, and he was never much for following rules or living up to his obligations."

"That sounds like him," Rom muttered.

"None of us understood how he was able to do what he did. He could control his demon naturally, without the technology."

Rom wiped the sweat from his brow. "How?"

Ramirez shook his head. "I don't know for certain, but it had something to do with a genetic mutation called the kaimira gene. Elements from beasts and meks were mixed in with his human DNA. That's what we were studying, and we would have figured it out if Diamond Teeth hadn't taken over."

Rom remembered the Tree Book. *Guardians of the Kaimira Code.* He thought of his father lapping syrup off the dirty floor. "Did the gene turn him into what he is now?"

"I don't know," Ramirez said. "What I do know is that, no matter how good someone is at controlling the demons, it's

still dangerous. You can melt down. You can die. I don't want to scare you, but you have to know the risks."

None of this was making Rom feel any better. "What do you mean 'melt down'?"

"If you are able to conjure a demon, you still have to control it. Controlling it requires balancing the human, beast and mek elements inside the demon. A good demonsmith balances the three elements in order to fight. Some demonsmiths lose control. The mind gets overwhelmed and crashes in order to save itself. Sometimes it's too late, and the tech surges into the demonsmith's brain. Changes it."

Rom thought of the fleeting image he had seen in the Tree Book: his father, seemingly unconscious, surrounded by indifferent attendants.

"For good?" Rom asked.

"Don't worry about that now," said Ramirez. "We don't even know at this point if you can conjure a demon."

"How will we know if I can do it?" Rom asked.

"You'll either be able to do it or you won't. That's how we'll know."

Ramirez looked around the room again. "We had a society striving towards the betterment of the world, and now it's become a den of drunken gamblers trying their best to stay out of the Grotto."

"What's the Grotto?"

"I can only imagine what it has become now. It's where the losers go, and the losers' families, and anyone who crosses Diamond Teeth. Some of my friends are still in there, slaving away to keep this place running."

"Doing what?"

"Who do you think powers Diamond Teeth's guard demons? The losers, working in shifts, barely alive. They melt down constantly, but Diamond Teeth keeps them working until they drop for good."

Ramirez looked as if he wanted to say more but changed his mind. "We'd better get some rest. We won't have long before your first match, and it's going to be a challenge." Ramirez paused, and the sound of the drums filled the silence. "I know you want to rush off without thinking and rescue your sister, but that won't work. You'll have to trust me. This is the only way to get her back."

After Ramirez left, Rom tried to rest, but he was too frightened to relax. He'd grown up hiding from beasts, and fighting them whenever he had to, but this was something else. Mek-beast hybrids, more powerful than any beast or mek alone. An underground society crammed with people, each one with an angle. Rom had never been in such a crowd.

He remembered the clump of black wire Riley had dropped. He checked his pocket to make sure it was still there. If he could somehow find his sister and escape, he wouldn't have to fight. It would be like it was before, with the two of them getting by just fine. Riley could finish her puppet, and they'd put on a show, telling the buzzers the crazy story of how their parents met: their father, an arrogant young trans‑ porter, risking his life daily delivering messages; their mother, from a nomadic desert tribe, imprisoned in the Demon Caves; their father had betrayed the cave dwellers as well as his own tribe to rescue her.

There has to be some way out of this room, Rom thought. He started by examining the furniture. There was a single bed with a gold frame. A mattress stuffed with feathers that Rom, after a lifetime of sleeping on floors and in bedrolls, found uncomfortably soft. Rom ran his hands over the crim‑ son silk sheets, pillows and feather‑stuffed blanket. He pulled the mattress off the frame onto the carpeted floor and searched underneath. Nothing.

Near the bed was the long bench that Ramirez called a divan. Its frame was also gold. Rom kicked a cushion covered in a yellow silken fabric. He didn't exactly expect a secret doorway to open underneath, but he wanted to be sure. A marble‑topped table stood in one corner of the room between two chairs made of dark wood. Lions, bears and other beasts had been carved into the chairs.

A tall cabinet with drawers and a desk completed the fur‑ niture in the room. Rom sat on the cushioned chair in front of the desk and searched through all of the drawers. They were empty except for a bunch of black robes like the ones worn by the boy with the shaved head. Rom tried to feel behind the cabinet, but there wasn't enough space, and it was far too heavy to move.

Instead, Rom ran his hands over every inch of the soft red carpet and the gilded walls. There was nowhere left to search, and nothing else in the room except for a heavy gold chandelier topped with lightbulbs made to look like candles.

The door opened slightly with a soft knock. Rom hurried to the entrance, but no one was there. At his feet, however, was a golden tray filled with covered dishes. He opened the first to find a steaming pile of roasted beast flesh and wondered how they got meat – and the bird feathers that stuffed the blankets. Did Diamond Teeth send hunters to the surface?

Another plate had fresh corn, and there was a golden jug filled with cherry juice. The smell of food made Rom realize how hungry he was. He took the tray to the table, set it down, and tore into the meal.

While he ate, his thoughts turned to the Tree Book. It had shown him a glimpse of what might have happened to his father; perhaps it could help him find Riley, or even tell him something about the kaimira gene. He dug it out of his pack and ran his hands over the surface. He remembered all of the times his father had read to him about Dragonfly, Lizard Girl and the others. He remembered how his father had warned him to behave because Dragonfly and Lizard Girl were reading about him, too, and Rom had always laughed, never believing it. As he opened the book now, however, he decided to try something.

The book pulled open as easily as before. The word *Breaker* appeared on the left side. Rom got up and made sure the door was securely locked.

"How to get started," Rom muttered, picking up another ear of corn. "Well, I can try writing something," he mumbled while he chewed.

On the blank page, he wrote with his finger: *What am I doing?*

He was surprised when a voice answered, accompanied by a line-drawn image of a girl's face in the corner. The picture was moving! At first she spoke in a foreign language, but then the sounds scrambled and unscrambled, and she was speaking English. *How am I supposed to know what you're doing?*

Rom raised his eyebrows. She was responding to him!

He wrote:

They've taken her.

Hybrid demons made of liquid metal.

And I've agreed to fight.

CLOUDWATCHING

When Mei woke the following morning, she strained to hear the sounds of her mother humming as she made breakfast and her father wrestling with the vines in the garden. Instead, she was met with the racket of children playing nearby. The smell of meat drifted through the air, and her bed felt like it was gently falling. Mei opened her eyes and saw the tightly woven bamboo around her. She felt the pulse of heat from the burner above and the bite of the cold wind from the crack in the canvas. She remembered. She was nowhere near Luo Ye.

She stood up and stretched. The sight of the Sky Village flying towards the sunrise snatched the breath from her lungs. The balloons looked like hills stretching towards the horizon, their bright colours dulled in the early light. Each one contained a family and a story. Hundreds of villagers stood on ropes between balloons doing tai chi in perfect unison – one bare foot on the rope, the other raised, then one arm raised, before slowly shifting to a different position. It was as if the wind itself kept a silent tempo.

How could they move like that without falling, Mei wondered. And how could their movements be so perfectly synchronized? No one seemed to be leading. Throughout the previous day, many of these people had bickered about trades, how much water to feed the soya beans they grew in crop baskets, and other matters central to the village's survival. But there was nothing but harmony in the silent hours of the morning.

Mei watched the land pass below as the other children played. The younger ones swung on the ropes, and the teenagers played with bags full of seeds. When someone dropped a bag, everyone watched it fall, and they launched into a rhythmic chant that drifted across the valley:

> T'chee, t'chee, there goes the ball.
> Let air bear you well for earth.
> Sometimes to grow you have to fall
> That spring bring seeds to birth.

Though Mei had no interest in watching anything fall to earth, she found herself humming along with the tune and realized she already knew it. Her mother used to sing it to her when she tended to Mei's scrapes and bruises. Mei had never thought about what the song meant, but it always made her feel like everything was going to be all right, no matter what had happened.

Mei would have liked to play, but even if she could bring herself to go out on the ropes, she did not know how to approach these children. Their games were so strange, and they seemed so at home on the ropes. Mei tried to tell herself there was nothing to it. Her mother had taught her rope walking on the clothesline outside their home. Wasn't that the same? But this time, she had no one to catch her if she fell, and the distance to earth was vast. The thought of mocking laughter and shouts of "land walker" as she fell were almost as terrifying as the prospect of plummeting to her death.

The breakfast balloon was upcurrent. Mei could smell cooked flesh, and she guessed it was the wild pig Ai-ling had caught. The smell reminded her of the time she and her father had come across a dead pig in the nearby fields. Her father had guessed that the beast was lost and had wandered too near mek territory; the meks had chased it into human lands and, as was their way, had scorched the entire area to kill the lone animal.

Mei couldn't bring herself to try the beast flesh, but she was curious about bird eggs, so when her turn came she requested a bowl of whipped pigeon eggs. They were surprisingly light and creamy. She ate silently, while Ai-ling's parents, energized by their early morning exercise, discussed their duties for the day.

Ai-ling slid into the balloon from above. She wore a close-fitting silk dress and matching silk slippers, both the colour of ripe cherries, and a feather tiara. Mei thought she looked beautiful, but she said nothing.

"Where are you going?" Mei asked.

"Going? I can't go anywhere," Ai-ling answered. "Today's a special day."

"What sort of special day?"

Ai-ling whispered, "It's bad luck to talk about it. You'll find out soon enough. In the meantime, I need you to do me a favour."

Ai-ling handed Mei a map made of coarse paper. As Mei looked at the terrain, it changed before her eyes.

"This is a flowing map, Mei. One of the few bits of science we have from before the wars. It shows the land as we pass over and the names of villages and other details. It will be a great help when you are cloudwatching."

"Cloudwatching?" Mei asked, still staring at the map. She had heard of the wonderful tools humans had before the wars, but she had no idea that any still existed. She held it gently, half expecting it to send an electric shock through her fingers.

A pigeon flapped towards the basket and landed on the edge. Mei shrieked and took a step back. Ai-ling ran her palm along the cooing pigeon's back and removed a piece of paper from its curled foot. She let the pigeon eat seed from her palm.

"Ewww," Mei said, disgusted and fascinated. She stepped closer. The pigeon was grey, almost the same colour as metal, but with spots of shiny purple and green on the neck. "Isn't the beak sharp?"

"If you're pigeon food, it is." Ai-ling looked at the note.

"What's that?" Mei asked, looking at the slip of paper.

"It's a message. I'm a Cloudwatcher. It's my role in the village."

"What does watching clouds have to do with birds?"

"Cloudwatchers are the news gatherers of the village. We have human contacts on the ground, and they send us gossip, stories, warnings, anything they think we should know. It all comes to me, and I try to make sense out of it and turn it into knowledge for our people."

"It's your job?" Mei asked. Her father had mentioned that the sky villagers were information traders. Mei needed to find out more.

Ai-ling nodded. "I'm not much good at it. I can't communicate with the birds the way your mother could. I'll never forget the way she did that. None of us will." She patted the bird once more, whistled, and opened her palms. The bird flew off in the direction it had come. "This is special seed. It keeps them healthy and enhances their homing abilities so they can find us no matter where we are. It also saves them a trip to the ground, which can be pretty dangerous."

Mei wanted to find out more about her mother and the birds, but she was afraid of looking like she knew less about her own mother than the sky villagers seemed to. "I thought the Sky Village didn't care about land walkers."

"Just because we don't involve ourselves in the affairs of land walkers doesn't mean we don't care about them," Ai-ling said. "And we trade the information for supplies, so our survival depends on knowing what's happening on the surface."

"What does that note say?" Mei asked. "Is there anything about the mek army that attacked my village?"

"It's a weather warning." She handed the slip of paper to Mei. "A storm coming this direction, but it's far from our path." Mei studied the message, wondering what the Sky Village would do if a storm hit.

Another bird swooped in and landed on the edge of the basket. Mei stepped back, then steadied herself.

"Give it a try," Ai-ling said, handing the bird and some seed to Mei. The bird twitched but did not try to escape. She ran her palm across its back and held her hand in front of its beak. It pecked at her palm, and she dropped the seed, afraid the beak would cut her.

"The beak's not very sharp," Ai-ling said, giving Mei more seed. "Try it again."

Mei let the bird peck seeds from her palm. It tickled, but it was fascinating to be so close to this beast, to feel its slick feathers, its warm body and its beating heart. She had never touched a beast before, and she was surprised at how similar they were to humans. Mei whistled and the bird flew off.

The message read: *The Scimurai have been spotted on the western border. Yu Yuan, Xin Lu Village.*

Mei handed the message to Ai-ling. "I don't understand. Who are the Scimurai?"

"This is worrisome," Ai-ling said quietly. She looked up at Old Hug, an arching platform hundreds of feet across, like two massive arms hugging the clouds. Held aloft by dozens of balloons, Old Hug was always at the centre of the village, and it was the designated spot for parties. Today, it was where the Sky Council had convened. "And bothersome. It's the third sighting."

"Who are the Scimurai?" Mei asked again.

Ai-ling cocked an eyebrow at her. "I'm amazed how little your parents have told you about your family history."

"My parents never tell me anything," Mei admitted. Her face flushed, but at least her ignorance was out in the open now, at least with Ai-ling. Now, perhaps, she could ask questions about her mother more freely.

"The group was formed more than a century ago by a man named Hiro," said Ai-ling. "Some called it a cult, but they were really just a group of warrior scientists who wanted to save Japan from its obsession with technology. The government called them traitors and tried to wipe them out, but when the Trinary Wars began, the Scimurai were the only ones who knew how to fight the meks."

Human warriors destroying meks! But what did they have to do with her family? Mei didn't know, but she hoped they were after the mek army, too. "They sound like they're on our side," Mei said.

"Just because they fight meks doesn't make them good. In the decades since the Trinary Wars, they've caused more harm than good among the human villages and tribes. They don't care who gets hurt. Some say they behead mek sympathizers."

Mei wondered who could possibly sympathize with meks. "Do you know what they're after?" she asked.

"Sky only knows. I'll just say that when they are spotted, it's best to keep an eye out for danger. Whether they are the fire or the smoke is something even the elders can't agree on."

Mei scanned the horizon for more birds. "What do the Scimurai have to do with my family?" Mei asked.

"Maybe there are some things better left unsaid, for now," Ai-ling said. "I don't often think before I speak, and it has got me into trouble more times than I can remember. Perhaps you are too young to know these things."

"Not you too," Mei snapped. "I'm not too young."

Ai-ling smiled. "All right. In that case, you won't mind taking over as Cloudwatcher while I'm away."

"Me? Cloudwatcher? But I'm..."

Ai-ling finished Mei's sentence. "Too young? You can't have it both ways."

Mei resented the trap, but Ai-ling was right. If she could get over her fear of touching the birds, she might be able to learn more about these Scimurai, or sightings of the mek army. Her father had said it was the best way for her to help him find Mother.

And it felt nice to be trusted with a role. Cloudwatcher. "I'll try my best," Mei answered.

"I know you will," Ai-ling said. "You'll present what you've learnt at the next Sky Council meeting. Don't forget to tell them about the Scimurai and the storm."

Mei looked eagerly into the sky for signs of incoming news as Ai-ling leaped out of the basket and scuttled across the ropes, two large bags under her arms.

As soon as she'd gone, Feifei struggled out of the pouch and flew in circles around the basket.

"Finally decided to wake up?" said Mei. She watched her pet flutter in the breeze and wondered how she would interact with the birds. Feifei nuzzled Mei's cheek until she giggled.

While Mei waited for more messages, she opened the Tree Book and flipped though the pages. She was still afraid of the rumbling Animus voice, but she wanted to know more about her mother, and find out if anything had happened to Breaker.

"Hello, Tree Book?" she said. "Are you there? Can you show me my mother again?" Just as before, spiralling symbols appeared in the corner. It was Animus. Colours swirled and slashed across the page, forming shapes and then pictures. As the image settled, Mei recognized the scene – she was looking at the Sky Village. The image zoomed in closer, and Mei saw herself holding the book with Feifei flitting around her head!

"Why are you showing me myself? I want to see my mother with the mek army." She turned the page.

The mek army was marching through rice fields, burning them as it went. Mei studied the area carefully. There was a river in the distance – yes, it was definitely a river. And on a hill, a high tower of some sort, with a tiger painted on the top.

Mei was surprised when Breaker's line-drawn face appeared in the corner of the page, replacing the swirling symbols. Mei was still amazed that he was real.

Dragonfly? Did you fall out yet?

"What?" Mei shouted. "How can you ask such a thing?"

Sorry, he said. *I was joking.*

Mei remembered from the stories that Breaker had a terrible sense of humour, always joking about morbid things like being ripped apart or eaten. Mei always thought it was his way of acting brave after being chased around by beasts. She enjoyed this about him when she thought he was only a character. She'd have to get used to it now that she knew he was real.

"Are you OK?" she asked.

I've been better, Breaker said, *but I'll live.* He told her what he'd learnt about the kaimira gene. *Listen, I think it's dangerous. And I think Animus is connected to it.*

"All I know is that it knows where my mother is, and if it can help me find her, I'm going to use it."

What are you going to do if you find her? Take on a whole army of meks by yourself? Maybe Animus is just trying to trick you. I don't trust that voice.

"I can't just leave my mother locked up in a cage. You wouldn't do that with Riley."

You've got that right.

"But I'm just floating around up here with these people who don't care. She could be dying. I don't even know what meks do to humans."

Breaker grimaced in the drawing. *I've only heard stories. It's not pretty.*

Mei braced herself. "Tell me. I want to know."

I heard that meks are kind of haywire. The humans they capture, they make them fight beasts and watch mek performances.

"Those are just stories," Mei said. Why would meks do

such ridiculous things? Weren't they supposed to be logical?

There was a rustle as Feifei dived into her pouch. Mei felt a pinch on her scalp and realized a pigeon had landed on her head. She shook her head violently, and it flapped away and circled the basket, looking for a place to land. Mei blinked at the passing clouds, allowing her eyes to readjust. Birds surrounded the perimeter of her basket, and others circled the balloon, trying to land. Mei panicked and shrieked, looking in all directions for a place to hide. But they were everywhere, their sharp beaks pointed at her, loose feathers blowing across the basket. There was nowhere to hide. She swallowed, closed her eyes, and took a deep breath.

"Wait a minute," Mei said, placing the book on the stool. She gathered messages quickly, petting each bird once, praying it wouldn't bite her, and feeding it a few seeds before sending it off again.

She looked at the pile of notes. Had she been absorbed in the Tree Book that long? A gust of wind scattered the messages all over the basket, and some flew over the edge. Feifei darted from her pouch and went after them, tiny limbs reaching, and managed to save most of them. Mei hoped the others were wedding announcements and nothing about the Scimurai or the storm. She looked eastward at the sky, which looked clear as far as she could see.

After the messages were recovered, Mei stacked them on the open pages of the Tree Book and read them aloud to

Breaker, in case he could offer some insight. There were several more mentions of the Scimurai. Mei read these messages twice, hoping to understand more than the words told her. Breaker wasn't much help, though he was particularly curious about Hiro.

The last messages were from several small villages. Meks and beasts were on the move, and battles were breaking out across the region. The last message stated: *The people of Luo Ye, Xin Lu and several other human villages have been taken prisoner by meks. The mek army has been spotted moving east towards Tiger Tower.*

Dragonfly! Breaker said. *Didn't you say your mother was near a tower with a tiger? Maybe that's the place. They're moving east.*

The Sky Village was also heading east! The meks had several days' head start, but the Sky Village would catch up with them soon. And when they did, Mei would have to be ready.

HEALTHY, HAPPY,
STRONG AND WISE

Ai-ling returned soon afterwards, with her parents. Mei told them everything she'd learnt from cloudwatching, hoping the Sky Council might agree to go after the mek army, but Ai-ling kept looking away into the distance. She did not seem to hear a word Mei said, and her parents just nodded, smiled and patted Mei on the head.

As Ai-ling tidied the basket, her mother shot up from her chair so violently that the entire balloon rocked.

"It's that rogue, Jun!" she shouted, pointing at a large balloon speeding towards them, propelled by short blasts of smoke and green fire from a small windmover attached to the basket. Mei counted six men inside, one wearing a silk robe as brightly hued as Ai-ling's dress.

Ai-ling's father disconnected three hook ropes while Ai-ling's mother pulled on a fourth and yanked their basket out of the path of the charging balloon. The balloon careered past, and Mei could see the laughing eyes of the men inside. They looked daring and good-humoured. But who were they?

"Hurry! They're turning around!" Ai-ling shouted. They pulled ropes so that their balloon veered to the side, but they were not moving fast enough this time. The other balloon was charging hard, all swishing ropes and boisterous shouts as it whooshed through the air towards them.

"Hold on to something, Dragonfly," Ai-ling said. "This could get bumpy." She put her arm around Mei's shoulder and grasped the handle just as Jun's basket crashed into a corner of theirs, knocking Ai-ling's parents off their feet. One of the men hurled a rope, and it hooked the basket near Ai-ling's hands. The men laughed as they pulled on the rope, bringing the two baskets closer together.

The man in the bright robe reached across the gap for the handle Mei was holding. His eyes caught Mei's and he grinned, revealing crooked front teeth. Mei felt embarrassed. Despite his teeth, the man staring at her was the most handsome of the group. He seemed much too clean-shaven to be a rogue.

As he reached further, he nearly fell out, and his friends snatched him by his belt to drag him back in.

He shouted, "You're not getting away from me, Ai-ling. I'm not leaving here without you."

Ai-ling's father shouted back, "Over my dead body, Jun!" The men in the basket laughed.

"If that's what it takes, sir," one answered.

Ai-ling's mother hooked the invaders' rope to a barrel of seeds and, with Mei's help, managed to heave it over the edge of the basket. Its weight jerked Jun's basket downward, nearly capsizing it, and Jun was knocked overboard. For one terrifying moment, Jun free-fell through the air, his limbs flailing. Ai-ling gasped. Jun caught the rope at the last second, his legs kicking beneath him. His friends pulled him back inside and cut the barrel free. It disappeared into the fog below.

Jun stood up in the basket, still grinning. "You're worthy opponents, venerable old ones, but I'll take what I've come for." Jun held two stuffed bags high over his head and tossed them into Ai-ling's basket. One broke open next to Mei's feet. Inside were red envelopes stuffed with currency that had lost its value a century ago.

Ai-ling's mother shouted, "No amount of money will buy our precious daughter, you snaggletoothed scoundrel. Go home."

Jun responded, "I have no home unless Ai-ling is with me. I would rather jump into the rice fields below us, into the jaws of the earth, disgracing my wind-friendly feet with the touch of the unyielding ground, than leave without your daughter." Mei almost laughed at such melodramatic language, but something in Jun's earnest tone and sensitive eyes stopped her. This was clearly a prepared speech, and he seemed to mean every word.

His friends were silent now, watching the exchange. Jun grabbed the rope and threw it back into Ai-ling's basket, hooking it firmly. Ai-ling covered her mouth, but Mei saw the corner of a smile.

Jun climbed onto the rope and walked across it, stopping halfway between the two balloons. He looked down at the fog, then shouted to his friends, "Cut the rope." His friends began singing, their voices breaking at the high notes:

> As wind is to the bird
> As language to the word
> As music to my song
> Without you, I'm all wrong.
> Give me a shove, give me a push.
> As I fall, hear the whoosh,
> My rosebush.
> As wind is to the wing
> Please, love, hear me sing.
> My voice may crack and sway
> But I mean it anyway.
> Give me a push, give me a shove.
> I'm like a dizzy dove,
> So in love.

One of Jun's friends held out a small pillow on which lay a slim jade knife. With great care, he severed the rope from their basket. Jun grabbed the rope as it fell, swinging down so that he hung directly below Ai-ling's balloon, holding tight.

"Ai-ling, I am at your mercy," Jun shouted over the wind. "Unhook the rope and be done with me. Or invite me into your home, into your heart, into your family, and save my life." Ai-ling looked at her parents, waiting.

They spoke in unison. "The decision is yours, daughter. We pray that we've raised you healthy, happy, strong and wise, and now you will choose your own life." Confused, Mei looked from parent to parent and then to Ai-ling for some clue as to what was happening.

"Mother and Father," Ai-ling answered, a tear running down her cheek, "you have raised me healthy, happy, strong and wise, and now I choose to begin a new life with this man I love." She tugged strongly on the rope. Her parents stood behind her and helped pull, and Mei joined the party and pulled with every bit of strength she could muster until Jun was in the basket. He smoothed his robe and ran his fingers through his hair, grinning widely.

Ai-ling's father manoeuvred the balloon so that it was directly beneath Old Hug. The giant platform had been decorated with paint and colourful streamers. Birds circled above in impressive formations, putting on a show for the villagers. Two giant falcons the size of hang gliders dived together through a circle of smaller birds, then levelled out as the circle spread like ripples of water. The smaller birds flanked the two hawks, and the entire flock flew through the Sky Village, weaving in and out of the net of ropes.

Ai-ling turned to Mei. "I told you today was a special day. Jun and I are getting married! We chose to wait for your arrival because I wanted you to be my feather girl."

"Me?" Mei asked, trying to make sense of this bizarre situation. What did a feather girl have to do? Land dwellers' marriages were much less complicated affairs.

"You are our good-luck charm, Dragonfly, and now our fortunes will be linked for ever with yours." Mei blinked back tears as Ai-ling placed a crown of small feathers on her head. She could tell from the excited faces surrounding her that this was a tremendous honour. Ai-ling reached to hug her, and Mei held her tight, surprised by how good it felt to be part of a family again.

FEATHER GIRL

Ai-ling's mother served tea and fruit as Jun and his friends joined the party.

Mei was startled by the sound of a thousand explosions. A bamboo yacht suspended from four balloons lurched up next to them, long strings of fireworks trailing like a crackling comet tail. Inside, an old woman waved. She was tall and straight with a shock of silver in her black hair.

"Old Su, you're just in time," Ai-ling's father shouted. "Come, have some tea."

Old Su shouted, "A cup of tea with old friends is what separates us from the beasts and meks."

Ai-ling explained, "Old Su is Jun's mother. She was also your mother's caretaker after your grandparents passed away." Old Su tethered her balloon to theirs and climbed aboard.

"Greetings, my new family. Ai-ling, you look like a thousand sunrises." She turned to Mei and studied her for a moment. "So, you are Pei-shan's daughter. Such pretty hair. But I see a storm behind your eyes."

Mei kept her gaze on the elder and gave a quick nod.

"Little Dragonfly," Old Su continued, "we're glad to have you back. Don't you worry about your mother. She's stubborn as a mountain top. She'll make those meks sorry they crossed her path." Mei couldn't help but smile, imagining her mother getting the best of a group of meks.

Old Su took the cup of tea Ai-ling offered her.

"Thank you, daughter-to-be," she said to Ai-ling. She took a sip and looked at Mei again. "I hope you enjoy our fresh air, and be careful not to fall out! Gravity is the invisible arm of the earth monster hungry to grab and eat you!" Her shoulders moved up and down as she laughed.

Not funny, Mei thought. Old Su's sense of humour was as bad as Breaker's.

The three elders convened in the centre of the basket, drinking tea with lotus seeds and red dates, as the couple kneeled in front of them. At the bidding of their elders, the couple paid homage to heaven and earth, then the Kitchen God, and finally their ancestors. Jun lit sticks of incense and inserted them into bowls. A cloud of fragrant smoke wafted around them. Mei watched, her arms wrapped around the bag of feathers Ai-ling had given her, imagining herself as a bride, her hair piled high, wearing a traditional silk dress, her mother next to her, smiling.

I wonder where Father is now. Has he found Mother and the other villagers? Has he been captured?

Mei backed away to the edge of the basket so she could look down. Below, a river's beige waters were smooth as glass, and a string of boats travelled down the centre. *It must be the Yellow River,* she thought. Her mother had talked often about it, like it was something greater than a river, a thread that bound all of China together – even its past and future.

Mei stared down into the river, imagining her fingertips slicing through the freezing water as she swam all the way home, to the ruins of her village.

"Dragonfly," Ai-ling said, touching Mei gently on the shoulder. "The feathers."

Everyone was looking at Mei, amused smiles on their faces. Ai-ling directed her to hand one brightly coloured feather to each person in the basket, starting with Ai-ling and Jun, who knelt in the centre, then everyone else, who formed a circle around the couple.

When Mei was finished, they all lowered their heads.

Old Su cleared her throat and began to speak. "You know you've grown old when you're always called on to speak first," she said. "But one good thing about being my age is that my memory is long, and if there's one thing those of us with long memories are good for, it's reminding people how difficult our struggle has been so they won't forget how lucky we are and will pass our rituals on to new generations."

They held their feathers towards the centre of the circle so that they touched, forming a crown over Ai-ling and Jun.

"Ai-ling and Jun. Before I bless your union, it's my responsibility to remind you that we exist today only because your elders found a way to survive the tragedy that befell the lands below us. It's up to you, your children and your grandchildren to uphold the ways that have preserved us."

Ai-ling and Jun nodded.

Old Su continued. "The Sky Village is more than a collection of balloons tied with ropes. It's the villagers weighing us down, and the fire pushing us up. It's the birds protecting us from meks and feeding from our grain. It's the cold, thin air filling the empty spaces between our homes. It's our babies and those on their last breath, and the joys and hardships that fill the space between. It's Low Watch and High Watch, and ten thousand eyes between, always watching our brothers and sisters below, but keeping to ourselves. And at the heart of everything are our young families. You, Ai-ling and Jun, must be the hook rope, connecting all."

The wedding party raised their heads and opened their eyes.

"I've rambled long enough!" said Old Su. "I wish you the best of luck on behalf of the entire village and all of the ancestors who have passed away. You make us all proud. Let's get on with the celebration! I'm hungry!"

As soon as the ceremony ended, a beaming Ai-ling hugged Mei. "We're going up to Old Hug so the other villagers can tease us while the cooks get the banquet ready."

Mei was eager to be part of this celebration. What other strange foods and snacks might they have? What songs and dances had they developed? Would any of them be the ones her mother had secretly taught her?

Mei bravely followed the others up the rope ladder to Old Hug. It was already crowded. The balloons sagged with the weight, but others were being inflated to keep the platform afloat. Wide tables covered with treats lined the circular dance floor. Ai-ling was drawn into a gauntlet of hugs, and Mei wandered off by herself, sampling from the tables: dumplings made from the wild boar – Mei still couldn't bring herself to eat them, though they looked lovely; tiny pigeon eggs painted with scenes too small and detailed for the naked eye; turnip cakes cut in the shape of kites. Large cauldrons of soup boiled between the tables. Plates of seed were placed around the circle, and birds of all kinds crowded around them.

As Mei was peeling the shell of a pigeon egg, she saw Sumi approach, flanked by two other girls. "We heard you can't walk on the ropes," Sumi said. The other two giggled.

"In my village we don't have to walk on ropes," Mei said. "We live in houses, not balloons."

"Houses are stuck to the ground," Sumi said. "Balloons can go anywhere."

"Do you even know how to operate a balloon?" Mei asked. If she was going to put up with this kind of rudeness, she could at least try to get some information. How to operate a balloon was something she would need to know.

Sumi glanced at her two friends and grinned. "You can't learn balloons until you're seventeen," she said. Then she added in a whisper, "But I know how already."

Seventeen? Mei couldn't wait five years. She needed to know now, in case they found the mek army. She didn't bother to say goodbye to Sumi and her friends as she slipped away from the festivities and returned down the ladder to Ai-ling's balloon.

The balloon's heating element was high overhead, near the opening, and Mei had to balance on two stools to get a closer look. The controls looked simple enough – a lever and a few buttons for adjusting the heat inside the balloon, and then a small windmover hanging from the side of the basket. She put her hand on the lever, just to get a feel for it, and imagined herself pushing the buttons, pulling the lever, speeding low across the landscape in search of her parents.

She opened the pouch and allowed Feifei to flitter out and land on her hand. She stroked the creature's soft fur, soothed by Feifei's tiny purr. Feifei buzzed around like a mosquito, far more agitated than usual. Mei pulled the lever down slightly, and the flame increased just enough for the basket to strain against its hook ropes.

"That's just silly," she said. "Down means up." She pushed the lever back up, and the balloon settled back into place.

"Easy enough," she said, satisfied with her mastery of ballooning. "Should we do it now, Feifei? Just take off? We might not get another chance?" She scratched her pet's belly with the tip of her finger. Her father would be furious that she was even thinking about it. She wondered whether she was capable of doing something so bold. Breaker would do it, she was certain.

"I have to get some supplies," Mei told Feifei. "You'll have to stay inside your pouch, so you don't make a scene and get us caught."

Feifei chattered angrily and crawled up Mei's hair, dancing around on the top of her head to avoid Mei's grasping hand.

Finally, Mei gave up. "Fine, you don't have to go in the pouch. But how are we going to hide you?"

Feifei leaped off Mei's head and circled her a few times, then landed on her palm. She spread her wings out wide, so that they just covered Mei's hand. Then the wings stiffened so that Feifei looked like an unusual hair clip. Mei smiled and lifted Feifei to her head. Feifei hugged her braid, tight as a clasp.

As Mei prepared to climb the ladder to Old Hug, thinking about how she might gather food without rousing suspicion, a hook rope bit into the basket inches from her hand. Mei jumped back with a shriek. The intricately carved wooden hook looked like a small dragon biting the edge of the basket.

Sumi pulled up alongside the basket in a small balloon, stopping a few metres away.

"Come here," she said in a mischievous whisper.

Mei looked up warily, expecting a trick.

"Hurry," Sumi said, her whisper now bordering on a shout.

"How?" Mei asked, looking at the rope. She already knew the answer.

"What do you mean, how?" Sumi asked. She sighed and scrambled across the rope, flinging herself over the edge of Ai-ling's basket and landing with a thump next to Mei.

Sumi thrust out her hand, revealing a miniature hot-air balloon as long as Mei's arm, with a dragonfly embroidered across the fabric. She handed it to Mei, with smiling eyes that betrayed her serious manner.

"Let's play kites!" Sumi said.

14
HIGH WATCH

Kites?" Mei took a closer look at the miniature balloon and realized it was made of paper-thin cloth with the finest of strings trailing out from the basket base.

Sumi leaped over the side of Mei's basket and walked a few steps onto the rope. She looked back at Mei.

"Are you coming?" Sumi asked, a puzzled look on her face.

"Can't we play kites from here?"

"Of course not. We have to get up high." Sumi was almost across the rope. Mei put her hands and a foot on the rope, her knees shaking. She looked down. A herd of beasts racing across a grassy plain looked like rolling pebbles. She stepped back into the basket.

"What's the matter?" shouted Sumi.

"I can't do it," Mei said, her voice trembling. She was too shaken to hide her fear, and tears welled in her eyes.

Sumi looked astonished. "Of course you can. Everyone can. Just do it. Don't look down."

Mei tried again, but terror gripped her. "I can't. Just go without me."

Sumi looked embarrassed for the new girl. "Land walkers!" She shook her head. "Wait a second. I have another idea."

Sumi ran back to Mei.

"Dragonfly, we'll go with the emergency back-up plan. You don't have to walk on the ropes, but we'll need to go through Old Hug," she said.

Mei looked at the dragonfly embroidered on her balloon.

"Did you know my mother called me Dragonfly?" she asked.

"Everyone knows," Sumi said, scrunching up her face. "Your parents stole you away from us when you were a baby. The old folks whisper about it with frown wrinkles in their foreheads."

"My mother didn't steal me. She's my mother, so I was hers to take." Sumi's blunt honesty was a surprise. Why did everyone here seem to know so much about her?

"By the way," Sumi continued, "my friends call me Morning Bird."

Mei was far from ready to consider Sumi a friend. "Why do they call you that?"

"Grandfather is Morning Man, and I help him make the morning meal. And I have to chase the birds away from human food, so I'm Morning Bird."

"Have you lived here your whole life?"

"Of course. I was born here. Grandfather left land walking during the Trinary Wars. So are you coming or not?"

Mei wanted to ask more questions, but Sumi was already halfway up the ladder.

"Right behind you."

They climbed up the ladder to Old Hug and hid behind a row of rainwater barrels. The wooden platform curved hundreds of metres in both directions like a giant boomerang, spotted with squat pagodas. A throng of villagers had already gathered, and others were on their way. Children played tag, and adults congregated around Ai-ling and Jun. They appeared to be having a contest to see who could give the most drunken, rambling toast. Morning Man was giving it his best.

"Nobody's looking this way," Sumi whispered loudly. "Hurry." She scuttled across the platform, ducking behind barrels and crates. Mei followed, wondering what would happen if they were spotted.

They sprinted from one barrel to the next until they were out of sight. As they raced down the centre of Old Hug, people emerged from below and dropped from ropes and ladders connected to balloons above. They were joining the celebration and paid no attention to Sumi and Mei.

The girls arrived at Morning Man's balloon and crept up the ladder into the basket.

"Won't your grandfather get angry?" Mei asked.

"He's busy toasting Ai-ling and Snaggletooth. It'll keep him busy for hours. He loves being the centre of attention, even if he acts like he doesn't."

"But won't we get in trouble if someone sees us?" Mei asked.

"That's an understatement," Sumi said. She grabbed one of the ropes and unhooked it from the next balloon. The balloon jerked, and Mei was certain they would fall. Instead, they floated up.

Sumi grinned the way she had when Mei first saw her. "Let's race to the top."

"What? I don't know how to fly a balloon."

"Just do what I was doing," Sumi yelled as she jumped out of the balloon and into a smaller one just below it.

Mei's balloon kept rising. Mei stared at the controls, paralysed. She was trapped. Then, she recognized her opportunity.

"I can do this," she said to herself, remembering how quickly she'd figured out the controls earlier. She turned the lever to lower the flame, and the balloon slowed a bit, allowing her a moment to get her bearings. She let the wind push the balloon a few feet and then turned the heat up again. The balloon floated skyward.

Before she could congratulate herself, however, Sumi shouted from the other balloon, "Dragonfly, watch out for the seedbaggers."

Two balloon lengths above her, Mei saw a tight web of ropes, with teenage boys playing around the centre. They kicked the small bag of seeds back and forth while clinging to ropes with their hands. The only open area was directly in the centre, and it looked barely large enough for a balloon to pass through. Mei grabbed at the controls, but she didn't know which one to use. She panicked at the thought of crashing into the boys.

"Move! Get out of the way!" she cried, but the wind carried her words in the wrong direction. A foot off to either side and she would hit the ropes, knocking the seedbaggers into the sky.

She pulled the lever slightly, and the balloon tilted right, but too far. She shifted the lever again, and the balloon veered sharply to the left. Just as the balloon reached the web, she shifted it into place. As it passed through the centre, the boys waved and shouted "sky racer" and "gravity slayer", which Mei didn't know how to take. Were they making fun of her for not knowing how to operate a balloon, or applauding her for making it through the tight gap? A few clutched the side of her basket and held on, shouting more names at Mei, and then jumped off, grabbing the ropes below as they fell, cheering and giggling all the while.

A minute later, the girls arrived at the uppermost layer, Sumi's balloon beating Mei's by seconds. Sumi threw a hook rope to connect her balloon to Mei's and scrambled over. Mei wobbled a bit, trying to find her balance.

"Congratulations," Sumi said. "You made quite an impression on the seedbaggers."

Mei was still trying to calm herself. "If it takes almost committing murder to get a boy's attention around here," Mei said, "I'll just keep my distance."

Sumi grabbed a rope ladder that was suspended in midair, leading to a large balloon directly above them. "That's High Watch. It's the highest point in the village. There's another one, Low Watch, below." Sumi climbed up the rope without looking back. Mei paused and gulped, then climbed after Sumi. Finally, they reached High Watch, where a man sat on a stool gnawing absentmindedly on dried cuttlefish.

"Hi, Master Watcher," Sumi said. "Can we go up top?"

"Your grandfather will Kitchen Moon me if he finds out, Morning Bird."

"It's Gicheon Mun," Sumi said, giggling, "and you know he doesn't practise the fighting arts any more."

"Once a master, always a master. I've seen him kicking the air and cutting words in the sky with a bamboo stick."

"That's just his way of exercising. Come on, Dragonfly has never been up here."

"Ah, Dragonfly." A look of sadness came over his face.

"Things haven't been the same here since your mother left. The birds grow more troublesome every year."

Master Watcher looked Mei up and down, shaking his head a bit. "You are the image of your mother. All right. Go on up," he said, waving his hand at them. "Don't let anyone see you!"

"Only the high birds can see us up there," Sumi responded, already letting the balloon rise higher, with but a single rope connecting them to High Watch.

Master Watcher shouted, "The birds have been acting strange lately, and I've spotted flying meks in the area. Keep an eye out."

As they rose straight up in Morning Man's balloon, far above High Watch and the hundreds of balloons below it, Mei felt sick, and she ducked down in the basket. *Don't look down,* she told herself.

"Dragonfly, you're just like a baby bird," said Sumi. "With fuzz instead of feathers, afraid of up and down."

"I climbed all the way up here, didn't I?" Mei demanded. She stood up as the balloon continued rising. It was one thing to be down lower with balloons and ropes all around, but it was quite another to be at the top, where the sky stretched out in every direction like an endless ocean of air.

When they were several balloon lengths above High Watch, Sumi attached bamboo cylinders to the bottoms of the kites, and she and Mei threw them into the air and let them rise until they looked as small as bats.

"What are the containers for?" Mei asked. It had grown colder, and Mei wished she'd brought a warmer vest. A cold gust ripped past, shaking the basket.

"You'll see," Sumi said with a grin.

Sumi beamed up at the kites as they disappeared into a small cloud. After a moment, she looked at Mei and said, "I heard some of the elders talking. They said meks killed everyone in your village."

"They're not dead," Mei snapped. "They've just been captured. And my father will find them. You shouldn't listen to rumours!" More quietly, she added, "My father will save them."

Sumi stared at Mei unfazed, her mouth pursed. She lowered her eyebrows. "So, can I ask you something impolite?"

"Why not," Mei said. She tugged at her kite, and it zoomed out of the cloud and into view.

"I've heard land walkers are afraid of heights. Are you afraid of heights?" She tugged her line, and her kite levelled next to Mei's.

Mei hesitated. She wasn't sure she wanted to share any more with Sumi, but she didn't have any friends here. And something about Sumi's forthrightness made her seem ... if not friendly, then at least easy to understand. "I don't like heights, but I can deal with them. What I'm afraid of is falling."

Mei saw a look of recognition in Sumi's eyes. Sumi glanced around and spoke quietly. "That's a common nightmare in our village, especially among younger children. But it's not something to talk about. You dream you're falling through the air and there are no ropes or anything to grab, and the earth monster's green face is racing up at you!"

Mei thought the dream sounded terrifying, but Sumi giggled and pulled on her kite. The sky villagers saw the earth the way Mei saw the sky, as a strange place where you can discover faces and other shapes if you look hard enough.

The fog and clouds had cleared, and even from this height, Mei could see the ground. It was still frightening to look down, and Mei felt nauseous. They had just crossed into desert lands, where the wrinkled ground was the colour of rust.

Sumi pointed at a string of mountains capping a crater. "That one looks like Grandfather." She giggled until her face turned red.

The mountains did seem to form a deeply wrinkled forehead above a sour and sunken face, and Mei couldn't help but laugh.

"It's even his skin colour," Mei said.

"The colour of rust," Sumi said. "But don't ever say that to him. He'll think you're calling him a mek."

Mei thought about the meks she'd seen her father fight, and the army of meks the Tree Book had shown her. All of the different shapes and sizes were fascinating, but it was frightening to think there was no way of reasoning with them. Once they were on a mission, they would continue until they succeeded or were destroyed.

"Have you ever seen a mek?" Mei asked.

"The birds keep them away," Sumi said. "But I did see some once, in the distance, when a few balloons landed for repairs. And if you use Master Watcher's far-seeing glass, sometimes you can spot them in the air."

"I've been chased by meks," Mei said.

"I don't believe you. You'd be dead or captured. Hey, look over there." She pointed at another patch of mountains, a colour between green and grey. She began tracing the shape with her finger. "That one looks just like a mek."

Mei traced the rest with her finger. "I can see the small head."

"With horns," Sumi added. "Sometimes they wear pieces of the beasts they kill." Mei found this hard to believe. Sumi was probably just trying to shock her.

"And the big shoulders," Mei said as she continued tracing the figure with her finger. "One long arm that goes to its feet, and another short arm."

"With pincers at the end," Sumi said, pointing at two curving lines of green. Remembering the kite, she looked up and began pulling it in. Mei followed, and soon the kites were back in the basket.

Sumi pulled the bamboo cylinder off her kite and showed it to Mei. Inside was finely crushed ice. "Cloud ice," she said. "When it gets unstuck, it's called rain!"

Mei pulled the container off her own kite. Sumi sprinkled a dark red liquid over hers, then Mei's. "Cherry juice," she said.

It was the most delicious thing Mei had ever tasted. She was so absorbed in the fluffy texture of the ice that it was a moment before she noticed Sumi had gone silent and pale. She was pointing out at the sky.

"Look over there." A flock of birds had just started circling high above. "And over there." Another flock was flying towards them. As Mei studied them, she could see they had claws almost as large as their bodies, and the sun glinted off their wings.

Feathers don't shimmer like that, Mei thought, *only metal.*

Meks.

15

PROTECTION OF THE BIRDS

The birds and the meks converged and circled one another. A mek scout separated from its group and headed towards Mei and Sumi. Before it could get far, the front row of birds – an eagle, a hawk and three sparrows – split from their flock and dived on the scout mek, tearing it into nuts and bolts, then returned to formation.

"Something must be wrong," Sumi whispered. "The birds never let them come this close." She was breathing hard.

Mei felt Feifei's grip on her braid tighten.

The two flocks hovered, as if waiting for the other to make the next move. Mei ducked into the basket, trying to hide, but she could not take her eyes off the scene in front of her.

As if by a silent command, the meks narrowed their formation into the shape of a dagger and flew into the birds, dividing the flock in two. Their metal claws ripped into the larger birds and hurled the smaller ones across the sky. Then the dagger veered around for another attack.

The birds abandoned their formation and dived, surrounding the meks in a shroud of flapping wings and snapping beaks. Mei stood, forgetting her terror, lost in the scene as she watched wires and feathers fall from the sky. Her whole life she'd heard stories about the Trinary Wars, which had raged for decades. But that was before she was born. Now she was witnessing an actual battle.

Seeing it now, in front of her, she wondered why the beasts and meks had started fighting again. And why had they started fighting in the first place? What had started this conflict that had forced humans into hiding? She'd heard the myth of West Wind, the scientist who'd nearly destroyed the world. But what was the real story?

A single mek separated from the battle and sped towards the girls.

"It's coming right at us!" Mei shouted.

Sumi shouted back. "The birds are supposed to protect us!"

Mei grabbed the lid of a bamboo rice barrel just as the mek dived at her, its metal claws and teeth glinting in the sunlight. The mek slammed into the lid, knocking Mei onto her back. Sumi shrieked as she backed towards the edge of the basket. The mek rose again into the air and faced Sumi, extending its razor claws as it hovered.

Mei held the bamboo lid tight, like a shield, but she knew she needed something large to kill the mek. The bamboo barrel was far too heavy.

She clenched her fists, and her nostrils flared. Her blood felt hot as it pulsed through her body. Feifei trembled in her hair. Mei had never been so angry, or so scared, or felt so alive.

As the mek dived on Sumi, Mei lifted the rice barrel with a grunt, held it over her head, and slammed it down over the mek, trapping it inside. Sumi looked up at Mei in astonished silence. Mei could hear her own heart pounding in her ears, the adrenalin surging through her veins. She wanted to uncover the mek and rip it to pieces.

She felt so strong now, supremely powerful, as if she could dive from the basket and fall a mile to the ground, land on her feet, and take out an entire mek army.

As the mek thrashed inside the barrel, Mei calmed herself, allowing cold logic to order her brain. She looked around the basket, seeing it only as geometric shapes, wind speeds, and trajectories racing through her mind. Feifei relaxed as she clung to Mei's braid.

"Mei, are you OK?" Sumi said in little more than a whisper. Mei stared at her friend, but saw her only as a potential obstacle to the task at hand. But what was the task? It buzzed in the back of Mei's mind, just out of grasp.

The mek quieted, and Mei was able, somehow, to sense its brain. The cold single-mindedness, the passionless efficiency. Sumi, standing in front of her now, seemed like little more than a beast, sweating and breathless. Was this human creature, weak and fearful, going to interfere with Mei's task?

What was the task? Like clearing weeds from a field, Mei pushed her feelings completely out of the way. Then she saw what she had to do. Free the mek.

She pushed the barrel over, and the mek rose into the air and hovered in front of her. She held her arm out, and it landed there gently, its razor claws retracted. Mei hummed a few mechanical notes, completely without melody. The mek hummed the exact notes back at her.

"Dragonfly," Sumi whispered. "The birds."

Mei looked up. They were surrounded by eagles, sparrows and other birds, gliding slowly in a close circle. They had apparently won the battle, as the mek forces were nowhere to be seen. The birds hovered, staring directly at Mei and the mek on her arm.

The largest of the eagles was clearly the leader. Its wings stretched out so far they cast a shadow over Mei. Something in the way it looked at her caused a shift inside her, and she was suddenly frightened. She screamed as she realized what was on her arm. She heard a tiny shriek from Feifei. Mei tried to shake off the mek, but its metal claws dug into her flesh as it leaped into the air. The large eagle grabbed the mek as two other birds ripped at its wires with their beaks and talons. The mek went still, its eyes dull, and the eagle let it drop, its gaze still on Mei.

The birds faced Mei again. She could feel their violent fear of her like a terrible itch across her whole body. They had seen her communicate with the mek. They were ready to destroy her, and she them. Mei closed her eyes as this new, intense feeling enveloped her. Feifei's body began growing warm, and then hot, and Mei felt a tingling sensation spread across her scalp and down her back, like when her mother brushed her hair so long that her head felt like a waterfall.

I'm Mei, from Luo Ye Village. I'm human. I'm the daughter of Pei-shan and Kai. I'm Mei. I'm their little Dragonfly. As these thoughts swam through her mind, she imagined her mother humming the old songs. She felt weak and scared, but slowly began to feel like herself again.

It was too late. The birds dived at her, their talons and beaks ready to destroy her. As soon as they touched her, though, they shrieked and bounced off. The smaller birds fell unconscious into the basket, and the larger ones reeled into the sky to regain their senses before diving again.

Mei felt a force emanating from Feifei, and she knew that the tiny creature was somehow protecting her. But Feifei's grip weakened as the attack continued. Sumi tried to help, but the birds drove her back. Mei grabbed the bamboo basket lids and smacked what birds she could, but they were everywhere.

Feifei's grip relaxed, and she fell to the floor of the basket. The tingling sensation stopped, and Mei felt suddenly vulnerable. The large birds honed in for another attack.

Then they dived, pinching and scratching her scalp and neck with their beaks and talons. Mei screamed just as she heard the thwap of an arrow, and then another, and another, followed by a screechy squawk. Then there was silence. She looked up just as the eagle leader, its wing pierced by an arrow, dropped from view. Morning Man stood in a nearby balloon, bow in hand, shouting.

Mei knew something profound and terrible had just happened, but she couldn't make sense of it. She just wanted to be away from this horrible place, back on the ground, safe with her mother and father. She bent down to look at Feifei, who was unresponsive but still breathing. Mei hurriedly scooped her up and put her gently into the pouch.

Morning Man threw a hook rope and raced across it to their balloon. He seized the controls, and the balloon plummeted downward so quickly it felt as if they were free-falling. Mei and Sumi clung to the edge of the basket. It finally jerked to a stop, tossing the two girls to the floor.

Morning Man glared at them and spat a few stern words to Sumi in Korean, then he scurried across the ropes in the direction of the Sky Council.

The girls looked at each other.

"He's angry," Sumi said. "I'd better go alone."

"Are you going to get in trouble for stealing the balloon?"

"It's not so much that. He's angry that I went with you. You've got beast and mek in your blood, like your mother," Sumi said shakily. "Grandfather told me to stay away from you. He said you were going to bring trouble. I should have listened to him!"

Mei left the balloon, stunned. It didn't make any sense. What did he mean she was part beast and part mek? And her mother, as well? Morning Man must be making up these lies, Mei thought, just to keep his granddaughter away from the land walker.

Back in her balloon with the Tree Book open in her lap, Mei had so much to ask that she didn't know how to begin. The symbols swirled in the corner as she waited for the rumbling voice of Animus. It had said it was human, animal and machine. Did that mean that she was like Animus? The symbols disappeared and were replaced by a drawing of Breaker. He was in his bed with the book on his lap. He looked like he hadn't slept in days.

"How is it possible for us to have mek and beast inside us, Breaker?"

Ramirez says the gene is from some old science, back before the Trinary Wars. My father had it, and that's why he could demonsmith without the tech. It's also why he lost his mind.

"Morning Man says my mother was able to communicate with the birds. But why is this happening to us? What if we can't control it, Breaker?"

In a few hours, I have to conjure a demon for the first time. So I guess I'll find out.

16

THE AVENUE

Diamond Teeth arrived at his office flanked by guard demons and the boy with the shaved head. Rom was exhausted. He'd been up all night talking with Dragonfly. They'd come up with a lot of questions, but few answers.

"Ready, killer?" asked Diamond Teeth.

"I'll do whatever you want," Rom said. "But not until I see that my sister is OK."

"You don't trust me?" asked Diamond Teeth.

"You kidnapped my sister and are holding me prisoner."

"But I've been pretty up-front about all of that."

"I need to see her," said Rom.

Diamond Teeth shrugged. He nodded to the boy with the shaved head. "Bring her in, Aiko."

It seemed like a long time before Aiko returned. He glared at Riley as he led her into the room. Her arm was scraped, and her hair was dirty and tangled. She looked as if she'd been crying.

Rom lunged for her. He wasn't going to let them steal her away again. At the same moment, Riley picked up her foot and slammed it down on Aiko's. He yelped and let go of her arm.

So he wasn't as tough as he looked, Rom thought.

Riley kicked Aiko in the shin, then ran towards Rom, tears mixed with the anger in her eyes. She hugged Rom hard. She was shaking.

Diamond Teeth's demon guards sprang into action, effortlessly pinning Rom to the ground and dragging Riley across the room.

Diamond Teeth laughed. "She's like an evil little monkey. She must have inherited some beast tendencies from your father, huh?" He looked around as if anyone besides him would find this amusing.

"Are you OK, Riley?" asked Ramirez.

"They won't tell me what's going on," said Riley. "They're keeping me in a room all by myself. The fake light makes me feel sick."

"Three meals a day and a clean room is hardly torture," said Diamond Teeth defensively.

"It is if there's nothing to do," said Riley.

Rom shot her a look that he hoped she understood as "keep quiet and stay safe". It was clear he couldn't break her out of here by force. He'd have to be clever and didn't want her screwing it up with one too many smart comments.

Diamond Teeth frowned. "All right, that's enough family face time." He nodded at Aiko. "Take her back. If she attacks you again, let one of the demons drag her around by the hair for a while until she learns some manners."

Aiko pulled her through the doorway.

"Let me go. Leave me alone!" Riley shouted. "Rom!"

There was nothing Rom could do. He stood with clenched fists, his knuckles pale, his eyes on the carpet, as her screams faded away. For the first time in years, he felt completely powerless. His body shook, and his fingernails cut into his palms as he tried to control himself. "You'd better hope nothing happens to her," Rom said.

Diamond Teeth jabbed a fat finger at Rom. "*You'd* better hope you can demonsmith," he said. "The Grotto can be a rough place for a little girl."

Rom, Ramirez and Diamond Teeth left the office and passed through a series of cramped tunnels. Electric lights illuminated the path at regular intervals. Ramirez tried to stall, pleading for food, drink and a bit of time to rest after the bruising journey, but Diamond Teeth ignored him. Ramirez had to jog to keep up.

They emerged from the last narrow tunnel and into a wide underground avenue. It wasn't much brighter than the tunnels at first, but off in the distance were more lights than Rom had ever seen in one place. At first, only a few stray people milled around or slept on the street, but the area ahead, beneath the blazing lights, teemed with people.

"The Avenue," Diamond Teeth said. "Where fortunes are made."

"And lost," Ramirez mumbled.

The streets were lined with buildings in much better condition than those aboveground. Balls of light the size of pumpkins dangled over even the tallest buildings, illuminating every inch of the Avenue. Everywhere there was activity: people, tents, noise, music spilling from the buildings and onto the streets.

Above the caves, in the beast-run streets of Las Vegas, the few people who had remained were little more than eyes peeking through boarded-up windows, dressed in homespun rags. But the cave residents dressed in luxurious finery in the fashion of Diamond Teeth. The men wore garish top hats, bejewelled capes and lacy sleeves. The women wore long dresses that bustled when they walked. Others, ragged newcomers who had clearly travelled long distances, took in the sights with wide eyes. New arrivals exchanged weapons and preserved food for copper nuggets, which they carried in ornate bags of leather or silk.

People hurried in and out of shops, taverns and the game houses that ran the length of the Avenue. Rom was impressed. No wonder everyone wanted to come here. All that was above was filth, hunger and attacking beasts. This was a real city, like the ones in books. The buildings, most of them the colour of gold and studded with diamonds, flashed in the electric lights. They had real glass windows – no cracks, no grime – through which you could see cave dwellers hunched over gambling tables drinking fermented fruit juice.

A few large cages dangled over the street. Inside were live beasts, trapped and angry. They were cleaner than the beasts Rom had encountered. Their fur shone in the electric lights, and they were ornamented with ribbons. It was a reminder that humans were in charge down here. The gamblers occasionally stopped to stare and shout insults, but they never got too close. Such a thing would have been unimaginable up above.

As the trio made their way down the cobblestone street, activity paused. Sun-starved men removed their hats and bowed to Diamond Teeth. Ashen-faced ladies fanned themselves melodramatically, as if overwhelmed in the presence of a figure as powerful as the sparkly toothed gangster.

Activity didn't stop for long – the caves were about winning and losing, and at this moment, as in all moments of the

day, there were games to be played. The bags of copper nuggets rattled throughout the length of the Avenue, where as far as the eye could see, clusters of gamblers shoved each other to get a better view of the dice, or wheel, or whatever it was that decided their fortune. The more formal games of chance took place inside the buildings, while on the Avenue itself countless makeshift variations occupied the crowds. Nothing was too insignificant to bet on. Rom watched as anything and everything became a game of chance. Would a caged rat scratch itself if left alone on a plate for thirty seconds? Would a strong, sneering fellow shout if a needle was poked into his body? How close could an unfortunate "volunteer" get to Diamond Teeth's nearest guard demon before it attacked? Every so often, Rom would spot one of the gamblers on his knees, indifferent to the hard cobblestones and the crowds swirling around him. Rom didn't understand what was wrong until one such man in a soiled blue velvet topcoat muttered, "I'm finished. I'm done for." The man didn't protest when two of Diamond Teeth's demons dragged him away.

"Are they taking him to the Grotto?" Rom asked.

"Where all of the big losers go," said Diamond Teeth. "He's out of the game."

Rom moved along, swept up again in the pulse of activity. The damp air smelled of smoke and roasted meat. His stomach growled.

They walked for fifteen minutes, and the activity showed no sign of letting up. It seemed so pointless to Rom, all of this movement over nothing more than the accumulation of copper nuggets. "What are they gambling for?" Rom asked Ramirez.

"For more nuggets, to buy all of the luxuries the caves have to offer," he answered, pursing his lips. "Some do win big, but most lose everything eventually."

"The stakes are high," Diamond Teeth interrupted. "That's what makes it exciting." The discussion was over.

Eventually, the crowds thinned, and the noise level dropped from a roar to a murmur. The buildings here were filled with darkened windows. Signs hung over the doorways, illuminated by crude torches. ROOMS FOR RENT. HARD MONIES ONLY. One sign was especially honest: DIRTY BUT CHEAP. This was where the gamblers slept, Ramirez told Rom, when they grew too exhausted to stand. Guttural snores rumbled through the open windows.

The path curved left and became a wide, dark tunnel. Diamond Teeth seemed to swell in anticipation as they walked, and Ramirez stopped his pained grunts. This street was narrower, the only illumination coming from the candles lining the walls, throwing billowing shadows across the floor and ceiling. The few residents on the street were silent, kneeling and bowing in front of the candles, staring at Rom and Diamond Teeth with upraised eyes as they passed. What were they praying for? Rom wondered. Luck? Or nuggets?

An enormous cavern glowed at the end of the tunnel. Ramirez put a protective hand on Rom's shoulder as they approached. Rom looked up and noticed the old man's head bowed reverently. His lips moved silently, mouthing a chant. "We give freely of our humanity to control the demons. Control the demons. Control the demons," he said. "And rise above the beasts."

THE PIT

Torches and candles of various sizes lined the circular arena. Tiers of stone benches rose high to the ceiling, chiselled into the cave wall. Rom could not even see the top of the massive cavern. He spun around, looked up through the flickering shadows at the empty benches, and imagined the room filled with shouting gamblers. Of course, he had no idea what it would entail, but he'd seen the creatures in action. He could only guess what sort of damage they could do to one another in a fight.

"This used to be a special place," said Ramirez.

"Still is," Diamond Teeth said.

Rom searched the arena for the demon he would try to control, but there were no hybrids to be seen.

"Take him to the Pit, Ramirez," said Diamond Teeth. "Let's see what he can do."

"Let me have that triggit," Ramirez said.

Rom handed it over, and Ramirez placed it in the centre of the ring. "The demon will form around it," he said. "At least I hope so."

Ramirez led Rom past the edge of the arena and down a narrow corridor to the Pit, which lay below the first tier of the arena's seating and out of view of the spectator seating.

Rom stepped inside and saw two stone chairs in the centre. The walls were bare. There was no sign of the newtech Rom had expected until Ramirez plucked a helmet from one of the chairs. It looked as if it had been pounded out of a sheet of thin black metal, and it resembled something an ancient gladiator might wear, but for the tiny wires that covered it.

Rom settled back into the hard chair so that he was looking up at the dark ceiling. "How am I supposed to control something that isn't there?" he asked.

"You're going to conjure it," Ramirez said, palming the helmet. "The technology uses a pattern that's already inside your head, something you probably don't even know is there. Then it grabs molecules and atoms from the air and puts them together based on that pattern."

Rom sighed. "But how do I get it to do that?"

"The demon already exists inside your subconscious. The technology just turns it into flesh and metal."

"So this thing is inside me," Rom said. He thought about what it might look like. Strong, fierce and courageous, he assumed, but also fast, and clever enough to outsmart his opponents. "If I can conjure it, then how do I control it?"

"The helmet," Ramirez said, handing it to Rom. "If you have the gift, you'll know what to do. You'll feel it. The helmet is just a tool; the real power is in your mind. If you can't—"

"We haven't got all day!" bellowed Diamond Teeth.

The helmet felt cold in Rom's hands. He placed it on his head and pulled the visor down.

At first there was only darkness. Rom panicked. How would he know whether he had the gift of the demonsmiths? What would Diamond Teeth do to his sister if he didn't?

Slowly, the black gave way to a burst of colour. Rom could sense a new intelligence emerging inside his own, forming itself out of his own secret thoughts – a mixture of hope, fear, even his nightmares. He could feel it digging and prodding as it formed. He had hoped to be in control of his demon's creation, but it was a struggle just to hold on to his own identity. A sharp pain tore through his mind, and Rom cried out. He was losing himself, drifting away from consciousness, and something else was taking over. His head throbbed and felt like it was inflating. He was certain that his brain would rupture, that he would fall into oblivion and this new thing inside him would seize control.

Just as Rom was sure the pressure couldn't grow any larger, the feeling morphed into a cool tingle that raced down his spine all the way to his feet and back up again. The blur of colour snapped into focus. He was looking at a dirt floor, but with eyes that were not his own.

Rom twitched and the floor was replaced by a view of the candles lining the edge of the arena. Rom was seeing through the eyes of a battle demon.

This is more than newtech, Rom thought. *Way more.*

"Steady!" said Ramirez. "Keep it steady! You're doing it, but your demon hasn't finished taking shape."

Ramirez's voice seemed far away. Rom tried to ask what the demon looked like, but he only succeeded in making the demon's jaw wag. It was dizzying, and Rom felt he might be sick. Just a thought, an instant, and the demon would move. It was, in one way, no different than moving your hand. Except the proportions were all wrong, and Rom had no idea what thought made what part move.

"Not one of the mightier specimens I've observed," said Ramirez.

Rom tried to ask what he meant, but he just made the demon's mouth move again.

"I wonder why it keeps moving its mouth like that," Ramirez continued. "These hybrids are engineered for fighting, not talking. Though this one doesn't look like much of a fighter."

Rom tried to tear the helmet off, so he could see how his demon had turned out, but when he tried to move his arms, his demon fell face-first into the dirt floor and then toppled over on its left side. Rom felt an ache along his own left side.

Somewhere in the distance, he could hear Diamond Teeth barking like a walrus. "This is your fighter, Ramirez?" he howled.

Rom heard Ramirez's soothing voice beside him. "Easy, Rom. Focus on your instruments. Remember that the demon is controlled by achieving a balance of human, mek and beast. Do you see the triangle on the right? It will let you know how well you're balancing. That bar on the left will tell you how much power your demon has."

Rom looked at the screen before him. Two symbols flashed on the ends of his field of vision: a bar of bright green light on the left and a flashing green triangle on the right. Around the triangle were three symbols: ⌘ ✝ ⚕. Rom jerked his eyes and he felt the demon lurch to its feet again, then crash to the ground. This time, Rom felt the pain along his right side.

"You're blowing it, boy!" shouted Diamond Teeth.

"Easy, Rom," urged Ramirez. "Don't listen to him. No one figures this out their first time. Very few figure it out at all. It's clear that you have the gift. What we need to see now is whether or not you can learn how to use it."

The demon's senses were unimaginably sharp. Rom could smell gamblers from as far away as the Avenue. The residue of sweaty bodies from thousands of fights was masked slightly by scented candles. He also detected smoke and burning circuits. The Pit had another smell, very faint: burnt human hair.

Through the hybrid's eyes, Rom saw Diamond Teeth circling the arena. He willed the creature to get up. It lurched off the ground, but when his thoughts turned to Diamond Teeth, the demon crashed with a thud. It did not hurt as badly this time, however, and Rom had figured something out. He had been thinking like the demon, as if its body were his own – up until the moment when he saw Diamond Teeth's mocking smile. In order to control the demon, Rom realized, he needed to ignore his anger at Diamond Teeth and let the demon's beast and mek aspects surge – striking an elusive balance necessary to fully control the demon.

Rom closed his eyes and breathed, telling himself that when he opened them he would no longer think of himself as Rom, but as the hybrid lying in the dirt. He would smell what it smelled, feel what it felt, and move as it moved. He would *become* the demon.

He pushed the creature up on wobbly legs and scanned the arena. He saw Diamond Teeth circling the ring with an ugly scowl. The giant candles flickered beside him, and shadows danced across his sinister face. Rom tried not to think about what had been done to his family. Diamond Teeth was only prey, and Rom was a predator.

Rom heard Ramirez say, "Maybe that's enough for one

day," but the voice was muffled, far away – as if part of a dream. Diamond Teeth skittered to the left, stumbling over his own feet.

Rom ignored the controls flashing in his vision – the bar, the triangle. He concentrated only on the form in front of him and the need to eliminate it. The demon's legs tore through the sand. Its jaws snapped and its muscles tightened. All other thoughts disappeared. Power surged through the demon's body. Rom felt the need to survive, to eliminate, to sink teeth into flesh. The demon picked up speed and leaped, every fibre of its form – and Rom's – united in the single animal instinct to kill its prey. Diamond Teeth, his face distorted in a terrified grimace, fell as Rom charged.

18

MELTDOWN

Rom heard heavy breathing. Was it his own? What had happened? His limbs were jumpy with fear. "Ramirez?" he called. He whipped his head back and forth. The room was a blur.

Rom's focus returned, and he saw Ramirez holding the helmet in his trembling hands.

They were still in the Pit. "I had to stop you," Ramirez said. He sounded worried. Rom would have thought the old man would be proud of him; not only had he conjured a demon, but he'd figured out how to control it – all on his first attempt. Rom was only disappointed he hadn't killed Diamond Teeth.

Images flooded his mind. He recalled the scene in the Tree Book where men had gathered around his fallen father after a battle. He felt again the thrilling rush of speed. But he couldn't remember the last seconds of it. "What happened?"

"I've never seen anyone gain control that fast, Rom. If I hadn't pulled the helmet..." Ramirez extended a hand to help Rom out of his chair. "You have the gift, all right."

Rom was proud he'd been able to demonsmith, but something wasn't right. Those sensations he'd felt just before Ramirez stopped him had overwhelmed him completely. He'd thought only of destroying. He'd been thinking like a beast. He'd seen the effects on his father, but he hadn't considered the risk of losing his own humanity, and what that would mean for Riley.

Had he injured Diamond Teeth? That was not likely to help him get Riley back. His head was throbbing. As soon as he stood up, pain shot through his sides. He felt dizzy and put a hand on Ramirez's shoulder for support.

"Where did the demon go? Is it dead?"

Ramirez shook his head. "Its body dematerialized. But its pattern is inside you, and it'll stay there until you conjure it again."

"How long will I feel it there?" Rom asked. He could sense the thin thread of the creature's emotions – that overwhelming physical rage – still running through his body.

"For the rest of your life," Ramirez said, frowning. He helped Rom over to a bench carved into the Pit. "Just take it easy. It takes a little while to get back to normal."

Rom did feel different, but he couldn't say exactly how. Then Diamond Teeth was standing in the doorway, his suit covered in sand. He staggered into the room like an injured bear. Rom expected the worst – some new punishment for Riley because he'd been unable to control himself – but the gangster flashed a sparkling grin. "I told you my gut is never wrong!" He limped over and handed Rom his triggit. "You're a killer, kid. An absolute killer."

SKY COUNCIL

The cloudwatching pigeons had abandoned the Sky Village. Feifei was still weak and slept most of the time. The Sky Council was in its second day of secret meetings. And Sumi was avoiding her.

There was nothing left for Mei to do but flip through the Tree Book, searching the terrible images it showed for clues to her mother's location and talking to Breaker about the kaimira gene.

Breaker hadn't been himself since he had summoned the hybrid demon.

I felt something when I controlled that demon. I didn't tell Ramirez about it because I was afraid he wouldn't let me fight, but just before he pulled off the helmet, I could feel the beast taking over. I don't want to end up like my father.

"At least he's not in a mek cage. We just need to figure out how to set Animus free. If we do, I think the Tree Book can help us. It's a tool. My mother used it. So did your father."

If my father used it, that's all the reason I need to do the exact opposite. And didn't your father tell you not to open it? Because of Animus, probably.

"That's because he thinks I'm too young to take on any responsibility."

Dragonfly, whenever something seems too good to be true, it usually is.

"What else can we do? We need help!"

"Ms Dragonfly?" came a yelp from behind her. Mei jumped and slammed the book shut.

She turned around to see Little Message, the apprentice drumliner, who always carried a small drum on a rope around his neck. The drumline was used to spread urgent announcements across the Sky Village. When a message needed to go out, Master Message or Little Message started it by beating a code in rhythm, which would be picked up and spread as villagers joined in, banging on bowls with chopsticks.

"I bid you hello, Ms Dragonfly," he muttered, looking down at his feet. "Old Su asked me to fetch you." He swallowed with some difficulty. "They want you to join the Sky Council meeting."

Mei knew she'd have to answer for the attack in High

Watch, but she still wasn't ready to face the Sky Council. Would they kick her out? Part of her wished they would, but the other part longed to be accepted. And now that she'd seen so much more of the ground below, the roaming bands of beasts, the mek settlements, she knew that battles seemed to sprout from nothing and bloom into blood-red flowers. The last thing she wanted was to be in the middle of all that conflict.

She followed Little Message to the edge of the basket. How did they expect her to get to the Sky Council meeting? She wasn't ready to walk across the ropes.

Little Message showed her to a bamboo chair bound to a wooden ring, which was looped around the rope. Strangely, the plain chair was decorated with paper flowers.

"It's the senior throne." Little Message's face grew red. "We use it for those too old to walk across the ropes. Old Su told me..." He didn't finish his sentence.

"It's fine, Little Message." She climbed into the chair as he held the hoop. He let go, and the chair zoomed down the rope, the distance of several balloons. Even in the relative security of the chair, Mei couldn't bear to look down. She clutched the chair's arms until her hands turned white. Old Su was there to catch the throne and help her out when she reached the large balloon where the Sky Council was meeting. Little Message had half run, half slid down the rope and waited there breathless, saying nothing. Old Su handed him a small bag, and he leaped onto a rope just below and ran out of sight.

"Well," Morning Man said, "shall we have our cloud-speaking, or will we allow all order to become chaos? Our Cloudwatcher must have gathered a few scraps of news before she brought the wrath of the birds down upon us."

Old Su just smiled at Morning Man and patted Mei's shoulder reassuringly. "Yes, we shall have our cloudspeaking. Our young Dragonfly has been hard at work and is eager to share."

Mei stood in front of the elders and other guests. After everything that had happened, they were asking her to report the cloudwatching? She had not been able to make much sense out of the pigeons' notes. She cleared her throat. "There were weddings and births and deaths," Mei started. She paused, looking at the faces. "More births than deaths." Old Su smiled, and Mei relaxed a little.

"The Scimurai have begun moving west, very quickly, as if they are hunting or being hunted." There was some contemptuous laughter.

"They are always hunting and being hunted," Ai-ling's father said. "They seem to have forgotten the difference between the two."

Old Su said, "What other news, Dragonfly?"

"Several reports of conflicts between meks and beasts."

Mei hesitated.

"Tell us what you're thinking," Old Su encouraged her. "Trust your instincts."

"There's a mek army. They've been spotted travelling east, a few days ahead of us. I think they're the same meks that kidnapped the people from my village."

The elders looked at one another sombrely.

Morning Man spoke. "What evidence do you have?"

"If you trace the path and calculate average walking speed, you can trace it back to Luo Ye a few days ago." Mei was proud of herself for figuring it out. But should she mention that she had seen the mek army in the Tree Book? She decided against it. "We should be able to catch up with them in two days."

The Council stood in silence. Finally Old Su spoke. "It seems our Dragonfly is more like her parents than we guessed." She looked at Mei. "Child, these are all bad signs. Our hearts still break for the conflict land walkers put themselves through. They are our family, our friends. But we've survived this long because we don't get involved, and get involved is what we can never do."

"But my mother – she was a sky villager."

"She gave up claim to that identity when she left. As long as she lives, your mother will be a land walker. It was her choice."

"But it wasn't her choice," Mei said. "She didn't choose to

love my father. It just happened." Her face felt hot, and she could tell by the circle of stares that she was shouting.

Morning Man spoke. "Don't speak about things beyond your knowledge, child. You think you can speak of love? You have no idea what we risked for her. When she abandoned us, we ignored all common sense and went back for her. And how did she repay that sacrifice? By leaving again, and taking you along with her."

Old Su raised her hand at Morning Man. "She isn't ready for that tale yet, Master Breakfast."

Morning Man grumbled. "This child has made us enemies of the birds and made a bird slayer of me. How long can we survive with her here?"

Old Su scowled at Morning Man, but then turned with seriousness to Mei. "Yes, it's time to discuss what happened in High Watch."

Morning Man interrupted, "We've been talking about it for two days. We know what happened. This one's mother had the kaimira gene, and the girl's got it in barrelfuls. The meks sensed the beast in her, and the birds sensed the mek in her, and both attacked."

Mei stared at Morning Man. "That's not how it happened," she said. "The birds were afraid of me. But I could sense that they wanted to understand me. And the mek, too. It thought of me as a puzzle, and I communicated with it somehow. And the birds tried to communicate with me, too, but I didn't know how. I just felt scared, and angry. That's why they attacked."

If she and Breaker really did have beast and mek inside them, she couldn't blame the sky villagers for being afraid. Everyone knew that beasts, meks and humans were natural enemies, starting from the moment of birth. Did this mean Mei was her own enemy? Could she trust her own feelings?

"Nonsense," Morning Man said, shaking his head. "There's no understanding birds or meks. The girl's nothing but a danger."

"Quiet, Master Breakfast," Old Su said. "We know your theories. It's time to hear it from Dragonfly's mouth."

Mei found the courage to speak. She related the events as she remembered them. When she was finished, she said, "Morning Man is right. I need to join my parents on the ground."

Old Su looked at Mei with surprise, then back at the elders. "Whatever has happened, and whatever danger it's put us in, the most important question is what is right for the child."

The council members nodded.

Old Su continued, "It is out of the question to give one of our own to the earth. It is not what we—"

"But she is not one of ours," Morning Man interrupted. "Not unless she undergoes the Learning of the Ropes and

then performs the Sky Dance to mend the rift with the birds."
It was clear that Morning Man found this idea preposterous.
Mei had no idea what any of this meant, so she just listened,
feeling like a seedbag kicked around by a cluster of children.

"Too dangerous," Old Su said. "It will take her years to
finish the Learning of the Ropes, and as for the Dance, that's
dangerous even for sky villagers. We haven't had a Sky Dance
in decades – not since Master Watcher accidentally killed a
young hawk."

"Excuse me." Mei was surprised at how small her voice
sounded next to Old Su's and Morning Man's. "What is the
Sky Dance?"

"Dragonfly," Old Su answered, "when a sky villager loses
favour with the birds, there is only one way to regain their
friendship. A ritual established long ago, by your grandfather,
called the Sky Dance. It's a way of communicating with the
birds without words, and of showing them you are one with
them."

"If I do the Sky Dance, will everyone be safe?"

Morning Man laughed harshly. "You'd fall in the first few
minutes, and then the birds would tear you apart on the way
down. Safer all around if we just drop you off in the next land-
walker village."

Mei gaped at him. How could he say such awful things to
her? But she couldn't help thinking he might be right. Maybe
it would be better for everyone if she left the Sky Village.

"Dear Mei," Old Su said, "if you were to survive the Sky Dance, there is a strong possibility the birds would forgive what happened in High Watch. But it's far too dangerous for a child."

"And impossible for a land walker," Morning Man scoffed, "who has to be transported across the ropes on the senior throne."

Mei scowled at Morning Man, looking him straight in the eye.

"It's not my fault the birds and meks were fighting. I didn't start the Trinary Wars. I just wanted to save Sumi. Why do you have to blame me for everything?"

As Morning Man opened his mouth to speak, the balloon jerked in the current. The gathered Council members didn't flinch in the least, but Mei grabbed for the side of the basket without thinking. She forced herself to look over the edge, past the clouds below. Hundreds of beasts of all species were marching together through the ruins of a human town, kicking up clouds of dust. In her nightmares she could never have imagined such a terrifying force. She realized, suddenly, how brave Breaker really was, facing these beasts every day.

"I'll do it," Mei said. She had no idea what she was agreeing to, but she knew she didn't have a choice.

Old Su looked at her gravely but remained silent for some time. Then she said, "I didn't want it to come to this, Dragonfly," she said.

"Are you crazy?" Morning Man burst out. "We're in danger *now*, and she'll never be ready for the Sky Dance."

"Then you shall be her teacher," Old Su said, pointing her walking stick at him. Morning Man choked, his eyes wide.

"I can't!" he exclaimed. "I've got responsibilities. I've got breakfast to make and Sumi to care for. She's enough of a job for three of me."

"And yet," Old Su said, "you find hours every day to sit in Low Watch spying on land walkers with your far-seeing glass."

Morning Man's face turned as crimson as a sunset.

"It will take years to train her properly," he said, "and we must do something now about our alliance with the birds. We must be judicious concerning matters of safety."

"Nonsense," said Old Su as she bopped Morning Man on the head with her stick. "Judicious is a good word, but it is often misused by cowards. The girl was born here, and leaving was not her choice. I agree we cannot wait, so we'll have the Sky Dance as soon as she's finished learning the ropes. You will have a few weeks at the most. Should she fall, then it is as fate would have it. Should she fail, we will take her to the next land-walker village and send word to her father. But if she survives and passes the dance, the birds will welcome her, as will we, despite the secrets that lurk inside her blood, and she will remain with us."

20
LEARNING OF THE ROPES

Mei spent most of her waking hours with Morning Man training for the rope-walking ritual.

"This is a serious matter," said Morning Man on the first day, "so I'll have no childishness. When a land walker joins the Sky Village, which thankfully is very rare, they have to go through the Learning of the Ropes. It usually takes years, and Old Su has given you a few weeks at the most."

"What happens if I fail?" Mei asked.

"Then you get a one-way trip back to land. The fast way or the slow way."

It was clear to Mei that Morning Man did not want to train her. Their first lesson was walking, which, Morning Man explained, required relaxed toes and confidence, neither of which Mei had.

"I saw some of the smallest children wear belts with hook ropes." Mei knew as she finished the sentence that she should not have spoken.

"You're asking for a safety belt?" Morning Man asked loudly enough for bystanders to hear. The adults looked away and the children sniggered. "Next you'll be asking me to chew your food for you like a mother bird!"

Mei glared at Morning Man's calloused feet as he laughed. "I'm sorry I don't have monster toes like yours, so I can grip the rope better!" she snapped. Morning Man's laughter stopped. She could almost feel him seething.

Then another adult nearby called, "She's right, old man! You've got talons like an ostrich!"

Everyone laughed, except Mei and Morning Man.

"Let's just get on with it," he finally grunted.

Mei couldn't bring herself to look him in the face. From then on, she decided, she would speak only when she had to. There were so many pleasant people in the Sky Village, and she was stuck with a crank who hated her and blamed her for everything. The sooner she learnt the ropes, she figured, the sooner she could get away from him.

Morning Man picked Mei up and put her on the rope just outside the basket. "Your mother really should have taught you this business. Her failure to teach you the ways of her people is even more shameful than her going off with that land walker."

Mei held tight to the side of the basket. *Mother did teach me,* she thought. *She just didn't say what the lessons were.*

"You'll have to teach your toes to hug the rope," Morning Man said, "but first we need to work on your balance. Those who grow up here don't belong to the ground, and so it does not call to them. For them, gravity is a dance. For people like us, born and raised as land walkers, gravity is the earth's silent echo, reminding us that we have no wings. Now, let go."

Mei struggled hard not to look down as she removed her shaking hands from the basket, but it was impossible. The earth loomed below like a giant mouth ready to swallow her. She wondered how Morning Man would manage to catch her if she slipped, then shivered as the answer struck her – he would let her fall. As Mei held her hands out and tried to catch her balance, she thought about who would miss her. Ai-ling might, but she would be too busy with Jun to think much of it. Sumi might miss her as well, but she already had so many friends who grew up playing on the ropes that she would soon recover from the loss. Her father might be sad, but she'd caused him so many problems that a part of him would probably be relieved. Only her mother, if she was still alive, would truly miss her. The thought of dying before seeing her mother again brought tears to Mei's eyes.

"You can't cry on the ropes," Morning Man said. "Take two steps backwards."

Mei wiped her eyes. "Shouldn't I learn to walk forward first?"

"We don't have the luxury of wasting time. If you can learn to walk backwards, walking forward will be easy."

"But I can't see anything."

"That's what your toes are for. Feel for the rope, then hug it with your toes."

Mei moved her shaky right foot back slightly, feeling for the rope with her toes. She found it and put her foot down. The spot they had chosen was protected from the wind by large balloons on three sides, but Mei felt a gust coming in from the open side, and she braced herself.

As she stood, her arms held out, she thought about the rope-walking games she played with her mother. When she was young, her mother had always walked with her, on a parallel clothesline, holding her hand in case she fell. Mei had always loved the game, especially when she made her mother proud by balancing properly. She was five the first time her mother let her walk alone. "Just imagine I'm next to you," she said. "I'll always be next to you."

At this thought, the tears came back, and Mei lost her balance. She flapped her arms, shifted the weight of her body, and tried to catch the side of the basket, but missed. As she toppled, screaming, she felt the rope slap into her body and managed to hook her left leg around it, which left her hanging upside down. She stopped screaming when she saw the earth below her, a blur of green and brown. It was too terrifying for sound. For the first time, she felt that gravity was calling up to her, telling her she had no right to be among the clouds.

"Girl, give me your hand." She strained to look up and saw Morning Man's sour face leaning over the basket. Mei reached for his hand, but it was too far away. "Fine, then, give me your foot." She stuck her right foot in his direction as far as she could stretch it. He grabbed it and hauled her back into the basket like a sack of grain. She felt a sharp pain in her leg. "Won't you at least try to focus? You've only got a few weeks, and you can't even get through the first lesson."

"I'm sorry," Mei said.

"Sorry won't get you far in the Sky Dance," Morning Man said. "It will get you yanked to a premature and no doubt dramatic death in the rice fields. We'll try again tomorrow."

Mei fumed in silence as Morning Man ambled across the rope towards his balloon. She felt an urge to cut the rope and watch him fall, and then tried to shake the violent image from her mind. How could she think such a thing? Could those terrible ideas have come from the mek inside her, or the beast?

Mei stroked Feifei's pouch. "I scare myself sometimes," she said.

21

BALANCE

Balance is not something you can just turn on and off," Morning Man said for the thousandth time. "It has to be present from the moment you wake up. Every cell in the body must be in balance."

Mei learnt to block out Morning Man's disgruntled presence and focus on the ropes. She found that if she closed her eyes and pretended to be walking on the clothesline at home, her mother nearby to catch her, humming soft, bright tunes to urge her along, she could keep her balance. But the first reminder that she was in the Sky Village – the sound of children playing seedbag, the creak of ropes as the village readjusted during the midday meal – sent her climbing back to the scowling Morning Man.

When Mei was finally able to walk backwards from one balloon to the next, she stood smiling and proud, as if her mother had been watching. Morning Man moved quickly to rope dancing. "It's one thing to maintain balance simply walking from one place to the next," he said, "and quite another when you are dancing in front of a flock of unruly birds with an eye to your demise."

Morning Man showed Mei a few steps. The exercise was a cross between a dance and a fighting art, with slow, graceful kicks and rolls. Her mother had taught her many of the moves, another of their secret games they had played while Father was away on an expedition. Mei had always suspected these games had something to do with the Sky Village, because none of her friends played them, but her mother refused to admit it, saying only that games are honey for the soul. Mei remembered the moves, but she had to relearn the footwork. At the beginning, she could barely perform a basic jump, much less a cartwheel kick. She tried pretending she was at home dancing with her friends from school, and after much effort she was able to stumble through to the end.

"This dancing tries my patience," Morning Man said. "It's nothing but a poor imitation of fighting. If you can keep your mouth closed, I'll teach you something useful." His sour expression did not change, but Mei detected the slightest trace of rebelliousness in his voice.

Mei nodded, and Morning Man began to move his limbs. He was almost cheerful as he swept his arms and legs gracefully through the air, now on one foot, now leaping and spinning with astonishing speed and force. As he went through the moves, he talked. Mei was not sure whether he was teaching her or talking to himself, but she listened. The art and philosophy of fighting had always been taboo in her village, because the elders didn't want to draw unwanted attention from the nearby mek territory. There were stories of nearby villages arming themselves, solely for defensive purposes, only to fall victim to devastating mek raids.

Violence was also frowned upon here in the Sky Village, which only fed Mei's curiosity.

"Why doesn't the Sky Village have any fighters?" Mei asked.

Morning Man stopped his movements and looked at her as if she'd just appeared out of thin air.

"It's a good question, Dragonfly," he said. "And a decades-old argument among the Sky Council. When anyone tries to show any common sense, Old Su says the same thing, that trained warriors go looking for a fight."

"You don't agree with her?" Mei asked.

"The people here don't look down often. And when they do, they only see what they want to see. It's a fiction to most of them, the battles they see, like pebbles on a Go board. But

I've been in those battles, fighting alongside men, women and even children, and none of them went looking for a fight."

Mei didn't know what to say. She tried to picture Morning Man in battle. Why had he left and joined the Sky Village?

Morning Man resumed his poses and movements. "Gicheon Mun," he said, "is about cultivating inner power. It is the gateway to heavenly energy. Strict practice will teach you to develop your own power in accordance with the principals of universal balance. It is a way to find harmony in times of increasing conflict, and to use harmony as both shield and weapon."

Mei recognized the movements at once. Her mother had practised them when her father was away, and Mei had played along, mimicking everything. Her mother had never explained the meaning or use of any of the exercises, but Mei remembered the feeling of calm and strength they brought. Could her mother have been a student of Morning Man?

Mei knew they were neglecting important lessons, but she liked seeing Morning Man in high spirits, and the familiar motions comforted her.

Morning Man introduced a second fighting style, this time using swords. In the Sky Village, swords were used only for decoration on Old Hug, and Mei wondered whether Morning Man would get in trouble for taking them. She had always loved the simple, lethal power of swords, but her father had never allowed her to hold one. Now she held the curved samurai sword in front of her, examining the chipped blade.

"This fighting style is called Hankumdo. Using the basic strike techniques, you can carve the characters of the Korean alphabet. Sumi is particularly good at this." He demonstrated, and Mei recognized more exercises her mother had taught her, using tree branches instead of swords. Mei knew the shapes back then and had guessed they were symbols of some sort, though she had no idea they were Korean characters. Practising on her own, she had changed them into Chinese and spent hours carving her thoughts into the breeze with a stick of bamboo.

"Did you teach this to my mother?" Mei asked.

Morning Man looked perturbed. "I can't be blamed for everyone who waves a stick around. Enough questions. Focus."

They spent much of the week in a secluded section of the village practising these fighting moves. When a villager wandered by, they hid their swords and resumed practising the dance.

Mei began to look forward to her training sessions. But it worried her that Morning Man had not taught her the dance.

"If you're fretting about dancing, then why have you let me waste my time all week?" Morning Man asked.

Finally, she asked him. "It's just that ... the Sky Dance—"

"You aren't going to pass the Sky Dance, Mei. The birds won't allow it."

"What do you mean?" Mei asked, bracing herself for another of Morning Man's insults.

"It's about time somebody levelled with you," he said. "Do you even know what it means that you were born with the kaimira gene?"

Mei shook her head. She had decided not to say anything about the Tree Book or Breaker, but she needed to find out what Morning Man knew. "Does it have something to do with the way I lose control over myself sometimes?"

"It has to do with more than that," Morning Man said, his expression suddenly sad. "It means you've got mek and beast in your genes, in your blood and bones, mixed in with the human. You got it from your mother, and she got it from her father. But in you it's much stronger, and it makes you dangerous, to yourself and to others. You're an abomination, and the birds have already sensed it."

Mei glared at him. What hurt the most was that she thought he was right. She felt like an abomination.

"But why me?" she asked. "Why Mother?"

"You should ask Hiro about that."

"The one who started the Scimurai?" Mei asked. "Isn't he dead?"

"Hiro doesn't die easily," Morning Man said, laughing bitterly. "Trust me on that one."

195

Morning Man clearly wasn't going to give her any more information, or even teach her the rest of the dances. "Then why have we been doing this?" Mei asked.

"Old Su is hard to argue with," Morning Man said. "And if I'm stuck with you until the dance, I should teach you something useful. You'll need to know how to fight when we send you on your way. Particularly if you disregard the wisdom of the Council and go chasing after meks."

TRAINING

Rom's body protested as he rolled over in the bed. The ache was as acute as a throbbing cut, but it was everywhere. He rubbed his arms and chest, trying to convince himself he would be all right, desperate for a few more minutes of sleep despite the pain.

He was just about to contact Dragonfly when Ramirez burst through the door. "What are you doing?" he demanded. "We're already behind schedule!"

Rom tried to listen, but he found it hard to focus. Everything looked different. Ramirez seemed transformed. All Rom could see was how weak the old man looked, his skin soft and vulnerable, his muscles sagging. Rom could push him over with one finger. He'd never had that thought before, so why did he have it now?

You're a killer. An absolute killer. That's what Diamond Teeth had said. Rom thought again of his father in the kitchen. Now Rom had accessed the beast within him. Was this his "gift"? Was this what he had inherited from his father – the ability to see and think like an animal?

Ramirez pulled Rom out of bed. "Do you think that just because you managed one demon move, you'll win the tournament?"

A breakfast of boiled oats, raisins and banana was waiting on the table. Ramirez paced back and forth while Rom ate.

"The other demonsmiths have been fighting for years," Ramirez said. "The lucky ones have trainers, and the others figure it out on their own. The more sophisticated demonsmiths are able to balance human, beast and mek, but most put everything they have into a single aspect, or even a single thought, fear or impulse. It makes them dangerous, but it takes its toll, and they don't last long."

"What sort of fighter was my father?" Rom asked.

"Your dad was an artist, the way he danced with his own feelings, turning them into weapons, taking it all the way to the edge and then pulling back. He was special, not like any of the others."

"So special he couldn't control it," Rom said.

"He could control it all right. He did things no one thought were possible. We'd been experimenting with demons a few years already before he came around. We'd found the triggits and knew they were part of some science far beyond what we could hope to understand. We managed to build some interesting gadgets out of them, then one of my men used a triggit to summon a creature like nothing we'd ever seen, a highly advanced beast-mek hybrid. We learnt how to summon and control them, and we used the fights to test them and to improve our ability to control them before taking them into battle above against the beasts.

"When your father showed up, he learnt quickly how to summon a demon without the technology. It was like he had the technology inside him, like it was built-in, natural. We studied him and discovered he had an unusual gene. It shared some characteristics with the basic elements of the triggit. We were able to make some major advancements in the demon-smithing science."

"The kaimira gene," said Rom.

"He said he was born with it, and that he was part of some grand story he didn't even want to try to understand. I'm not really sure about that – your father had what I would call a very casual relationship with the truth – but it doesn't matter. He could tap into human, beast and mek without aid from the technologies. Look, I don't know all of the answers, but I know that without your father, none of the advancements we made would have been possible. We'd been working ceaselessly down here, encountering one setback after another, and all of a sudden here was Jack, the answer to all of our problems. He was a fundamentally un-serious man who took his talent completely for granted. He didn't really follow any of our rules or, to be honest, care all that much about getting topside and taking the city back from the beasts. We'd started the fights by then, though, and he liked being the demon-smith no one could beat.

"That's about when Diamond Teeth came into the picture. He brought tremendous resources – men, weapons, food and all the supplies we needed for our research – and he offered to be our partner. I figured out pretty quickly that his true intentions were far less noble. But by the time he made his move to take control of the caves, the other scientists were in his pocket, and I fled to the surface."

"What happened to my father? Did he go with you?"

Ramirez shook his head. "I don't know how long he stayed, but I know he stayed too long. In the end, Diamond Teeth wouldn't let him leave. He had to escape."

It didn't make sense. "If he had so much power, why couldn't he escape earlier?"

"I don't know."

Rom kept his eyes on Ramirez.

"Rom, the truth is, he was hooked on it: the fighting, the gambling. After he lost your mother, he slipped."

"How do you know it won't happen to me?" Rom asked.

"I don't."

Rom and Ramirez trudged to the Battle Demon Arena for

training, past the blur of leering faces and the jingle of copper as the contests raged along the Avenue, punctuated by accusations and fights.

Rom drew attention along the walk to the arena. A lanky kid his own age bowed to him rather theatrically, his knotted hair sprouting from beneath a top hat. He was overseeing a tabletop ring in which two blind cave beetles battled.

"Care to place a bet?" the boy asked Rom with a smile, revealing two missing front teeth. The toothless smile sparked a memory of Myra, the girl who had swindled him out of the power cells. Before Rom could take a closer look, he was swept forward by the churning crowd and a determined Ramirez.

Two of Diamond Teeth's frilly-sleeved thugs guarded the door outside the Battle Demon Arena. "Practice still going on," one of them said in a rough voice.

"Can't we go in and watch?" Rom asked.

Ramirez shook his head. "Strictly forbidden. Demonsmiths aren't even supposed to talk to one another, much less watch one another train. Everyone trains in private with their sponsors."

They took a seat on a bench near the entrance and waited. Rom heard scuffling noises and the thud of footsteps. He watched people hunched over candles in the hallway, murmuring about taking Las Vegas back from the beasts. Ramirez had mouthed similar prayers before. Rom respected the idea, but he had lived above for his whole life. If they really wanted to defeat the beasts, what were they doing down here gambling and shouting at one another?

The sounds stopped, and soon the boy Rom had seen in Diamond Teeth's office emerged from the doorway. The sweat on his shaved head shone in the torchlight, but his walk was easy and confident. As he strode past, followed by his handlers, he did not look at Rom, who could not help feeling that this boy knew something that he didn't, something that would give him the upper hand in battle.

Ramirez and Rom made their way through the silent, empty arena. Rom was jittery but eager to start. Once inside the Pit, he grabbed his helmet and slapped it on his head.

Ramirez pulled it off. "Sit down."

Rom glared at his trainer.

"Look," said Ramirez, "I know you're eager to fight, but there are certain precautions—"

"You just told me I had to learn by doing. Give me that helmet so I can figure out how to win."

Ramirez frowned. "It's precisely that kind of attitude that I'm worried about. It's not about winning; it's about how you win. Forgetting that is how people get hurt. That's how your father got hurt, Rom. He got reckless."

"I'm not my father," grumbled Rom.

"I guess you can learn it on your own then," snapped Ramirez, throwing the helmet to the floor.

Rom blanched. Ramirez was always dithering about one

worry or another, but this time he seemed genuinely angry. Maybe the stress was getting to him, too.

"Sorry," Rom mumbled.

"Just focus on finding the human, beast and mek aspects within you. Feel them out, then try to balance them. Understand?"

Rom rolled his eyes. "No! You're not making sense. Have you ever controlled a battle demon?"

Ramirez's face grew red. "That's not the point. I know more about this science than anyone in the caves. Just because I don't have the gift—"

"OK, so balance and harmony. That's how you fight. Now tell me how to win."

Ramirez sighed. "The easiest way to win is to destroy your opponent's triggit."

"What will that do?"

"The triggit connects controller to demon. Crush it. Break the connection. You win. Simple enough?"

"I'm called Breaker," Rom said, grabbing the helmet and easing into position. "That's just the sort of information I can use."

The stone chair was damp with sweat. Rom pulled down the visor of the helmet and waited for the show to start. He felt the demon forming, conjured out of the atoms and molecules in the air. Rom was in no hurry to prove anything this time, so he took a moment to examine the demon he was controlling through its own eyes. He couldn't see everything, but what he did see – rusted hooves, exposed wires, decaying metal patches – did little to build his confidence.

He remembered a bucket of water he'd seen in the corner, kept there to clean the battle circle between fights. He brought his demon to full height and looked around as the arena came into focus. The bucket was still there, next to a wire scrub brush. He manoeuvred slowly towards it, then kicked it over. As the water collected into a pool on the arena floor, Rom was able to get a look at his demon's whole body.

The front half had the bulky build and horns of a rhinoceros, while the back half had the smooth lines of a cheetah. The demon was bluish and covered in faint spots. Patches of rusting metal covered random parts of the body, and wires sprung from unexpected places.

Could you look any less intimidating? wondered Rom.

The power bar was full and flashing green. The triangle was on the right, surrounded by the three symbols. He watched the triangle carefully this time. He thought once again of Diamond Teeth laughing at his demon, then cowering when it charged. Rom felt a renewed urge to destroy. The beast aspect of the triangle flashed red.

OK, time to balance. Rom thought of Riley, of how excited she got when they performed puppet shows. Diamond Teeth's poisonous smile kept creeping into his thoughts. Rom searched for a way to bat back the animal rage inside him. *Riley sleeping under a pile of blankets. Dad reading from the Tree Book.* The thoughts came in waves, and the red corner of the triangle dimmed.

Now we're getting somewhere.

The trick, Rom realized, was figuring out which type of thought – be it beast, mek or human – would get the demon to do what he wanted. If he wanted the demon to charge, as he'd done with Diamond Teeth, the beast aspect was a good choice. But how to return to human afterwards?

Rom imagined his little sister in the grips of the guard demon outside the Alamino Casino. With the surge of anger this image brought, the demon lurched forward and charged around the ring in all directions. But then Rom remembered his feeling of helplessness. The human symbol flashed. Guilt, one of the most human of emotions.

Then the guilty anger turned into something else, a desire to annihilate. Rom tried to pull back, but the rage kept building, replacing the memories with primal flashes Rom didn't know how to control. All he could feel was fear and anger. The demon was charging around the arena so fast that Rom could not make out its surroundings.

"Balance!" Ramirez shouted over and over. The voice seemed to come from a great distance, and then disappeared completely.

AIKO

Rom crawled out of bed, but his muscles ached and his vision was blurry. How had he got back to his room? He couldn't remember anything of the training session other than the blinding speed. He blinked a few times and looked around for Ramirez, but the old man was nowhere to be found. But sitting atop the table where Rom took his meals was the boy with the shaved head, Aiko, looking just as serious as he had in Diamond Teeth's office.

"You're not supposed to be here," said Rom, remembering Ramirez had said that demonsmiths were forbidden from interacting with one another.

Aiko leant forward. "Are you going to turn me in?"

Rom raised himself up on his elbows. "How did you get in my room?"

The boy jumped off the table with a smile. The missing front teeth created a gap in his smile that changed the severe cast of his face entirely. What was it with missing front teeth?

"Oh, I have my ways. You shouldn't worry about me so much right now, Breaker. You have problems of your own."

Rom wondered how he knew about his nickname. "Who are you?"

"Lots of problems. Too many to consider," Aiko said. "Your friend went to speak with Diamond Teeth ... I mean Mr Julius." He smiled again. "If I had to guess, I'd say he went to talk about your little meltdown out there."

"Meltdown?" Rom vaguely remembered Ramirez using the term.

"You don't remember a thing, do you?" Aiko said, shaking his head. "Happens all the time. Usually not so soon. You gamble? Play cards?"

Rom shook his head. His vision was still blurry. "What's a meltdown?"

"You don't gamble? You're in the caves, Breaker boy. There's no getting out. You should have some fun while you're still all human. That demon really got you, didn't he? Way I hear it, you were all beast when you melted down. You were raging around that ring. Out of control. Big, bad, Mr Beast." Aiko hopped up on the marble-topped table and growled, waving his arms and collapsing into a fit of laughter. When he got control of himself, he jumped to the floor. "Seriously, you don't play cards?"

Rom sat up and rubbed his eyes. *All beast.* Right now he felt like a worn-out human being who needed more sleep. "Don't you have a hole in the wall you can crawl back through or something?" Rom mumbled.

Aiko laughed. "We're all living in holes down here, buddy."

"Then get out of mine."

"You're rude, Mr Beast. You always treat your guests like this? Some people forget, but we try to keep it civilized down here in the caves. Maybe I need to go into the reminding business?"

Rom was unable to suppress his smirk, though he knew it would only encourage Aiko. Maybe he should try to get some information out of him.

"Everyone talks about demonsmithing," said Rom, "but no one can tell me what I'm supposed to do."

"What you're supposed to do is figure it out for yourself, Mr Beast. Human, beast, mek. Easy, like juggling. If you lose it, you crash. Everyone loses it eventually. Everyone melts down. That's why you don't see many old demonsmiths. How about a game? Any game!"

Rom ignored the request, focusing on Aiko's scattered advice. "Can you die in the fights?"

"Not usually. I mean, some people do die, but that doesn't

happen very often. You'll just lose what makes you human. It's *worse* than dying, right? Your mind goes mek or beast. Going mek is bad news, Breaker. You got no feelings any more. You're cold. Never happy, never sad. Just flat, you know. And beast? That's even worse. You'll be roaming the streets on all fours, howling at the moon." Aiko gnashed his teeth. "Ah-ooooh!"

Rom thought of his father in the kitchen. Then he thought of Riley. "Do you know how to get to other places in the caves?" he asked.

Aiko smiled again. "Where do you want to go?"

"I want to see my sister," said Rom. "Long curly hair, likes to stomp on other people's toes?"

Aiko pulled up a chair, scowling. "Oh, her. Sure thing. So long as she's still alive, that's no problem at all. First, let's have a game."

"So long as she's alive?" Rom started, but Aiko just pulled a bag of copper nuggets from his robe and shook it.

Rom didn't have any money, but he was in no position to argue, so he traded his hunting knife for a few nuggets. Aiko produced a deck of cards from his pocket.

Rom learnt quickly that Aiko was a master. "I've been down here a long time," Aiko explained as he dealt the next hand. "I'm Diamond Teeth's champion, and I just keep winning. Better than the alternative. You have anything else to bet, Mr Beast?"

Rom was growing impatient. Ramirez would not be gone for ever. "Shouldn't we get going?" he asked.

Aiko smiled. "One more hand."

"Why are you even here? Just to rob me?"

Aiko put his finger to his lips, climbed up on the table, and pulled down the chandelier. He pulled himself up easily, then disappeared into the ceiling. Rom stared at the chandelier, cursing himself for being too distracted by roasted beast flesh to inspect the ceiling more closely. The chandelier came down once more, and Aiko popped his head out.

"You coming, Mr Beast?"

Rom pulled himself up into a crawl space so narrow he had to lie on his belly and shimmy forward on his elbows. He heard the sound of a match striking against a tinderbox, and soon the tunnel was illuminated by Aiko's torch.

They moved forward in the flickering light. It was cooler in the corridor, and the fresh air cleared Rom's mind.

Rom struggled to keep up with Aiko and finally squeezed himself through a twisting passage that emerged into a giant cavern. High above, through a round opening, he could see the stars, white holes punched in the black sky. He had forgotten how brilliant the night sky in the desert could be.

"This isn't where they're keeping Riley," he said.

"You're a quick one, Mr Beast. No denying that." Aiko's smirk glowed for an instant before he extinguished the torch.

"Hey!" Rom shouted.

The only sound in the cavern was the rush of wind far above and the gurgle of water from somewhere below. Rom tried to recall the way back. If he could find the wall, he could grope his way to the opening of the tunnel.

"Aiko!" he shouted.

There was no answer.

He got on his hands and knees. He crawled a few metres, then reached out for what he thought was the wall, only to grasp at empty space.

A chorus of laughter boomed from the other side of the cave. Rom recognized Aiko's laughter, but there were others there, too.

Matches ripped against tinderboxes, and soon the cavern was awash in smoky light. In addition to Aiko, Rom saw four others. The stringy-haired boy who had tried to get Rom to gamble on fighting beetles leant against the far wall inspecting his glossy shoes. With him were a boy and girl around Riley's age, with grey eyes and narrow faces, dressed in rags much like humans aboveground. The fourth was the girl who had swindled Rom out of his power cells. Myra. Like Aiko, she wore the plain black robe of the demonsmiths.

Rom pulled himself up off the ground and saw he was just steps away from the opening. He was covered in mud.

The boy in the top hat removed it and bowed once more. "Let us stop with the games, please. At the risk of parroting the phrases of a certain jewel-toothed buffoon, I will point out that there is no need to dispense with civility, despite the darkness that enshrouds us. I am Robertson, and this is Mica." Robertson pointed to the girl, who nodded ever so slightly. "And her twin brother, Leo." Leo gave Rom a half salute with his index finger. "You remember Myra, naturally."

"You all live down here?" asked Rom.

Myra smirked. "We're down here on a mission. We'd much rather be topside, swindling buzzer boys."

Rom was too busy piecing the situation together to address the insult. "You're transporters," he said. "My father was a transporter once."

"A good one, from the stories," said Aiko. "Speedy and greedy."

"Maybe a little too greedy," said Myra.

Rom glared at her. "Shouldn't you be off trying to cheat innocent people?"

"No one's innocent," said Robertson. "Not here, at least."

"My sister is," Rom responded. "She never did anything to anyone."

"I disagree," Aiko said, glancing at his foot.

"There are others like Riley," Myra said. "We've lost people, too."

Mica shouted, "Like Myra's brother Byron. He's—"

"Certain of our colleagues," Robertson interrupted, "are also in the Grotto." He gave Mica a sharp look.

Mica turned away, sulking.

"Tell me about the Grotto," Rom said.

"Bad place, Mr Beast," said Aiko. "Guarded by the demons. Where the losers go."

Leo added, "You might end up there if you melt down."

"*When* you melt down," Aiko said.

"Can you tell me—"

"We'll do better than that," Robertson interrupted. "As long as you can keep up." He winked.

With that, everyone blew out their torches. Rom chased the sound of laughter and feet against the stone floor. They were moving too fast for him to feel his way; his only choice was to trust his senses and run. He found that if he didn't think too much, he was able to jump over stones he couldn't see and evaluate where Aiko and the others were just by the way their laughter and shouts echoed off the cavern walls around him. He was aware that something had changed in him; maybe it was his experience with the battle demon.

Finally, the sounds stopped, and Rom joined the others as they stared at a giant gate some distance away.

Aiko nodded at the gate. "Grotto's in there. Got to get past the big gate."

"And before that," said Robertson, "one faces the guards." He pointed to the walls lining the passage ahead.

Rom peered into the darkness. There were holes carved into the walls, lit by dim torches, with a demon perched in each. "Observe," said Robertson. He rifled through the bag slung across his back and pulled out a triggit and a helmet. He put the triggit on the floor. The helmet was larger and even less elegant than those in the Battle Demon Arena. He attached two power units to the device and placed it on his head.

Rom eyed the power cells. They looked identical to the ones he'd traded to Myra. Before he could say anything, a demon materialized in front of Robertson. Four long, skinny legs supported the torso, but the upper body was that of a stringy-haired monkey, with long, hairy arms.

"Meet Shakes," said Robertson with a showman's bow. The demon scrambled across the rocks and towards the gate. As it approached, the guard demons slunk from their hiding spots – four, eight, sixteen. Shakes was surrounded.

Before the guards could move, Shakes dived at the one directly in front, biting and clawing, using its giant arms to rip the guard in two. It threw the two halves at two others, knocking them into the ones behind.

Several guard demons attacked at the same time, and Shakes leaped straight up, turned a circle and a half, and held a perfect diving pose on the way down. The demons waited, ready to pounce. Just as the demon entered the circle, Robertson tore off the helmet, his demon disappeared, and the triggit shattered on the ground. The guards lunged, smashing into one another.

Aiko laughed. "That's what I call style," he said.

"That's what I call cheating," Myra said. "And a waste of a good triggit."

Robertson was pale and sweating. Rom could tell, despite his bravado, that the helmet was taking a toll. "The purpose was to make a point."

"Is it dead?" Rom asked.

"No, of course not," Robertson said. He handed his helmet to Leo. "But he is going to be angry next time I conjure him. Shakes hates fighting."

Rom suspected it was Robertson, not Shakes, who didn't like fighting. A demon had a mind of its own, but that mind was connected intimately with the human master.

Aiko pulled another helmet from his bag, attached two more power cells, and handed the helmet to Rom. Rom recognized the symbol on the power cells – there was no question they were the same ones. He looked at Myra, who smiled back at him and shrugged.

"It's your turn, Breaker boy," Aiko said.

"What about you?"

"You'll see Myra and me in action soon enough, Mr Beast."

Leo put his helmet on Mica, dropped a triggit to the floor, then grabbed her hand. The twins closed their eyes and concentrated, and before them appeared a demon even larger than Robertson's. The two-headed hare rested on its haunches, a metallic turtle shell covering its back.

"Meet Boomer," said Aiko.

They all stared at Rom silently, waiting. Rom took the triggit out of his pocket and placed it near Boomer. He put the helmet on, and immediately felt a needle of pain push from one temple to the other. The pain spread to his gut, then all the way down to his feet. He thought he might throw up, or faint, or both.

The pain faded as soon as Rom's demon materialized, but now Rom was afraid. He had already melted down twice. And he had no way of knowing whether these helmets were safe, or if these people were on his side. But if Riley was inside the Grotto, he was going to need friends. And information.

Rom had no choice. As the two-headed demon lurched off towards the gate, his own followed closely behind.

24

THE GROTTO

Aiko whispered, "Think small, right." As the two demons neared the remaining guards, the twins' demon Boomer splintered into dozens of small parts. Each small piece then morphed into a tiny copy of the demon before scampering away in all directions. Only one of the tiny Boomers paused and looked back at Rom's demon.

Myra spoke. "Have you ever felt divided, Breaker?"

"Every day of my life."

"Think about that. Try to *feel* it again, not just remember. Let yourself splinter, then grab hold of one of the pieces."

Rom focused on how he had often felt with his father. He wanted to hug him, but he wanted to knock him out, too. Divided. Splintered. He remembered the last time his father had left. He'd sneaked out early carrying a small pack. Rom had pretended to be asleep and watched his father through a half-closed eye. He'd wanted to follow him, to trade, roam and fight beasts. But who would take care of Riley? As Rom watched his father saunter into the distance, it was as if he was being ripped in half. It had taken every bit of strength he had to stay still, then check on Riley, and then make breakfast.

Rom's demon exploded, pieces flying into the air in all directions. The pieces formed tiny demons as they hit the ground. He tried to focus on one of them, to re-establish his connection, but they were so small, so slippery. They ran in all directions. At last, Rom was able to push his thoughts into the nearest copy, and it paused and turned around.

In an instant, Rom could see through the eyes of this tiny demon. Small rocks looked like boulders, and Aiko was a giant.

He sensed Boomer sprinting off towards the gate and sent his demon after her.

The guards weren't programmed to look for such tiny trespassers, so Rom's demon and Boomer passed undetected through the gate and into the Grotto.

Rotting debris and rusting scrap lined a muddy path. Rom looked around at a single strip of shacks made of mud-splattered canvas and rusted metal. Inside the shelters, pale forms in tattered clothing huddled around fires for warmth.

The smell of rotten food and greasy torch smoke was thick in the air. It felt like a village of ghosts.

Rom had grown used to the chanting, the pounding drums and the shouts of gamblers in the caves. The eerie silence of the Grotto magnified the ominous creaking sound in the distance.

Rom saw a family arguing in one of the shacks. Two children clutched at each other's hair, snarling. "Give it back!" one shouted. A crust of bread dropped through the dark. A gaunt man on all fours grabbed the crust of bread with his teeth and devoured it in one bite.

Rom's demon struggled to breathe in the fetid air. Rom thought of the cavern where they'd started, the glimpse of open sky. He thought of Riley. He had to get her out of this place.

All around, humans were labouring, making many of the items enjoyed by the gamblers. A group made candy necklaces. An emaciated woman glanced around and bit into one. As the pieces fell around her feet, a guard demon dragged her through the mud towards the centre of the Grotto.

Two tiny demons scurried in the same direction. The creaking sound grew louder, accompanied by cries and moans that sounded barely human. The demons emerged from a cluster of huts and stopped. In front of them was an enormous wheel made of tech scraps and wood, the gnarled spokes of which were pushed by countless humans. Some of them growled and bit at the air as they pushed, reminding Rom of his father. Others pushed in silence, their eyes dull. These were clearly the people who had melted down. This must be what Aiko meant about going beast or mek. Their faces were stark white and wet with sweat despite the chill. They shuffled forward, pressing the wheel with trembling arms. The sound of the wheel in the silent Grotto was like shrieking to the sensitive ears of Rom's demon. The sound was all but unbearable.

Rom wanted to turn away from the horror, but he forced himself to stare. He needed to try to understand why the wheel was there and how it worked. The people pushing the wheel were all wearing helmets like the ones used for demon-smithing. The helmets were thick with tangles of wires that ran the length of the spokes to a black hub that looked like a section of the trunk of an impossibly large tree that had been struck by lightning. Some black bark was visible, but the top was splintered and rotting. Lights and more wires were lashed to the hub. The lights pulsed as the wheel churned. More wires led to a hole in the wall.

One man with eyes as dead as bolts stumbled and fell and was immediately dragged away by two guard demons. His face was without emotion or hope. Moments later, the woman who had tried to eat the candy necklace was herded towards the wheel. The fear in her eyes reminded Rom of a cornered coyote. She snapped with her teeth but the guard demons just smacked her forward.

Boomer and Rom's demon used the shadows for cover. Guard demons were everywhere, patrolling or guarding groups of workers.

"Please, not the wheel!" the woman said. "I'm losing it. I can feel it. I'll go beast if I do one more shift." The guard demons snapped their jaws near her hands, and she hurriedly connected the wires to her head and began to push.

Rom felt a sharp pain as Boomer head-butted his own demon, urging him to move on. They stole across the shadows, under the feet of those pushing the wheel, then slowed to keep pace with a young boy. Boomer snapped ferociously at the leg of his pants, trying to get his attention. The boy bent down as he walked. Boomer continued to tug. Finally, the boy looked down and opened his mouth as if to say something. He said nothing, but Rom noticed the gap where his teeth should be. He was one of them.

The boy's face had no expression. He stooped to examine the tiny demon, and Rom saw a flicker of recognition – the boy had seen Boomer before. A smile inched across his face, and then he trembled violently. When the spasm subsided, his face was once again completely blank. He straightened and resumed pushing the wheel.

Rom could see the twins' dejection in the way their demon's four ears dropped. But they continued through the shadows, past the wheel, and towards a group of humans making paper flowers, the kind that decorated the hats of the more garish

gamblers. Careful to avoid the guards, Boomer waited until a worker dropped a flower, hopped to catch it before it landed in the mud, then scrambled away as the clumsy worker was dragged off by the guards.

The two demons arrived at a small patch of dirt littered with small, plain tombstones. In the far corner of the graveyard, Boomer stopped and placed the flower next to one of the stones. The name *Byron* was cut unevenly into the stone.

Byron. The name of Myra's brother. He'd died in the Grotto. Rom thought of Riley again and felt his stomach clench.

Boomer hopped across the graveyard towards a small hut, the entrance of which teemed with demons. Then she charged.

Rom understood at once. Boomer emitted a high-pitched shriek, a sound much too great for her tiny body, and then veered back into the shadows. The guard demons launched after her, leaving the hut's entrance unguarded for a few seconds. That was all Rom needed. He sent his demon through.

Rom recognized Riley at once – the shock of black, curly hair, the small, tense body huddled into a ball, the defiant frown.

He had no way to communicate with her, but he had to be sure she was OK before turning back. His demon crept over, slowly, and he watched as her frown turned into a look of disgust and then amusement.

"I thought you were a rat. But look at those horns. You're some sort of tiny rhinoceros mek. Did you come over here to stab me?" She laughed.

Rom knew the tiny demon wasn't exactly imposing, but did Riley have to laugh?

Rom made the demon shake his head.

"Is that a no?" Riley said. "You want to keep me company?" Her voice broke. "The guards don't let me talk to anybody."

Rom moved his demon closer. Just about everything in the hut was broken. Rom was reminded of his own habit of breaking things when he was angry and hoped Riley wasn't following his example.

"I thought if I broke enough stuff, they'd send a human in here, and I could find out what's going on. But no luck. All I get is you."

His demon rubbed his head against Riley's hand, careful not to poke her. It felt weird, but Rom hoped it might cheer her up.

"I don't know where my brother is," Riley said, scratching the demon's head with her finger. "No one will tell me if he's OK." A tear tracked down her dirty cheek.

She scooped the demon into her palm and examined him. "I like your spots. Can I call you Spot?"

Rom wished there was a way to make the demon speak for him, so he could let her know that he was trying his best to rescue her. He turned around just in time to see two guards pounce. He leaped away from Riley. Then everything went black.

Rom shook his head. Aiko had removed the helmet, but Rom still felt the sharp pain.

"I need to get Riley out of there," Rom said.

"Slow down, Mr Beast," Aiko replied.

Myra was looking eagerly at the twins. "Did you see Tick?"

"He didn't even recognize us," Mica said. There were tears on her face, and on her brother's. "We have to bust him out."

Robertson nodded. "We'll need at least a dozen demon-smiths and helmets."

"You'll need a lot more than that to take over the Grotto," said Rom.

"We're not taking over," Myra said. "We just need enough to bust Tick out. And your sister, too, if you'll help us."

Rom and the twins bent down and snatched their triggits from the places where their demons had dematerialized.

"The big wheel," Rom said, "what is it for?"

"The Demon Wheel," Aiko said. "Power generator for the caves and the demon guards. Drains people like power cells and sends the power to Diamond Teeth, so he can control the guards."

"What would happen if the wheel were destroyed?" Rom asked.

Robertson laughed. "You are an ambitious thinker, if not very realistic."

Aiko jumped in. "Destroy the wheel, the lights go out. The demons disappear."

"But it would take an army to accomplish that. We're only interested in rescuing Tick." With that, Robertson blew out his torch, and the others followed suit. Rom heard them scatter, but this time there was no laughter.

Rom crawled back towards his room in darkness. Though he made a few wrong turns, he was finally able to find his way. While he squirmed forward through the dank mud, he thought about Aiko's friends. He didn't trust them any more than he did Aiko, but he couldn't help but think they were all after the same thing. And they had shown him Riley. He needed help sorting out his thoughts. He needed to talk to Dragonfly.

Back in his room, Rom opened the Tree Book.

"All right, book. Time for a little help."

Immediately, the voice of Animus shouted, *Let me out!*

"I want to talk to Dragonfly."

Two Guardians can free me. Three can restore me.

"If you have so much power, why can't you free yourself?"

Incorrect. Two Guardians can free me. Three can restore me.

"How about this," Rom responded. "You tell me what you plan to do if we free you."

Incorrect. I am Animus. Free me. I will be your vengeance.

"Can you show me Riley? Then I'll think about freeing you."

Incorrect. Free me and I can help you.

"Let me talk to Dragonfly!"

The page went blank.

Rom stared. There had to be more than that. Where was Dragonfly? He needed to talk to her right now, but she must have had her book closed. He wrote her a note.

Dragonfly,

So much has happened. I don't know where to start. I have to get Riley out of here, and fast. I have to win. The beast aspect is so strong in me, and it's hard to balance, but it's the only way. If something happens to me, just remember that. You have to learn to balance the beast, mek and human. If you want to survive.

Breaker

The thump of drums echoed through Rom's quarters as he tried to sleep, the uptick in tempo just noticeable. The day of the battle approached.

25

THE STORM

Mei waited for Sumi near the string of balloons where the children had their lessons. Word had spread about the attack at High Watch, and now almost everyone avoided her. Even the adults seemed to always be on their way somewhere when Mei came around. Morning Man, she realized with surprise, was the only one who still looked her in the eye.

She wanted to get Sumi alone and explain. With Ai-ling away on her honeymoon, she was Mei's only friend.

Sumi came from the instruction balloon with two friends. When she saw Mei, an uncharacteristically nervous expression crossed her face. Thunder rumbled in the distance. Just as the girls looked to the sky, it began to rain.

"This wasn't announced on the drumline," said one of the girls. She looked at Mei with a smile that was just a little too sweet, and Mei knew that the girl blamed her for the unexpected weather. "Maybe your Cloudwatcher friend was too busy playing with meks."

"She's not my friend," Sumi said, her cheeks red. "We'd all better get home." She glanced down at her feet as if she wanted to say something to Mei, then hurried off with the two girls.

Mei held out her hand to let a few cold drops hit her palm, then stuck out her tongue to collect a few more. She wasn't going to let Sumi and her friends upset her.

She heard the creaking of ropes as the Sky Village made a sharp turn. Balloons crashed together and others strained against their ropes as the village adjusted to the new direction. Directly west, she saw a dark storm cloud, lightning flashing from within. The balloon felt ominously fragile as it rocked back and forth in the gusts of wind.

Back at her balloon, Mei found Ai-ling and Jun, who had returned prematurely from their honeymoon. Ai-ling looked panicked.

"Mei," she said, sounding desperate. "Did you get word of this storm during your cloudwatching?"

"The pigeons have stopped coming," Mei said.

"Why?" Ai-ling said. "The pigeons have been our closest allies for almost a century."

Mei opened her mouth, trying to find the right words.

Jun approached them, a sober look on his face. "The storm is close, and we need to brace the village."

The elders were gathered in Old Hug, giving orders through the drumline. It was too late to reverse direction, and they were over mek territory, so there was no hope of landing and waiting it out. Still, the elders shouted orders, and the village became a hive of frenzied activity as its citizens secured their homes. They were already using every windmover at their disposal to push the village out of the storm's path. Villagers deflated the smaller, more vulnerable balloons and crowded onto the larger ones below Old Hug, which would function as a giant umbrella.

Mei helped as best she could, pulling ropes and packing balloons into larger baskets. She comforted frightened children while herding others who saw the storm as a chance to play dangerous games on the ropes. In the chaos, Mei raced across the ropes, carrying infants from one basket to the next. She realized that she'd mastered rope walking, and just in time. The winds pushed at her from all sides, but there was so much to be done that Mei forgot how terrified she was supposed to be.

As Mei delivered two infants to Old Hug, Old Su stopped barking orders long enough to give her a nod. Mei felt proud – and a little embarrassed. She headed back into the storm, working until all of the villagers were gathered in the cluster of secure balloons.

*   *   *

The nose of the storm was upon them now. The baskets rose and fell in the current like driftwood in the sea. Ropes creaked. Water slashed and swirled through the air, stinging cheeks and pelting balloons. Jun and his friends volunteered to head above High Watch armed with power-charged kites to catch the lightning. Mei saw Ai-ling's smile fade as he told her, and her face turn as grey as the approaching clouds.

When the storm hit, Mei and Sumi were in the same balloon. Morning Man had also volunteered to catch lightning, and Sumi watched his balloon anxiously.

"It seems so dangerous up there. Couldn't someone die catching lightning?" Mei asked.

Sumi looked at Mei. Tears welled up in her eyes as she pushed through the crowd to the opposite end of the basket.

Ai-ling patted Mei on the shoulder. "I guess she never told you. This is how her parents were killed."

Mei felt like throwing up. She'd said a terrible thing, but how could she have known Sumi was alone in the world, just like her? Well, Sumi did have Morning Man, but Mei didn't exactly envy her that. "How did it happen?" shouted Mei over the howling wind.

"Her father and grandfather volunteered, and her mother didn't want to let them face the danger alone, so she went, too. It was a bad storm – positive lightning, the worst kind – and we lost three of our four high balloons. Seven good people were stolen by the storm."

"She never said anything." Mei looked for Sumi through the whorls of rain. "How did Morning Man survive?"

"He shouldn't have," Ai-ling said. "He fell."

Suddenly, the balloon listed sharply to the left. People clutched at one another to keep from falling, and children wailed. Mei saw a flash of lightning high above the balloon. "I'm so scared," she said.

As if in response, a clap of thunder ripped through the air. "I'm sure this storm won't be so bad," Ai-ling said. She tried to smile, but Mei sensed her fear. "Besides, Jun has more than his fair share of wits. That's one reason I married him. I just hope those daredevil friends of his don't do anything foolish."

Ai-ling was called away to tend to some of the younger children. Mei stood alone, watching as the dark clouds consumed the lightning catchers and then the other balloons around her.

She felt helpless. Crowded onto balloons beneath Old Hug with the other villagers, there was nothing left to do but wait out the storm and hope that Jun and Morning Man survived. She peeked into her pouch. Feifei's colours were vibrant again, but she still lay unmoving.

What would Breaker do? Everyone thought it was her fault the Sky Village was heading into a storm. She'd done everything she could to help prepare, but now she felt useless. What would Breaker tell her to do? He'd probably tell her to *tough it up* or *stick it off* or some phrase in his language that meant to have courage and to be strong. He wouldn't over think it, like her. He'd probably go out there and face the storm and catch lightning. He'd do whatever he could to help Jun and Morning Man, so that afterwards he could face Ai-ling and Sumi.

Mei stared at the cloud that swallowed the lightning catchers, and the figures inside, standing ready with their kites. What she was thinking was complete insanity, she told herself. How could she possibly help? She would probably be killed. Worse, she might put someone else in danger. There was no logical reason to join the lightning catchers.

But maybe there was more to thinking than just logic. She'd had a hand in getting them into the crisis and ought to try to get them out. And after what had happened with the flying meks, maybe this kaimira gene of hers – whatever it was – maybe it would help her help the village. If Breaker could conjure and control a demon, surely she could do something. She waited for a moment when no one was looking in her direction, then slipped over the edge of the basket.

SPOT

An owlish man with a pale, pinched face entered the room, bearing a towel, some scissors and a razor. "Shaved heads for fighters in the tournament," said the man. "It's the rules."

Rom felt like the drummers were inside his head. He had thrashed all night in bed, listening to the tempo of the drums grow faster and louder. People on the crowded streets had joined in the noise, striking pipes and banging rocks together in celebration of the biggest gambling event of the year: the annual battle demon tournament. Rom dragged himself out of bed. Last night's tray of untouched food sat atop the marble table, next to his breakfast. A black robe lay folded on the chair in front of the cabinet. He pulled it on and sank down onto a velvet-covered stool. His hands and legs tingled. There was a sticky, foul coating in his mouth and throat that made it difficult to swallow. He couldn't look at the food, much less eat it.

While the man snipped at Rom's hair, Rom stared at his red-eyed reflection in the mirror and tried to convince himself that he was a champion. He thought of Dragonfly and the courage she had already shown. He thought of Riley. His curls drifted to the floor while the old man cut and shaved.

"Doesn't look like you slept much last night," the man said.

"Why do demonsmiths have to shave their heads?" Rom asked. The drums were so loud it was difficult to converse.

The man grunted. "The helmets can burn your hair if you get too worked up." He ran the razor along Rom's head. "Think you've got a chance to win?"

Rom didn't answer. He just stared at his reflection. As his mass of tangled curls fell away, he was shocked to see how much he looked like his father.

Ramirez came in shortly after. He rubbed his hand over Rom's head. "You look sickly and three years younger than you did with that rat's nest on your head."

Rom squirmed away. He knew the insult was an attempt to loosen him up, but he wasn't in the mood. Rom was fighting for himself and Riley now. If he won, it would be his victory, not Ramirez's.

The two made their way through the caves. Eager faces lined the path to the arena. People wore the very finest garments of silk, lace, velvet and leather. They had been brushed to shine in preparation for the tournament, and jewels flashed in the electric lights.

Celebratory smells hung in the air: roasting beast flesh, vats of stew, and a pungent glogg made of plums, apples, raisins, spices and fermented fruit juice that boiled in pots near every doorway. Rom tried not to look anyone in the eye, but he saw Leo and Mica. They bowed at him with a theatricality they must have learnt from Robertson, then ran off down the Avenue towards the arena. The drumming had been synchronized, but as Rom and other fighters passed the lodging district and turned towards the Battle Demon Arena, the rhythm broke. The drummers played as fast as they could, none in time with the others.

As he walked down the hall to the arena floor, an icy calm descended over Rom. He forgot the drumming, and Riley, and all of the rage that had consumed him in the days leading up to this one. He saw the crowd as a million swirling parts, atoms dancing in space without order or direction. In less than an hour, the fight would be over. Rom would win or lose.

Rom made his way into the arena without betraying emotion. Torches illuminated the battle circle, and the drummers pounded with animal fury. Above them, as high as Rom could see, were members of the cave's elite: sponsors whose demonsmiths had won in previous years, and whose luck was still running high. The men wore top hats and gripped their lapels like barons while the women fanned themselves.

The crowd was a single, undulating monster with thousands of faces, emitting one deafening roar. Rom was the centre of everyone's attention, but he had no interest in the audience. He kept his head down.

"Walk a circle around the ring," Ramirez whispered. "Keep your head up, smile, show some confidence."

Rom walked around the ring, but he kept his head down and refused to smile. When he had finished, his opponent emerged, shedding the black robe to reveal an elaborate costume: a mask of liquid metal, complete with sharp, curling horns, ruby eyes and a fanged mouth that reminded Rom of the wolves aboveground.

He strutted around the ring with raised arms. The crowd cheered. The demonsmith came to Rom's side. He lifted the mask just enough to reveal a gap-toothed smile. Aiko.

He shrugged at Rom, then danced out into the ring to posture for the ravenous crowd.

Aiko must have known they were going to battle. Why else would he have made the secret visits? Aiko had wanted to size him up, intimidate him, or both. Rom spotted Aiko's gang in the crowd: Robertson, still in a top hat, the twins Mica and Leo in matching lavender silks, and Myra in a long, frilly dress. Rom was ready to stare down their smiling faces, but they all wore nervous frowns.

A great roar emerged from the crowd as Diamond Teeth strode into the arena in a red silk suit and hat studded with diamonds and rubies, carrying a jewelled cane.

The crowd bellowed and cheered, and Diamond Teeth raised his hands and flashed his wicked smile. He pulled his hands down with the ritualistic grace of a matador swinging his cape, and the crowd quieted.

Diamond Teeth pointed to the fighters.

"Bow," whispered Ramirez.

Rom and Aiko bowed in unison.

Diamond Teeth shouted, "Why do we fight?"

"So we may conquer!" chanted the crowd. Rom noticed that Ramirez was shouting along with the rest, though his heart didn't seem to be in it. Rom wondered if these people really wanted to conquer the beasts aboveground. Surely these hybrid demons would succeed if Diamond Teeth allowed it.

"Who must we conquer?" shouted Diamond Teeth.

"The beasts!"

Diamond Teeth lowered his arms and the crowd fell silent once again. Four massive candles, wider and taller than Diamond Teeth himself, marked equal intervals around the perimeter of the fighting circle. In the silence, Diamond Teeth went to each one, paused for a moment and hung his head, mumbled something unintelligible, then lit the candle.

"What's he saying?" Rom asked Ramirez.

"At one time it was a chant to remind us of what the fights were for, but now it's just a way to froth up the crowd so they gamble more," whispered Ramirez through gritted teeth.

Rom looked at Ramirez. In spite of everything, he had some sympathy for the old man.

When the fourth candle was lit, Diamond Teeth raised his hands again.

"I give you Aiko, and his demon, Muddy, fighting newcomer Breaker, the son of the one and only Jack Saint-Pierre, and his demon..." He looked over at Rom. "What's your demon's name, Breaker?"

Rom's mind raced. It hadn't occurred to him to give the demon a name.

"We don't have all night," Diamond Teeth shouted.

Then Rom remembered Riley and the name she had given to the tiny demon. It's not what he would have chosen, but there was no time.

"Spot."

"Spot?" Diamond Teeth asked. He turned to the crowd. "I give you Spot!" he shouted.

He used his cane to draw a circle in the centre of the arena. When he finished, he made a slash down the centre.

"Your triggit," Ramirez said.

Rom followed Aiko to the centre of the ring. Both handed

over their triggits, and one was placed on each side of the slash.

The crowd let loose. It was time to battle.

Before Rom could follow Aiko into the Pit, Ramirez stopped him. Rom struggled to get free – more of Ramirez's advice would only distract him from his purpose. But Ramirez gripped Rom's shoulders tight and spun him.

"Rom," he shouted, struggling to be heard above the din. "You're such a good young man." Ramirez looked as if he might cry. "If anything happens, Rom ... just, I'm sorry. I am so sorry."

Rom felt his stomach churn. The crowd grew restless and stomped their feet. There was nothing to do but fight. Rom made his way into the Pit, where he strapped the helmet to his head and lowered himself into the chair. Aiko flopped into his chair and caught Rom's eye. "Meltdown," he mouthed slowly, before snapping down his visor with a grin.

Rom ignored him and lowered his own visor. The power bar on the left and the balance triangle on the right both glowed brightly as Rom tried to conjure Spot. Nothing happened.

Then Ramirez was next to him. "Just focus. Concentrate. Push the crowd out of your mind."

"It's not working," Rom said. "Is it possible to conjure a demon two days in a row?"

Ramirez lowered his eyebrows and shook his head. "It takes some recharging, couple of days at least. Why? We didn't practise yesterday."

Rom liked to keep his secrets, but in desperation he told Ramirez everything about the gang and last night's trip to the Grotto. The old man just listened, gripping the side of the stone chair until his knuckles turned white.

"Absolute stupidity," Ramirez spat. "This isn't a game. What if your demon doesn't appear? The crowd will tear you apart."

Just then, Spot flickered into view, looking less than energetic. Ramirez glared at the demon, then at Rom. "We'll talk about this later," he said, stepping back.

Rom brought Spot to his feet, and the demon began to circle. Rom heard the jeers of the crowd. He turned and looked for Aiko's demon. *Let's see how his hybrid looks,* he thought. *Maybe they're all a little junky.*

Aiko's demon, Muddy, came slowly into view. He was nearly twice as big as Spot, with long, thin metal legs and a robust body covered in spikes. His long tail had a spiked ball at the end. Muscle rippled across the surface. His metallic head was all jaw and fangs, with gleaming red eyes and two long, curling ram's horns. As Rom watched, Muddy reared up on his two hind legs and swiveled his spectacular head.

The crowd exploded with applause. Drums crashed.

Spot's keen sense of hearing amplified the sound, and Rom's ears throbbed.

Muddy circled with a light-stepped grace the lumbering Spot could not possibly match.

Rom's mind raced. Muddy was faster and stronger. And Aiko was cleverer.

Rom needed a strategy, and fast. The only real tip Ramirez had given him was to destroy the triggit, which would sever the connection to the demonsmith. Muddy wore an armoured chest plate, and Rom guessed it protected the triggit. Rom tried to push his doubts away, but already the human aspect of the triangle was glowing a dull red.

Muddy charged, and Rom felt the wind knocked out of him as the horns slammed into Spot's side. He landed hard. A surging terror rose in him and told him to flee. Rom tried to get Spot up. His power bar had dropped by half.

Muddy charged again. Rom braced for the impact, but at the last second the demon stepped aside. Its tail whipped in a circle, and as it came towards Spot, the spiked ball morphed into a hideous mouth of snapping fangs. Spot shrank back. The ball came at him again, this time in its original form. It slammed Spot in the side, knocking him down. Aiko wasn't even targeting Rom's triggit; he was just toying with him. Rom's power bar dropped to a quarter. Out of the corner of his eye, he saw Muddy strutting around the arena. He heard the crowd above him. He was going to lose.

Rom struggled to breathe. The animal terror had distracted him from his doubts, but he was in no position to congratulate himself. The fear threatened to overwhelm him, pushing him to run, to escape. He swivelled his head, but Muddy was nowhere to be seen.

A cold, rational voice emerged: *Look above and behind you.* Before Rom could react, the hybrid's jaws were clamped around his chest, over the triggit. Rom was unable to move.

Do something! Do something! Rom struggled to balance his thoughts.

The crowd smelled victory now. Those who had gambled on Aiko jumped up and down, and the cavern resounded with the rhythm of their stomping feet.

It's over, Rom thought. He thought of Riley. *It's over.* The human aspect of the triangle flashed red.

As the jaws closed over his triggit, Rom heard the sound of the chest plate crunching. The pressure was unbearable. He wanted to scream. He heard the crunch of what must be the triggit and felt a shock in the back of his skull. Spot's body went limp, and his eyes rolled back. Rom was blind. The fight was over.

Why, then, could he feel Muddy relaxing his jaws? Rom was still somehow connected to Spot. His vision returned, and he could see the controls in his mind. The power bar ticked up. The triangle flashed green. Cold rationality spoke to him: *calculate a victory; do not jump up in a blind rage.* A whirl of emotions came over him, blending together. A brute instinct to survive. A desire to save Riley. A comprehensive understanding of Muddy and his weaknesses. For the first time, all three aspects were in harmony. Could he control the demon without the triggit? Ramirez had said his father could control his demon naturally, without the use of technology. Did Rom have the same ability?

Muddy let go and reared up again on his hind legs, his metal jaws snapping, growling at the crowd. Muddy's tail whipped around above his body. The spiked ball morphed into a distorted face that taunted Spot with a mocking sneer. Copper nuggets changed hands in the seats, and there were disappointed groans from those who had taken a chance on Rom.

Rom's power bar continued to tick up, and he plotted his move. He had learnt from his fall. He had to destroy Aiko's triggit. He needed to use all three aspects to do it – force, calculation and will.

Rom shifted his eyes until he could see Muddy posturing for the crowd, back turned to Spot. Rom waited. The triangle pulsed green. As Muddy turned back around, Spot leaped. Time seemed to stop as Rom felt his demon's body high in the air, suspended. The shocked crowd fell silent. As he descended from his leap, Spot spread his jaws wide. He crashed into Aiko's motionless demon and clamped down on his chest. Rom felt the spiked tail crash into Spot's back.

The two creatures tumbled to the sand with a thunderous crash. When the cloud of dirt cleared, Spot still had Muddy by the chest. The crowd erupted.

Rom knew he could win if he held on. Muddy strained beneath him, but Rom just bit down harder, anger surging through him like electricity through wire.

Rom's triangle flashed red on the human and animal sides, and his mind raced. He struggled to adjust his thoughts. He focused on the creature flailing beneath him, brutal cracking sounds emanating from the metal body. He was going to break the triggit and hear the crowd roar. He bit harder, embracing the rage, savouring the moment of certain victory.

Spot's jaws closed with a final burst of strength, and the triggit shattered. Muddy dropped lifeless to the ground, then disintegrated.

Rom clenched and unclenched his hands as he took a deep breath. His sides and back throbbed with pain. He had avoided a meltdown. He'd won. His thoughts raced to Aiko beside him, and he lunged out of his chair, legs unsteady, pushing Aiko's keepers out of the way.

Ramirez stared at Rom with wide eyes. The old man was pale, his lips quavering. "How did you..."

"Aiko?" shouted Rom.

"We'll know soon," Ramirez said.

"Aiko?" one of the keepers repeated.

Aiko jolted up but kept his eyes focused on his hands.

Rom felt his stomach lurch. Had his opponent gone mek?

"That was so cheap," Aiko whined. He looked up, and his eyes were clearly human. "How did he do that?"

Rom, relieved and exhausted, moved away to avoid answering the question. The truth was, he had no idea.

27

BETRAYAL

The next morning when Rom woke, Aiko was there, along with Robertson, Myra and the twins.

Aiko said, "You been out for two days, Mr Beast. Getting your beauty sleep? Even two days won't help you there. You're looking even worse than your demon."

"I thought losing your triggit would humble you."

"You can gamble for anything in the caves," Aiko said, fishing a shiny new triggit out of his pocket and holding it up. "Especially if you're the best gambler around."

"Leave me alone," Rom said. He glanced at the twins, who were poking around the room, while Robertson and Myra made themselves comfortable on the divan. "Why are you all here?" he finally asked, though he didn't expect a real answer.

"Friendly visit," said Aiko. "Make sure you didn't go beast overnight."

"And that subject remains unresolved," added Robertson. "You were snoring like a warthog."

Rom glared at Aiko. "I thought the losers went to the Grotto," he said.

"I predict," Aiko said, ignoring Rom's statement, "that when you melt down there'll be a lot of snarling and begging for table scraps. You pick out a dog name yet?"

"I was thinking Aiko," said Rom.

Mica and Leo giggled.

Aiko laughed, too. "I'm still high in the rankings. Not a loser yet. I'd say we can both be on top, and get anything we want. Gold, jewels, all the food we can eat, whatever. What do you want, Mr Beast?"

"I want my sister back."

"Boring. You should think big. Like how you can get us *all* out of here. Your sister. Tick. Maybe even a few half-brains if you're the generous type."

It occurred to Rom that Aiko was just as nervous about losing as he was. "Why should I help you when you tried to make me lose? That's what that night was about, wasn't it? You wanted me to summon Spot so I wouldn't be able to when I fought my first match. Well, it was a waste of time."

"About that," Robertson said. "How exactly did you manage it?"

"Can you do it again?" Aiko said. "Here, in the room. Without the triggit or the helmet?"

The twins chimed in, "Can you, can you?"

"If I do, will you leave me alone?" Rom asked.

Aiko opened his eyes wide in mock disbelief. "Only thing worse than a sore loser is a sore winner."

"I believe," Robertson said, "that we have a deal."

Rom cursed himself for making the suggestion. He wanted to talk to Dragonfly, but he needed to get these characters out of his room first. He had no idea whether he could summon Spot without a helmet or a triggit outside of the arena.

The drums had started up again. The sound made Rom think of rocks cracking against teeth. He closed his eyes and tried to picture Spot: the long horn and muscular shoulders, the goofy expression, the sleek flanks and cheetah spots. He tried to forget the protruding wires and rusty slabs of metal. Maybe if he didn't think about them they wouldn't appear this time.

He opened his eyes, and there was nothing. The gang stood around him, waiting. Aiko tapped his foot.

Rom tried again. His mind was jumping all over the place. Riley. The gang. The deafening crowd in the arena. The Tree Book. Instead of trying to push the thoughts away, as he might have done before, he let them all crowd into his mind. He acknowledged each one and then let it go until he felt a sense of calm.

He imagined Spot – not the physical Spot, armoured and ready for battle, but the thread of personality Rom felt while seeing through Spot's eyes. Alongside the courage, bravery and hope, there were other traits, like stubbornness, eagerness and a fascination with new things. Rom let those qualities fill his mind.

Rom knew from the gasps in the room that it had worked. But when the twins giggled, and Aiko started roaring with laughter, he didn't want to open his eyes to see what disaster of a demon he had conjured.

There, on the floor, where he had expected Spot – or even a new-and-improved Spot – was a pup no taller than Rom's shin. The infant Spot stood there bashfully, looking around at everyone.

As embarrassed as he was, Rom knew that this was the real Spot, no longer enhanced for battle by Diamond Teeth's technology. This demon was just a pup, vulnerable and in need of Rom's protection.

"This is a travesty I have no time to witness," Robertson said. "Come on, let's go." He pulled down the chandelier and disappeared, the others trailing behind him.

"But he's so cute," Mica said, just before she shimmied up.

Rom flopped back on the bed and looked at Spot. This was the killing machine that was supposed to win Riley's freedom? What if Spot appeared in this form in the arena? The crowd would get a good laugh, and Rom would join his sister in the Grotto.

Spot took a step forward and fell over onto his side. Rom sighed. "He can't even walk properly. I don't have time for this."

A platter of cold mashed potatoes, green beans and more roasted beast flesh waited next to the bed. Rom ate quickly, then grabbed a torch and his tinderbox, pulled down the chandelier, and climbed up the cord.

He paused when he heard Spot yelping below. "Oh, great," Rom moaned. He couldn't risk Diamond Teeth finding Spot. He'd have to take the little thing with him.

As they made their way along the crawl space, Spot struggling to keep up, Rom thought about what it would be like to escape the caves with his sister. He'd seen the stars. There had to be some way out.

Rom came to the end of the crawl space and emerged into the larger cavern, where the sun shot through the opening in a glowing pillar of light. Rom stumbled forward with Spot in his arms, closed his eyes, leant his head back, and let the full force of it envelop him. He couldn't remember feeling anything as glorious as that sudden warmth. Spot emitted a deep, contented rumble. Rom remembered what it felt like to run through the streets, legs churning, sweat popping off his forehead, the brilliant sun shining in the sky.

Reluctantly, Rom left the circle of light and explored. The cavern was round, stippled with stalactites and stalagmites – glistening like wet clay in the sunlight. The stream gurgled past, filled with blind white fish that pooled in the darkness. As Spot tried to spear a fish with his horn, Rom scanned the cavern for other openings and found one across the way. It was much larger than the crawl space, and he was able to walk upright with room to spare. It was silent. Rom, with Spot padding softly behind, followed the path until the sound of a bellow stopped him stock-still. It was Diamond Teeth.

Rom snuffed out his torch and dropped to his knees. The voices drew closer, emerging from far off, but clearly audible.

"He's not ready." The voice was as unmistakable as the subject of the conversation. Ramirez.

"It's too late. If the kid melts down, so be it."

"*When* he melts down," said Ramirez. "He's pushing too hard, and he won't listen to me."

Diamond Teeth laughed. "Have a little faith, Ramirez. Just keep pumping him full of talk about balance and harmony. It's a bunch of nonsense, but the fighters do last a few weeks longer when you've been lecturing them. Look at how far the other Saint-Pierre got before he lost it." His speech broke off into gasps of laughter.

"He's got the gift, and he's got it strong, Julius, but he's melted down twice. You know what will happen. He's not ready."

"It doesn't matter to me whether he wins or not," said Diamond Teeth. "All I want is a good show and plenty of betting."

"Please," said Ramirez. "Give him a month to train before the next fight. He'll still be able to compete in the final games. He won't make it that far if you start him off in the early rounds."

"Are you negotiating with me? Are you negotiating with *me*? That's funny, because usually people who want to negotiate with me have something to offer. This was just as much your idea as it was mine. Remember that, Ramirez."

"But think of the risk."

"You know, it's my strategy not to think so much about risk," Diamond Teeth said. "Because risk is everywhere. Take up above. Kid has lived for thirteen years up there, roaming streets controlled by packs of beasts just waiting for a chance to tear him to shreds. You think he hasn't always been at risk?"

Ramirez sighed. "Push him too fast and too hard, and he'll turn out like his father."

"I don't see the downside, Ramirez. That boy's father was the best entertainment we've had down here. Even after the meltdown. The gamblers ate it up."

"Don't you want to see him make it to the final game? The big one? This kid could tip the scales. Word will spread faster than a mek fire march. Tribes will come in from all over and gamble everything they have."

Diamond Teeth hooted. "And all this time I thought you were looking out for the boy. You're out to win the big one, same as everyone else. You're the real pig here."

Ramirez breathed out hard. His voice grew soft. "Living topside is impossible. I can't find supplies for my research without risking my life, and food is a whole other challenge. There's plenty I don't like about how you run things, but at least down here it's safe."

"I never thought I'd see the day when Ramirez started talking sense. But if you want your champion to make it to the final game, you should worry about coaching the kid instead of protecting him. Though, in my opinion, training is overrated. He'll figure it out or he won't."

"What about his sister? What happens to her if he loses?"

"You know as well as I do what will happen. And you'll go to the Grotto, too. There's valuable work to be done there, though the turnover rate is unfortunately high."

"The casualty rate, you mean."

"Don't exaggerate, Ramirez. Those suckers in the Grotto aren't dead. Not technically, anyway."

"They'd be better off if they were," Ramirez said quietly.

"Sacrifice is the noblest of gifts," Diamond Teeth said. "Isn't that what you used to say?"

"That was different—"

"And now you're going to have to sacrifice something if you want me to go easy on your boy."

There were a few moments of silence. Spot struggled to free himself from Rom's grasp. The little demon was far stronger than he looked.

Ramirez spoke again. "The boy you caught a while back trying to smuggle power cells into the caves—"

"Scary eyes, missing teeth. What about him?"

"He has friends here. They're trying to break him out." Ramirez went on to describe the gang, using every bit of detail Rom had given him, telling Diamond Teeth to look for scrawny kids with missing teeth, including his own champion, Aiko.

Rom leant back, his head pounding. So that was it. Ramirez had been in on it the whole time. Riley's kidnapping, the journey underground, the capture in the tunnel. Rom felt sick at the thought. How could the old man betray him? And how could Rom not have seen it? All this time, the only thing Ramirez wanted was wealth. He was no different than anyone else in the caves – worse, in some ways, because at least those other gamblers weren't using other people to get what they wanted.

Ramirez had stopped, and now Diamond Teeth was speaking. "So, they're trying to build their own little army. That is a useful piece of news. And because I'm a man of my word, I'll take it easy on Rom for the next few fights."

Rom raced back down the tunnel, dazed. How could he have been so foolish? He felt the anger welling up in him. He would turn it on Ramirez and rip him to shreds. He would—

Rom dropped the torch and gripped the wall, staring at Spot, who stood straight, looking a little more solid than he had back in Rom's room. Rom could feel the hybrid demon inside him now, the beast aspect surging through his mind, wanting to eliminate the threat. The shadows from the dropped torch boiled around him like bats. What was happening? Could he melt down even outside the Pit? Would he ever make it to another fight? Something red glowed from within Spot, as though the creature were on fire from the inside, feeding on Rom's anger, growing stronger and more beastlike.

Rom closed his eyes and breathed deeply. *Balance.* He tried to picture Riley. The way she acted brave but squeezed his hand when she was truly scared. He fished the black wire from his pocket and rubbed it. His rage faded. Spot's scarlet glow paled and became a soft blue light. Rom took a few more deep breaths and moved on.

By the time Rom climbed back into his room, the drumming was deafening.

Spot was larger – it wasn't Rom's imagination. The creature crawled into the corner, curled into a ball, and began snoring. Rom considered his demon. Spot was growing quickly, but what if he materialized like this in the next fight? He wouldn't stand a chance.

Rom needed to talk to Dragonfly. She had a talent for helping him sort through his thoughts and make sense of them. She was the only one who could understand what he was going through, the only one who talked to him in a way that felt genuine. And he had no reason to believe she would lie to him. But if Ramirez could betray him like this, maybe Dragonfly could, too. Rom opened the Tree Book and ran his finger along the page, forming letters, and then words.

Trust no one, Dragonfly. Not even me.

Why wasn't she responding to his messages? Was she angry, or had something terrible happened? Rom looked over to the corner where Spot had been, but he had vanished. Spot and Dragonfly were the two things Rom could trust in these caves, and now they were gone.

Rom pulled the blanket over his head and tried to sleep.

28

CATCHING LIGHTNING

Mei was soaked by the time she made it to Old Hug. The enormous structure formed a roof shielding some of the balloons below from rain. Wiping the water from her eyes, she traced the ropes from Old Hug to the high balloons, each of which held two people – one to control the balloon and the other to handle the kite. Morning Man was paired with the dinner chef, and they were struggling to keep their balance against the gales. Jun and his friends operated the rest of the balloons. Their reckless laughter carried through the wind.

Mei wasn't sure where to go. Then a small bolt of lightning ricocheted off the dinner chef's kite and hit him in the stomach, knocking him out of the balloon. As he fell, Mei bolted across Old Hug. The chef bounced on a mound of dirty laundry near the edge and would have rolled into the open sky if Mei hadn't caught him. He was three times her size, but somehow she summoned the strength to move him. Her heartbeat pounded in her ears as she dragged him to an area covered by a tarp. He was unconscious and unusually warm, but still alive. Mei cut the kite string from his wrist and tied it to her own. She reeled in the kite, hoping it wouldn't attract another bolt of lightning before she could climb up the rope ladder. Morning Man was struggling with the controls, cursing in Korean. When she pulled herself over the edge, he jumped back.

"Dragonfly? What are you doing up here?" he shouted.

"He's safe," Mei said. "Dinner chef. He's on Old Hug."

Morning Man looked over the edge. "A pity. He's such a terrible cook. Ah, but he is a great fisherman. Now go back down. This is no place for you."

Mei held her ground. "I'm already here, so you might as well tell me what to do. You can't do this alone, and I'm not letting go of this kite."

"This is no time to play hero," Morning Man said. He stared at her for a second before nodding. "OK, little warrior. Let me show you how to use this before you get us both killed."

Two strings, one cloth and one wire, hung from the kite. Mei held the cloth string while Morning Man connected the wire to a machine on a rubber platform in the corner of the basket. The machine's moving valves made it look like a giant heart made of copper.

"It's called a lightning harvester," Morning Man shouted over the wind. "It collects the lightning so we can use it to power our machines."

"What does the kite do?" Mei asked.

"It attracts the lightning and channels it to the harvester. It's a special design, with tiny windmovers on both sides, so if you see a stray bolt, a simple tug will send the kite where you need it to go, faster than your eyes can follow. It'll be easy enough to draw the lightning. Whether we can hold it is another question."

"You aren't sure it will work?" Mei asked.

"This is a positive lightning storm," Morning Man said. "They are rare, but they're ten times as powerful as negative lightning storms." Mei remembered what Ai-ling had told her about Morning Man's daughter and son-in-law – Sumi's parents – dying in a storm like this.

Mei launched her kite. It caught a current and rose up through the rain and wind, jerking the string roughly in her hands. The thin metal coils on the kite's head looked like elk horns as it charged the clouds.

"Watch yourself, Dragonfly," Morning Man said. "This storm's got a smell about it."

Mei heard Jun yelp and looked just in time to see a bolt hit his kite. The light flickered down the wet rope and into the harvester. Mei heard a loud popping sound, and the machine hissed.

"He'll be all right," Morning Man said. "He's been at this a few times."

Mei saw lightning jump from one section of the largest storm cloud to the next just before it hit her kite. She felt a violent tug and watched the electricity dance down the wire, then into the machine. The machine hissed and emitted a pulsing glow for a few seconds. Mei felt a rush of fear, and she did her best to control it.

Another bolt streaked in from the centre of the storm cloud, missing Mei's kite by a few metres as it shot straight down. There was a loud crash as the lightning punctured an empty balloon and then shattered a corner of Old Hug, sending debris into the crowded basket below.

"Watching the lightning is not enough," Morning Man called over the howling wind, glancing down. "You've got to move your kite to catch it."

Mei swallowed hard, trying not to cry. She'd imagined being a hero, but this was difficult, and terrifying. She could barely keep her balance in the wildly rocking balloon, let alone manoeuvre the kite.

Morning Man shouted, "No time for tears, little one."

"I'm not crying!" she shouted back, gathering her strength.

"And don't let another one get by you!"

A bolt of lightning streaked from the front of the cloud and hit Jun's kite directly. It travelled downwards in a tight spiral. Then the machine exploded.

Jun and his friend gripped the sides of the basket as pieces of the harvester flew in all directions. A hook rope was severed – if the other broke, their balloon would be sucked into the storm.

"Keep your eye on your own kite," Morning Man shouted through the wind. "They are twice your age and can take care of themselves."

Mei shifted her attention in time to see a small bolt bounce from one cloud to the next, heading in her direction. She hoped it would hit one of the other kites.

The bolt zigzagged closer, and Mei tugged hard to pull the kite into its path. The lightning struck the kite with crackling force, yanking the string from her hands. The bolt flew down the wire and into the machine. Mei closed her eyes, expecting the machine to explode. It hissed and popped, but the harvester remained intact.

Mei let out an exhilarated yip, but then she looked at her hands as her kite disappeared into the storm. At the same moment, an enormous orange ball of light moved towards Jun's balloon, white streaks of lightning trailing behind it like electrified braids. It smashed into their balloon, and the braids wrapped around it like tentacles, puncturing it on all sides.

Mei looked on, horrified, as Jun and his friend fell through the clouds and out of sight.

"Ball lightning," Morning Man shouted. "It's unnatural. I've only seen it once in my life."

"They fell," Mei whispered, straining her neck to see where they had gone.

"That's where growing up on the ropes comes in handy," he said confidently.

Mei looked back down to see that the men had already climbed into view on a single wet rope.

"We're almost through the cloud," Morning Man said. "Losing your kite isn't going to help matters. We'll have to move over to compensate for the missing catchers."

Mei felt powerless. She searched around, desperate to find a way to help. Then Feifei emerged from her pouch and flapped into the sky, her delicate wings struggling against the wind and rain.

"Feifei, get back here! You'll get hurt. You'll be sucked in by the storm!" But as she spoke, something amazing happened. Feifei's wings expanded. They continued to stretch and spread until they were as wide as a kite.

"Dragonfly," Morning Man bellowed, "what is that creature? What are you doing? Don't—I..." But his voice faded into the distance, until she could no longer hear him. A foreign thread of images and feelings had taken over Mei's thoughts. It was Feifei. Mei focused on that thread, followed it. Feifei wasn't thinking in words, but in images, equations, flashes. But mixed in with all that was something familiar and comforting – something soft. It reminded Mei of the time she spent with her mother, silent but together, not needing to speak, as if they communicated through the very air they shared. She sobbed now as she felt the same sort of link with Feifei.

"Go," Mei said.

Feifei took the end of a kite string and flew straight up against the harsh wind. Mei gripped the other end of the string, watching her pet fly deeper into the storm.

As Morning Man manoeuvred the balloon, Mei watched the lightning crawl inside the nearby cloud. She hoped this was the last layer of the storm. Her hands burnt from holding the string, and her arms were shaky and tired. She did not think she could catch any more lightning, and she was worried about Feifei.

She caught a glimpse of clear sky, but also a pulsing glow in the belly of the cloud.

"Keep an eye on that one," Morning Man said, confirming her fears. "It's holding its power. It will be a strong one when it shows itself."

"I know what I'm doing!" Mei shouted, mostly to bolster her own confidence. Mei stared at the glowing light, where a ghostly figure seemed to dance inside the cloud. She wanted to hide, but then she thought of Breaker. He would be brave, she knew. He would stick it out.

When the lightning showed itself, it moved at blinding speed. The bolt barrelled towards Old Hug, straight at the spot where Jun's two fallen friends were tending to the dinner chef.

Something was happening in Mei's mind. Symbols pulsed along the sides of her vision. Time slowed, and Mei saw events around her unfold in a complex web of patterns.

A circle with a crosshair moved over the lightning bolt, and Mei could see a black-and-white representation of the kite. She moved her wrists and arms like the nimble parts of a perfectly calibrated machine, and Feifei moved in response to intercept the lightning. The crosshair locked into place over the lightning bolt and began blinking. The last thing Mei remembered was a loud explosion.

She came to a few minutes later, Morning Man's face looming over her. His usual angry frown was gone, and his lips trembled.

"No doubt more sky-blasted science," he said. "You and that demon bug of yours. But we'll deal with that later. Let's get you to your feet. You caught the big one, Dragonfly, but Old Hug's taken some damage, and we're going to have to land for repairs."

"Aren't we over mek territory?" Mei asked. There seemed to be a thick pane of glass between her and her emotions. During those last seconds before the bolt struck, she had felt nothing – no fear, no guilt, no panic. Not even excitement.

"We're landing just the same. There's too much damage to repair with the materials we have." Mei thought about the terrifying meks in the mountains near her village, and those she and Sumi had seen from High Watch.

Even though Mei knew she should be afraid, she felt nothing, even when she saw Feifei lifeless on the basket floor, her wings charred. There was a steely coldness inside her, and the part of her that used to care seemed like a vague memory.

29

RILEY

Rom kept to himself for the next few days, refusing to see Ramirez or anyone else. His only comfort was Dragonfly, whose determination reminded Rom to focus on getting out, and Spot, whom Rom summoned when he needed a less opinionated companion. Spot had taken to breaking anything he could reach with his horn, and while Rom tried to train the demon to behave, he secretly enjoyed the destruction to Diamond Teeth's finery.

Gambling, speculating and arguing over the upcoming fights became the sole occupation of the cave dwellers. People lined up at makeshift stands to bet on which fighters would be matched, the length of the fights, and whether a demonsmith who melted down would go beast or mek.

Sixteen demonsmiths would compete for the championship. There was one fight per day; winning five fights earnt a contender the chance to battle the reigning champion.

No one was supposed to bother Rom, but security deteriorated as the tournament wore on. The barriers that previously separated the demonsmiths from the other cave dwellers crumbled in the chaos. Human guards could be bribed, and people were constantly pounding on Rom's door with desperate pleas for information. *Breaker, how you feeling? You ready for the next fight?* There were threats. *Lose the next one if you know what's good for you!* There was begging. *Just give me a tip, Breaker; it's my last chance. If you don't help me out, I'll end up in the Grotto.* Rom tried to ignore them, but it was maddening. Their voices slithered into the room over the sound of the drums.

Rom was about to get up and chase one such visitor away when a messenger came to his room with news that his next fight had been moved. It would be later that same day.

Rom's opponent was known for her powerful beast abilities. She wore an elaborate mask of leopard-patterned velvet that matched not only her cape, but also the dyed pattern of her buzzed hair. She growled at Rom as they entered the Pit. Rom was relieved when Spot materialized in full-size fighting form. But Rom could sense the real Spot inside the fighting demon, bewildered at being asked to battle. In previous battles, Spot had been joined in some way to the battle technology, which enhanced fighting instincts and limited others.

But now Spot was disconnected, no longer a tool, but a natural extension of Rom's own mind. Rom didn't rely on technology like the others to conjure or control. He still used a helmet, which provided the power bar and other instruments, and a triggit, to help him focus his power, but he was no longer in need of either.

Despite Spot's reluctance, the bond between him and Rom was far stronger than before, and they won the fight in two minutes, easily dodging the other demon's venom-fang attack. The girl hissed angrily at Rom as she was taken away.

Rom's third opponent was less catty, but no more effective. The oafish, terrified boy tried to mask his fear by holding his fists up to the crowd and dancing from side to side. He wore a costume inspired by ancient knights. A helmet covered everything but his eyes, and he wore a chain-mail vest and red velvet cape. The hapless boy beat his chest, and Ramirez snarled. "He's supposed to be a knight, a noble warrior from ancient times, but there's nothing noble about this display." His special move was the shield shell; he tried to spear his opponent with a great barb on his demon's shell. It took longer for him to parade around the ring than it did for Spot to snap the life out of his battle demon.

Rom's next opponent was known for her mek precision. She wore a mask of gleaming alloy and a necklace of blinking lights. Rom took her out in thirty seconds. Diamond Teeth exclaimed that it was one of the shortest fights in the long and distinguished history of the tournament. Rom himself was surprised by the incompetence of his opponents. After all, he was a just a novice. It shouldn't be so easy. But the crowd loved his efficiency in the Pit, and soon he was the favourite.

The fights went by in a blur, and though Rom and Spot grew more fierce and powerful with each one, Rom began to feel less engaged. He felt like he was hovering far above the spectacle, watching battles in which he had no personal stake. He was afraid of the rage he'd used to beat Aiko, certain that it would result in a meltdown or worse, so he tried to stay calm. In the arena, he kept his face set and stared straight ahead, tuning out both praise and insult. Everyone was using him for their own gain, and he found it easier not to feel anything. His only thought was to save Riley. Everything else was a tool or an obstacle. His face showed no expression, even in the most extreme moments of the fights. He thought less and less about Riley as his sister and focused on her as a goal, a prize that would enable him to stop this passionless march. To the crowd, Rom was a stone-faced killer, and the joylessness with which the new demonsmith annihilated his opponents had a signature allure. He was unlike any other fighter they had ever seen.

After the fourth round, there was a break in the tournament. The rest brought Rom back to his senses. He still had no strategy for rescuing Riley, but he had to see her again, to make sure she was still safe.

Rom made his way to the cavern, using tinderbox and torch only when absolutely necessary. He was skilled, now, at travelling alone in the dark. Once inside, Rom allowed himself the luxury of a few minutes staring at the open sky. The promise of being aboveground filled him with hope.

Rom traversed the tunnels around the Grotto, one after another, but found no hint of a secret entrance. He kicked the wall in frustration, but stopped when he heard a distant tapping noise. He held his breath as a guard passed through an intersecting tunnel.

It was hopeless. He could never break into the Grotto on his own, and Robertson and the others had shown that they couldn't be trusted.

He would have to summon Spot. It was the only way to find Riley.

Rom closed his eyes and tried to imagine the pup Spot, walking clumsily as he first had.

Nothing happened. He concentrated his thoughts on how he had felt in the ring. Afraid of what he would see, Rom opened his eyes.

Spot looked up and cocked his head. He was bigger and stronger because of the constant fighting. Rom could sense the demon struggling to control the violent urges that allowed him to win in the ring. Spot looked as if he might attack his own shadow, or even Rom.

"I know how you feel, Spot," Rom said. "But right now we

need to focus on rescuing my sister. I'm working on a plan, and I need to see that she's still safe."

Rom needed a way to communicate with Riley this time. He tried ripping a page from the Tree Book, but it wouldn't come free, and the wrinkles smoothed immediately.

"Stupid newtech," he muttered. "I need this page so I can talk to Riley."

There was a dull glow on the page, and a line crawled down one side, splitting a page neatly from the spine.

"Thanks," Rom said. He composed his note quickly, speaking the words and watching them appear on the page.

This time it was much easier to split Spot into pieces and take control of one before the others disappeared into the cave floor. But without the help of the gang's demons, it was much more difficult to navigate the shadows and dodge guard demons on the way to Riley's hut.

When Spot reached Riley, Rom saw that her hair was tangled, her face splotched with mud. A tear trickled down Rom's cheek, and he felt his human emotions overwhelm him. He craved the warmth of collapse, but he pulled himself back, as he knew he must, by flooding his mind with cool reason, trying to stay alert for any information that could aid in Riley's rescue.

Riley's face lit up when she saw Spot. She sniffled and wiped her nose.

"Spot, you came back!" Riley said. "I thought the guards

got you. You look more cuddly than you did last time. Where's your armour?"

Rom moved Spot closer and dropped the note next to Riley's foot.

"What's this? Bringing me a piece of rubbish?" She picked up the note and read: *Riley, this is Rom. I'm controlling this little demon, and I can see through his eyes. I'm working on a way to get you out. Are you all right?*

Riley looked down at Spot. "You better not bite," she said. She got onto the floor, on her stomach, propping herself up on her elbows so that her nose was a mere centimetre from Spot's face.

"The demons won't let me go anywhere, Rom, and people keep trying to break into my hut. Some of them act crazy, just like Dad did. They keep yelling and trying to rip off the door so they can get my food. The demons chase them away, but I can still hear them."

"I hope this works," Rom said to himself. He withdrew his consciousness from Spot, and he felt the demon scatter into atoms and molecules that spread through the air. Rom's consciousness was back inside his own body. He opened the book and saw his note to Riley mirrored on the page in front of him. Her face appeared in the corner.

Riley, try writing over my message on the paper with your finger.

Riley's handwriting appeared. *Your little pet disappeared. Just* vanished. *How are you able to do all this stuff? You found some kind of newtech?*

I'll explain it all to you later. You have to stay strong for me.

I was starting to think you'd forgotten about me.

I'm trying. Believe me.

Try harder. Please. She was crying.

Rom heard footsteps in the cavern.

Hide this paper, Rom wrote. *We can use it to communicate.*

OK, wrote Riley. She wiped her eyes with her dirty sleeve, leaving thin streaks of mud across her cheeks.

You trust me, don't you? asked Rom.

Riley only nodded.

30

Myra

The fifth fight session would begin in less than a day. Rom stayed in his room, listening to the roaring crowd outside and the ever-louder crash of the drums. The more chaotic the noise, the more he relied on cold logic to endure, analysing the demons he had faced in the past and calculating how subtle differences in demon anatomy related to individual fighters. If he knew his opponent, Rom now understood, he could find the demon's weakness.

He lay with his eyes closed, thinking only of strategy, when he heard the sound of a key unlocking his door.

Diamond Teeth strutted into the room, his cane tapping everything in its reach like a dog marking its territory. He raised his hands in a triumphant gesture and smiled. "How you feeling, champ?"

Rom's focus faltered. He was much better at controlling his mind now, but the presence of Diamond Teeth still filled him with fear and rage.

"I'm not a champ. Every match is a new chance to lose."

"Fair enough," said Diamond Teeth, taking a seat on the divan. "The way you're taking them down, though. I've got to tell you, son, you're a pleasure to watch. You're a natural, just like your father."

Rom swallowed. His father had betrayed him, as had Ramirez. At least Rom knew where he stood with Diamond Teeth. And the boss of the caves was the only human Rom knew who was powerful enough to do anything about the beasts. Rom was sure the demons could take the city back if there was a way to operate enough of them aboveground.

"What's the point of these fights?" Rom asked. His calm was returning, and this was an opportunity to get some answers.

Diamond Teeth laughed, but there was no amusement in his eyes. "You weren't satisfied by what Ramirez told you?"

"You know how wacko he is," Rom said. He knew he was playing a dangerous game now, but he was feeling fearless. "Balance. Harmony. I don't see how any of that can help."

"You're right about that," Diamond Teeth said. "Philosophical nonsense, but it does have its uses. Calming the nerves before a fight, and so on."

"Why haven't you used the demons to take back Las Vegas?"

Diamond Teeth looked at Rom intently. "I know you've been in the Grotto. You've seen my big wheel. Problem is, it doesn't work if you get too far from the caves. If I want to take the fight to the beasts, I'm going to need the right commander. Someone with the right talent, who can control demons without using gadgets." Diamond Teeth brought his fleshy face closer to Rom's. "Is that something you might be interested in?"

Rom felt that he had no choice but to persist. "I hate the beasts," he said. "We should be aboveground, and they should be under our control, and so should the meks." It was the kind of thing Rom had heard kids say a thousand times, trying to prove how tough they were.

Diamond Teeth put his hands on Rom's shoulder. "I'm glad to hear it, Breaker. You remind me a lot of myself."

The idea disgusted Rom, but he would do whatever it took to keep Riley away from the Demon Wheel, at least for a while longer. Of course, none of it would matter if he lost, but losing was not an option. "As soon as I get Riley back, I'll help you get Las Vegas back."

"I'll take that under consideration," said Diamond Teeth. "If you make it to the final match, I'll arrange a little audition." He rubbed his fleshy face and stood up. "I'm glad we had this little chat. You're shaping up to be a pretty good demonsmith. I mean that. You're learning to fight the right way, Rom, and I can see how much you love it. What's not to love? The chaos of battle. That delicious moment just before you crush your opponent. It's what you were born for, Breaker. I can see it in your eyes. That's where the power is. Ramirez can talk all he wants about balance, but balance never saved anyone from a pack of hungry beasts, and it won't save your sister. But you've figured that out, haven't you?"

Rom's stomach churned. He did love those things about battle. Maybe he was more like Diamond Teeth than he wanted to admit. "Right," he muttered.

"It's OK to want to destroy your opponents, Rom. It's how you win."

"Right."

By the time the next fight was set to happen, Rom was resolved to do exactly the opposite. He would strive for balance in the fight. He would keep all of the aspects – human, mek, beast – in check. More important, he would go into the fight with complete awareness. He'd relied too much on the beast aspects, but this time, he would allow himself to feel everything, and to use those feelings to win.

Rom kept his head down on the way to the arena, focusing on maintaining balance, and tuning out the crowd. He was sure he could win, but careful not to let himself revel in his confidence.

Then he saw his opponent.

Myra.

31

BYRON

Metal strips flowed behind Myra like a plume of feathers. Her shaved head was uncovered and unadorned, exaggerating her severe eyes. Rom knew she didn't want to fight any more than he did. He also knew that neither of them had a choice.

Diamond Teeth strode into the arena, holding up his hands, playing to the gathered gamblers. He was wearing a white silk suit, a red velvet cape, and a comically large gold crown that sat crookedly on his bald head. He swung his jewelled cane back and forth like a flag. The crowd thumped its approval. Then he lowered his cane, and they became silent.

Diamond Teeth pointed to the fighters.

"Breaker, and his demon, Spot, will now fight Myra and her demon, Dart."

Rom and Myra bowed towards the crowd and then each other. Rom saw the familiar smirk on her face. He knew she wasn't going down without a fight.

Diamond Teeth jogged across the ring and jabbed his cane at the crowd. *"Why do we fight?"*

"So we may conquer!"

"Who must we conquer?"

"The beasts! By controlling the demons, we will conquer the beasts!"

Rom moved into the Pit, followed by Ramirez, Myra and her handlers. He sank into the stone chair, pulling the helmet secure. He summoned Spot, who materialized larger and more powerful than ever.

The crowd erupted. "Breaker! Breaker! Breaker!"

Rom steered Spot around the ring, staying just inside the candles. He could feel the perfect balance of his triangle. The demon moved effortlessly as Rom surveyed the weapons at his disposal.

Myra's demon, Dart, formed in the centre of the ring. Dart was as lean as a greyhound, with shimmering flanks and thin, tall legs that would give her great speed. Her lioness head gazed across the crowd. She was all sleek lines, designed to move.

The two demons circled the ring, eyeing each other.

Rom could tell at once that Myra was an entirely different sort of fighter. The usual showmanship and superficial aggression of previous fights were absent. In their place stood a creature of subtle power and grace.

The crowd grew restless as the beasts circled, and Rom tried to compose a strategy. Diamond Teeth had promised an easy fight, but he had underestimated Myra. Rom needed to find a way to beat her without causing her any serious harm, protecting himself in the process.

He would need more than the mek mastery he had developed. He would have to rely on his human and beast aspects to win. He would have to risk melting down again.

For the first time since his fight with Aiko, Rom felt doubt. Spot's knees buckled.

Myra did not waste her opportunity. Her demon lunged forward and knocked Spot to the ground.

Rom felt a surge of terror, and his human aspect flashed red.

Dart charged again. The crowd roared, screaming for blood. Rom forced Spot up off the ground and sidestepped the charge. His animal instincts were activated now, but the flood of human fear still threatened to overwhelm him. He tried to find his mek logic, but there was no time.

Dart was far more powerful than Rom had suspected. Her movements were short and swift, with perfect efficiency and a dancer's grace. With one lightning-quick motion, the demon doubled back, caught Spot by the flank, lifted him into the air, and slammed him to the ground.

Rom couldn't breathe. He looked to his power bar. Half-strength. His triangle was in chaos. The human side flashed red. Bright red. The courage of the beast was fading. He was going to melt down.

Myra's demon roared down at Spot. She was going for the kill.

Too much human. Too many feelings. Let go.

There was no time to care. It was kill or be killed. *It's OK to want to destroy your opponents.* That's what Diamond Teeth had said.

Summoning all of his power, Rom launched Spot at Dart, pinning her to the ground so that she faced the crowd. Spot held the struggling demon down as Rom's power bar dropped. If Dart managed to break free, Spot would be nearly defence-less to a counter-attack. Rom felt a surge of rage, but he knew it would drain his power and leave him vulnerable.

Myra was trying to destroy him. Rom felt foolish for hoping he could win without hurting her. Battle was about hurting the enemy – and winning by any means.

He needed to try something else.

Rom made his move. He withdrew most of his consciousness from Spot's body, leaving just enough to keep the hybrid from vanishing. Returning to his own body in the Pit, Rom looked across at Myra, strapped to her stone chair, her face pale under the helmet. Ramirez and Myra's handlers were watching the fight, oblivious to Rom as he unstrapped himself and crossed the room. Meanwhile, in the arena, Spot was helpless, his power dangerously low, and Myra took the opportunity to reverse the move and pin him.

Rom whispered a single word in Myra's ear: *Byron.*

Myra's demon began to tremble.

The crowd chanted. "Breaker! Breaker! Breaker!"

Myra's demon released its hold. A hush fell over the crowd as Spot scrambled away and stood. In the Pit, Rom heard Myra shout, "I can't feel anything!"

Rom knew that it would end now. He let his rage flow through Spot's muscles. Controlling Spot was effortless. He charged. Out of the corner of Spot's eye, he saw Diamond Teeth standing in the front row. His gold crown had fallen off, and his face was red and wet with sweat. He was waving his cane.

Finish it, Rom thought. The animal pulse burst through his mind, and he gave in to the thrill of its fury. Spot rammed Myra's trembling demon. The fight was over.

Rom came to slowly this time, his chest heaving, his body and his mind pierced with pain. The Pit was in a commotion, but no one bothered with Rom. He watched as a cluster of people, including Ramirez, gathered around Myra's chair. He threw his helmet off and joined them.

They were trying to revive her. Rom pushed his way closer. Myra's face was blank, her eyes staring straight ahead, her twitching body covered in cold sweat. Rom staggered away from the scene. He didn't need Ramirez or anyone else to tell him that Myra had gone mek.

KILLER

I can't get the image of Myra's face out of my mind, Dragonfly. It looked so blank as Diamond Teeth's guards dragged her off to the Grotto. She used to have this smirk on her face, but now there's nothing.

I am a killer, and they love me for it. You should have seen the way they cheered. They wanted more. They treat me like a hero.

I'm scared of what I'm becoming. And I'm scared you won't want to talk to me after what I did. But I'm more scared of being alone with these thoughts.

I knew what it might do to her, and I still did it. Because I had to win. How many more fights until I become inhuman?

I can't risk becoming like my father, and abandoning Riley like he abandoned us. There won't be any more fights. The first chance I get, I'm going to get Riley and make a run for it. Spot will help. I'm going to bust into the Grotto, and this time I'm not leaving without her.

33

MEKS AND BEASTS

For the first time in many years, the Sky Village had landed. Hook ropes were disconnected and balloons floated free, descending like raindrops across the wide, dry earth.

Most of its inhabitants stayed close to their baskets, as if the earth might swallow them whole at any moment.

"I heard you did it," Sumi said, approaching Mei soon after the storm.

Mei said nothing, still wary.

"Good work with the lightning kites," Sumi offered with a smile. "Maybe you can show me some tricks."

"Sure," Mei said, smiling, "if you promise to teach me more about controlling the balloons. Morning Bird."

Mei felt herself breathing more easily. The girls roamed around camp, surveying the repair work. Sumi was walking as if she'd forgotten where her legs ended. Mei did her best not to laugh. Her reconciliation with Sumi was a relief. Having a friend again made her feel a little more normal.

"This is what they mean when they talk about the unyielding earth," Sumi said, stamping the ground with her foot. "It hurts my feet, and it's hard to stay balanced. I feel like I'm standing inside a big dish of dirt. There's no air except for up."

It felt good, finally having an advantage over Sumi, but Mei kept it to herself. The two girls saw Morning Man in the distance talking to Old Su. Mei and Sumi circled around and eavesdropped from behind some rice barrels.

Old Hug's main power unit had been destroyed by lightning. They couldn't get the Sky Village off the ground without a new one.

"There's only one place to get a power unit in this territory," Morning Man said to Old Su. "I'll have to take one from a mek. I'll go right now."

Old Su bopped him on the head with her walking stick. "You think you can take on the meks by yourself? In broad daylight? You're older than I am!" She shook her head. "You'll take at least three men with you, and leave after dark."

"There are no real fighters left in the Sky Village. I'm better off on my own."

Old Su raised her walking stick again, and Morning Man flinched. Then she slowly lowered it. "Fine. You're right. We need everyone here working on repairs anyway. And what mek would want to bother with an old walnut like you?" She paused long enough to let him know there was concern behind her jokes. "Take some extra weapons anyway."

Sumi whispered to Mei, "We've got to follow him."

"What can we do?" Mei said. "There are meks out there."

"I know my grandfather. He's crazy. And he misses fighting. It used to be his life. If he goes by himself, he'll look for a fight."

"We'll have to hurry," Mei said. Morning Man had grabbed a large shoulder bag and headed up the road without looking back. When he was almost over the hill, Mei and Sumi started after him, careful to stay out of sight. Sumi's walking began to improve, but she had yet to acquire her land legs, so Mei held her hand as they scurried clumsily through the bamboo trees. The path became steep, and Sumi's grip tightened as they passed near a waterfall. Morning Man stopped to wash his feet.

Sumi wrinkled her nose. "We can't drink out of it now," she said. "He's just polluted the whole water supply." Mei giggled, then covered her mouth.

Later they came up the edge of a hilly clearing so vast Mei could barely see the bamboo trees on the other side. Morning Man stepped just beyond the trees and crouched. He pulled a crossbow from his bag and began fitting a bow.

"Oh, no! What is he planning to shoot?" Sumi cried. They sneaked carefully past a series of large trees, stopping a few feet from Morning Man. Sumi put her finger to her mouth, and Mei held her breath.

"So it's both of you now," he said without turning around. "One's just as bad as the other, and both loud as moose. Sumi, I taught you better than to chase after danger."

"But I was worried about you," Sumi said, looking out from behind a tree. "What are you going to shoot?"

"Girls and their questions!" Morning Man hissed. He crawled further into the clearing and up an incline. Mei and Sumi followed, peeking through two boulders at the top of the hill.

Morning Man pointed to the horizon, where Mei saw metal shapes emerge into the clearing from a path on the opposite side – giant wheeled creatures, tiny crawlers and every shape, size and function in between.

"What should we do?" Sumi asked. Morning Man pulled a farseeing glass from his bag and put it to his eye before handing it to Mei.

"Look," he said. Mei saw a row of wheeled meks as big as houses, with huge arms reaching towards the sky, and square heads on strangely thin necks. Others were more humanoid, but with oversized limbs retrofitted with weapons.

"The first generation was built to serve humans," Morning Man said, "if you can believe it. The later generations, built by meks, seem to have lost the habit."

Sumi took the farseeing glass and peered at the army. "Looks like about two hundred."

Morning Man nodded. "One of those big ones will have the power unit we need."

"But how can we get it?" Sumi whispered. "There are so many of them."

Mei saw eagerness in Morning Man's eyes, but it faded when he looked at the two girls.

"We'll wait," he said.

They hid behind the boulders as the meks marched slowly across the dry earth, sending clouds of dust into the air.

The wind changed, and Morning Man turned his face towards the breeze and sniffed. He wrinkled his nose.

"What is it, Grandfather?" Sumi asked.

"Beasts," he said. He pointed to another hill in the distance, directly in the path of the meks. Several white animals with black spots crouched there, and others were approaching.

"Beasts here?" Mei said. "But this is mek territory."

"You're right," Morning Man said. "But they're here. The battles are starting again."

"Snow leopards," Sumi said. "And elk behind them. You can see the tops of their horns."

Mei strained her eyes to see. As more beasts approached the hill, she began to make out their shapes – desert cats, wolverines and others. Compared to the meks, they were disorganized, even fighting among themselves, but they began to settle as the mek army came closer.

The snow leopards stood in front, their tails brushing the sand, so low to the earth that Mei could see only their spots. Behind them two rows of wild horses pranced in place. A row of desert cats crouched nearby, much smaller than the snow leopards, with two rows of giant elks and antelope towering over them.

As they waited, Mei watched some of the desert cats impatiently pounce on one another's shadows. Occasionally, an elk stamped its foot near one of their tails and they fell back in line.

The meks halted just in front of the hill. Several small, round meks approached the front of the pack, their long arms waving like water hoses in the strong wind.

"Detector meks," Morning Man said. "They use them to sniff out beasts and humans."

Mei sensed that the desert cats were eager to attack the waving arms. One crouched low, tail twitching, paws kneading the dirt. But just as it leaped, an elk swooped in with its horns and knocked the cat several metres down the hill in the other direction. The cat rolled and landed on its feet. It shook the dirt off and took its place again, now still and ready.

Mei handed Morning Man the farseeing glass. His face and gestures reminded her of that desert cat. She could see how badly he wanted to rush into battle.

Mei knew that beasts were excellent hunters but not strong on strategy. The detector meks would surely have caught the scent of the beasts, but the wind had gathered strength, carrying it in the opposite direction. The wind, Mei knew, would help the Sky Village move more quickly out of mek territory. She thought about the villagers patching and refilling their balloons, the kids playing in the dirt, hundreds of lives depending on Morning Man and on this lucky change of the wind.

The larger force of meks marched slowly around the hill. The snow leopards pounced, flying through the air like arrows and landing on top of the large ones, their fangs searching for exposed wires. The desert cats followed, biting and clawing the detector meks' hoses and batting them around like balls. The elks and antelope closed in from behind, ramming meks of all sizes with their horns, flinging the small ones away, and overturning some of the others.

The machines, caught by surprise, seemed frozen and defenceless as they calculated their options for response.

The giant meks wheeled themselves into a circle as well as they could with snow leopards biting into their joints. Other large meks completed the circle around a group of smaller ones, who had crossbows, catapults and other projectile weapons fused to their bodies.

"Circling the wagons," Morning Man said. "The meks will win this one, but we may still get lucky."

"Why do they fight?" Mei asked. As soon as she'd said it, she knew it sounded foolish, but she wanted to know. It was something no one in her village discussed.

"Border disputes are the trigger," Morning Man answered. "But the real reason is hatred. Hate that goes deeper than bone, into the centre of every atom and molecule. You can feel it yourself, deep in your DNA, in your instincts, this fear and anger."

Mei understood. She'd felt that hatred in High Watch, when the birds had attacked. But she also knew that, for her, there had been more. There had been the sense that she could somehow reach out to beasts and meks, that she could understand them.

"But why did the Trinary Wars start in the first place?"

"The question of the age," Morning Man said. "Hiro once told me there was truth to the old legend of West Wind. He told me he knew her – he called her Zephyr – but that would make him twice as old as he looks. He says she wanted to use science to save the world, but nearly destroyed it instead. Whatever started the big wars, it looks like we might be in for another one. We're deep inside mek territory; the beasts travelled far to get here."

Mei thought about the images she'd seen of West Wind, with strange symbols blowing in the wind, and of the same symbols swirling in the corner of the Tree Book whenever Animus was present. Was there a connection?

The beasts were resilient in the face of the organized defences. The desert cats leaped into the centre of the fortified circle, further confusing the meks. The snow leopards had disabled two of the giants, and another was overturned and smoking. A few beasts lay still, but Mei could not tell whether they were dead or unconscious. She saw a hatch open on the back of one of the giant meks. Two humanoid meks loaded the unconscious beasts into it.

"Why are the meks taking them prisoner?" Mei asked. She remembered Breaker's claim that meks made humans and beasts fight one another as a form of entertainment.

"Trust me," Morning Man said, "you don't want to know."

The surviving detector meks waved their hoses, releasing a thick smoke into the air before heading off with the rest of the mek group. The wind had died, and the smoke filled the air between the two hills. The beasts broke into a run, the cats scattering at random, the elk and antelope fleeing in herds. When the smoke cleared, there were bodies of meks and beasts strewn over the ground. Mei stood up to get a better look.

"Wait," said Morning Man, his hand on her shoulder.

After a few minutes, some beasts began to stand, weak and disoriented. They headed off after their kin, leaving the dead beasts and broken meks behind.

"Stay behind me," Morning Man said.

"But they're dead," Mei said.

"There's no such thing as a dead mek," he said.

They walked slowly towards the battlefield. Two giant meks were on fire, and several smaller ones were in pieces. Another giant was overturned and damaged, but it still glowed and hummed. The air stank with the smell of smoke, scorched metal, the burning flesh of beasts unlucky enough to be caught in the flames, and the acrid remnants of poison released into the air.

"This one," Morning Man said, pointing to one of the giants. He took out his knife and pried open a hatch. Inside, a heart-size object pulsed with purple light. Morning Man protected his hand with his leather vest, then reached into the hatch, pulled out the object, and dropped it into his bag. The mek's glow died, and the hum stopped.

"We're going to have to run before the others get here," he said.

"Others?" Mei asked, looking around. Morning Man pointed at the horizon. Mei couldn't see anything through the gauzy layer of smoke.

"I feel them," Sumi said. "They're coming so fast."

"Too fast," Morning Man replied as he used his knife on another deactivated mek. This one looked like a giant eyeball with four massive wheels for limbs. Morning Man cut some wires and connected others, then opened a large hatch at the back of the eyeball.

"Hurry, get in," he said. Sumi jumped in with a grin, but Mei was wary.

"You want me to get inside that?"

Morning Man scowled. "Do you want to face their army? From the sound of it, there are several hundred meks coming this way." Mei remembered the flying meks from High Watch. She climbed in without protest.

They sped off over the field. Morning Man sat on top with exposed wires in hand, touching them together to command the machine. When they were just out of view of the camp, Morning Man stopped the vehicle and climbed out.

"We're not taking it with us?" Sumi asked.

"Take a mek into camp?" said Morning Man, incredulous. He turned to Mei.

"Dragonfly," he said, "what we're up against now, with the meks and beasts on the move – it's going to be the biggest fight of my lifetime, and I've lived a long time and seen some big fights."

He stuffed his hand into the mek's neck cavity and pulled out several wires. He held them against one another until they sparked.

"Those powers you have, I can't even begin to understand them. But one thing I know is that they're tied to your emotions. It was the same with your mother, but your powers are on a whole other level. Things have gone too far now with the birds, and the Sky Dance won't be enough. But if you can use your powers, we might have a chance."

He twisted the wires together, and the mek jolted forward and began to roll. "You're the only one who can remake the peace between the Sky Village and the birds. It's in your blood, in your kaimira gene. But if you aren't completely sure who you are, and what you stand for, you might just destroy us all."

The rolling mek began to smoke. Sumi and Mei stared wide-eyed as it caught fire and then exploded.

Mei could not respond. She knew she had a powerful ability; she didn't know she might hold the future of a whole people in her hands. How could Morning Man ask her to take on such responsibility?

Morning Man pointed into the distance. "There's a human settlement two days from here." He removed the mek power unit from his bag, then tossed the bag to Mei. "There's enough water and food here to last you that long, and some other items for trading. They're desert people, strong and friendly. You'll be safe there, and when I hear word from your father, I will tell him where to find you."

Morning Man was sending her away, after telling her the future of the Sky Village was in her hands? She was on the verge of becoming a true sky villager. And with the help of the Tree Book, she was finally on the trail of the meks who took her mother. How could he send her away now, to another village where she knew no one?

Sumi gaped at her grandfather. Mei looked in the direction Morning Man had pointed. She imagined a human village, in some ways like her own. Families, kids running barefoot on the hard earth, no risk of falling through the clouds to her death. She longed more than anything to feel safe. But was safety anywhere only an illusion now?

Mei didn't say a word when Morning Man and Sumi walked off, or when Sumi turned around and waved her arms, tears rolling down her face. She felt so alone. Even when they had gone a distance, Morning Man dragging Sumi's arm as she shouted in Mei's direction, Mei remained still.

She stood there as Morning Man and Sumi disappeared over the hill. She could faintly hear the sound of Sky Village kids playing in the distance.

Looking out over the desert, she put a finger in her pouch and stroked Feifei's head. Her pet was still motionless. Mei wished for the thousandth time that her parents would appear magically and take her home. But her mother was a prisoner of the meks, and her father was risking his life to save her, and there was nothing left of her village. No amount of wishing was going to change that.

She thought of her friend Rom, battling demons to rescue his sister, risking his humanity and even his life. These sky villagers had opened their homes to Mei, knowing the potential danger. Could she really leave them, now that the birds were no longer on their side?

She couldn't bring herself to run away. And to find her parents, she needed to build an alliance with the birds, so she could use their eyes and wings to search the world. But to win the birds' forgiveness, and their help, she had to perform the Sky Dance.

And then there was Ai-ling, and Morning Man, and Sumi, and Old Su, all too selfless to demand her help, but looking to her as their only hope. She had to help them.

Mei turned back towards the Sky Village and began to run.

Once they had the power unit, it didn't take long for the Sky Village to become airborne. The patched and inflated balloons rose. Villagers threw hook ropes back and forth to connect the baskets, and the ropes creaked as the village spread out across the sky.

They jerked to a stop. A metal spike bit into the basket near Mei's hand, and she looked down to see humanoid meks climbing up a heavy cable towards the Sky Village. Shouts of alarm turned into screams of terror as more hooks found their marks, and a platoon of meks climbed up from the dust cloud below.

34

A CHANCE WORTH TAKING

Rom wasn't afraid. He knew he was being followed as he entered the large cavern on the way to the Grotto, but there was nothing that Diamond Teeth or Aiko's gang could do to him that would feel worse than what he'd done to Myra.

Rom stopped in the slim pillar of moonlight and waited. The steps grew louder and stopped.

"Ramirez," Rom said, without turning around. The old man's walk and laboured breathing gave him away. "I'm not in the mood for a lecture right now. Trust me."

Ramirez spoke softly. "I know what that last fight must have done to you—"

"How can you know?" Rom snapped. "You tell story after story, but you don't know what it's really like."

"I know right now you want to go storming into the Grotto and get Riley. You want to destroy anything that gets in your way."

Rom turned to face him.

"Thing is," Ramirez continued, "you know as well as I do what's going to happen. It's just a dramatic way to commit suicide. The last fight got to you, and somewhere deep down you're feeling like maybe you don't deserve to be alive."

"I told you I'm not in the mood for a lecture." Rom turned away from Ramirez and looked up at the stars through the small hole high above. "Especially not from you."

"What's that supposed to mean?" Ramirez asked.

"I heard you talking to Diamond Teeth."

Ramirez was silent for a moment. "I told him what he needed to hear, Rom. And now I'm going to tell you the truth."

Rom rolled his eyes.

Ramirez continued, "I have a plan for destroying the Demon Wheel, but for it to work, you have to keep fighting, and you have to win."

"Why should I believe anything you say?"

"Because I looked out for you and Riley topside, and I've looked out for you down here. You're both still alive, aren't you? Doesn't that buy me a little bit of trust?"

Rom kept silent as he thought. It would be so much easier to go out in a blaze, giving everything he had to get to Riley.

He might even see her one last time before the guard demons destroyed Spot and then hunted him down. It would be easier, but it wouldn't be right. Ramirez knew these caves better than anyone. If there was any chance the old man meant what he said about destroying the Demon Wheel, it might be a chance worth taking.

"Go ahead," Rom said. "I'm listening."

35

JINX

The gamblers swirled like hungry vultures around a carcass as Rom made his way to the arena for his last match. Ramirez tried to push people out of their way, but they were two against thousands.

Eventually a troupe of guard demons fought its way through the crowd and surrounded Rom, providing an escort. The hallway to the arena floor was jammed with more raving gamblers. Diamond Teeth's demons had to remove people by force, flinging them into the crowds to create a narrow lane for Rom.

One of the gamblers grabbed Rom by the shoulders and hurled him inside the arena. Rom stumbled and tried to gain his footing, but he couldn't right himself in time and fell roughly to the sand. The crowd roared.

Rom pushed himself up and stood tall. Banners bearing his name in elaborate script whipped back and forth. People banged drums of wood, skin and metal. Torches flared everywhere. A miasma of smoke, sweat and fermented fruit juice hung over the arena.

Diamond Teeth made his entrance. He wore a purple suit studded with gold nuggets that matched his crown and cane. Over the suit he wore a gold cape, lined in fur, with a twenty-foot train.

Diamond Teeth danced to the centre of the ring, arms outstretched. He dipped right, then left as his entourage struggled to keep him from tripping over his cape. He swung his cane around at the crowd, bringing the simmer to a full boil before lowering the cane and bringing the throng to order.

There was still no sign of Rom's opponent. He looked to Ramirez for explanation, but the old man was looking intently at the guard demons that surrounded the arena. There were far more than usual, which meant there were fewer elsewhere in the caves.

Diamond Teeth jabbed his cane towards the waiting masses.

"Why do we fight?"

"So we may conquer!"

"Who must we conquer?"

"The beasts! By controlling the demons, we will conquer the beasts!"

"I can't hear you!"

"The beasts! By controlling the demons, we will conquer the beasts!"

Diamond Teeth lowered his cane, and the crowd fell silent once again. He slowly made his way to the candles. As he lit them, he shouted, "You all know that I am an honourable man. You know that I am unwilling to give you a poor championship." He paused as his voice echoed in the rafters. "That would be unfair to you, my loyal subjects."

A hot wave of nausea shot through Rom's stomach, scorching all thoughts of escape or victory. *You're in over your head. You don't even know who you're going to fight. There's no way Diamond Teeth will allow you to win. Even if you do, you'll never get out of here alive.*

Rom felt his mind wandering. But after weeks of fighting, he was able to control the urge, to stand at the brink and keep himself from falling – for now anyway. Still, there remained a part of Rom that wished everything would go black.

Diamond Teeth flashed Rom a smile as he continued. "This year has provided me with a challenge. Breaker has proven very difficult to beat. Not since his father's glory days have we seen such a spectacle in the arena. If there is no fighter who can match Breaker, then there's no game.

"Because I knew you would appreciate a good show, I had to work very hard to find my champion. For this match, there was only one who would really do."

Rom had trouble breathing. He willed himself not to

vomit on the sand. The crowd swirled in his vision. He searched it for a comforting face and at last found Aiko and the rest of the gang. Aiko glared at him; the others avoided meeting his eyes.

"Gamblers, thieves, scoundrels," shouted Diamond Teeth, "I give you the battle of a lifetime!" Diamond Teeth turned towards the entrance, and Rom looked in horror towards the shadows.

His father staggered into the open. Like an animal let out of its cage.

He looked even worse than he had in the kitchen of the burnt-out skyscraper. The simple, ceremonial black robes covered his emaciated frame, and his head was shaved clean. But his face was smeared with dirt, and he lurched and lunged with a crazed fury that was all beast.

"I give you Rom Saint-Pierre, otherwise known as Breaker, with his demon, Spot. And I give you the one and only Jack Saint-Pierre and his demon, Jinx."

The audience erupted.

"Who must we conquer?"

"The beasts!"

Rom noticed his father looking around in terror like a cornered dog.

Diamond Teeth drew the circle. Rom and his father tossed in their triggits. Neither needed them, but it was still part of the ritual.

Rom had to purge his emotions or be swallowed by them. A numbness swept over him as he drifted into mek thought. He would go through the paces of the fight. He would do what it took to win.

The two demonsmiths settled into their chairs. Without hesitation or ceremony, his father put his helmet on. Rom heard a roar. His father's demon, Jinx, was already forming.

Despite his cold confidence, a part of Rom hesitated. He knew that steely mek thought alone would leave him vulnerable. His father would fight like a beast, and if Rom wanted to defeat him, he would have to fight fire with fire. Rom called on all three aspects and held them at once.

Before Rom slipped on his helmet, he looked at his father one more time. This was the man who had played with him and Riley as small children, letting them ride on his back as he crawled around the floor, making funny beast noises. This was the man who had read to Rom from the Tree Book. Rom had turned Myra into a mek-brain, and it was possible he might kill his own father. His beast aspect loomed; it was fight or die, destroy or be destroyed. He let this instinct take root inside him – survival balanced with pity.

Rom slammed his helmet on and strapped it tight. He watched the power bar and the triangle come into view. The technical aspects of demonsmithing, once so foreign, were soothing now. Spot moved easily. Control was no longer conscious. It was instantaneous as the twitch of a muscle or the blink of an eye.

Rom observed his father's demon skulking around the ring, biding its time. The hybrid lacked the elegance of some of the others Rom had faced. His skin was bare and red with irritation in some places and furry in others, as if the demon had been tearing off his own coat clump by clump. Jinx looked like an oversized, armoured wolf with four metallic tentacles that twitched and jabbed, itching for contact. Its basic form was similar to Diamond Teeth's guards, and Rom wondered if Jinx had been used as a model. Jinx's fangs chomped at the air, revealing a mouth of sharp teeth and rusted circuitry that crunched and sparked with every bite.

Jinx presented a nervous front, but Rom suspected he wouldn't attack until he sensed the opportunity for a perfect kill, and so Rom took the offensive, hurling Spot forward. There was a thud as Jinx was knocked to the ground. Rom could hear the crowd shouting his name, but he didn't waste time gloating. Instead, he dived towards Jinx's chest and snapped his triggit in two.

Jinx sprung up and retreated. Like Rom, Jack didn't need the triggit to retain control. This was going to be a long battle.

Rom's power bar was still full. His triangle pulsed green on all sides. He felt the power of balance surging through him. Whenever doubt arose, Rom crushed it. *There is only survival.*

His calculations were cold and precise. He held his emotions at bay, balancing in a way he had never done before.

The two circled the ring while the crowd roiled above them, growing restless. Neither demon was willing to give way. Rom searched for weakness. His father's strategic abilities should have suffered when he went beast, but his demon was still far more powerful than any Rom had encountered. Rom felt himself getting impatient and realized his father was manipulating him. He was presenting a demon that was all beast, but he was fighting with mek precision.

Finally Jinx charged, sailing over Spot's head in a single leap. Rom turned Spot's head to see where the demon had gone, then realized his mistake. It was too late. The jaws were around Spot's leg, the tentacles holding him down. The crowd erupted.

Jinx sank his lupine teeth into Spot's belly, lifted him up, and slammed him into the sand with ground-shaking force. Rom watched in terror as his power bar plunged. Spot's body writhed under the pressure, searching for a way to break free. In the chair, Rom's body absorbed the blows, and he groaned with pain.

As his strength faded and the crowd roared louder, Rom wondered what he would become when he melted down. He would probably end up like his father, going through human motions but with the heart and mind of a beast. He tasted the sand of the arena floor and continued to squirm. It would all be over soon. For the first time in the battle, Rom's triangle tilted out of balance – the human aspect flashed a dull pink.

Rom choked on the injustice. All his life, he had been forced to fight before he was ready. He was sick of it. It was his father's fault. Even before the transformation, he had hardly ever been around and had done nothing to keep his family safe. Rom wanted to feel sorry for himself, to give into the human instinct, to let go and collapse.

Then he thought of Riley. He had to focus, for her. He let his beast rage fill him, even as his mind raced through strategies. There was only one strategy: *survive.*

With a sudden surge of strength, Rom swung Spot's paw and dislodged the jaws from his belly, then staggered back.

The crowd, who had been resigned to a swift kill, came alive at the thought of a comeback. Rom ignored them. Spot was hurt, and so was he – sitting in the stone chair, he struggled for breath, and his chest throbbed with pain. He was more terrified than he had ever been.

Rom knew Jinx was at full strength. While the demons circled each other once again, Rom watched his power bar edge up. His triangle was still in balance, but the urge to let go and escape into beast or mek thought was stronger than ever. Rom felt his legs bucking against the straps.

The demons were face-to-face now, perfectly still. They looked each other in the eye. The crowd urged them forward, wanting more action, but neither one moved.

Rom realized that his father had never been able to balance. He had the same powers as Rom, but he had always spun too far in one direction or another. Even when he was fully human, he'd never been able to balance his children with the rest of his life. There was always something calling him: a restlessness that never allowed him to be satisfied with his life.

Rom would win by doing what his father couldn't.

Jinx seemed almost to smile. It mistook Rom's pensive stillness for fear and made tentative, taunting dashes, feigning charges and then retreating.

Rom took off the helmet. He used all his concentration to hold Spot in place. In the chair, his limbs relaxed. Rom was communicating with Spot in a way that was so real and intense it was as if he had left his body behind and climbed inside the demon. *We need to do something we've never done before.*

Rom felt the demon accepting.

His opponent went into a crouch, staring at Spot, suspecting a trick.

Spot stayed where he was.

Jinx pawed the sand.

Rom focused only on holding the human, mek and beast aspects together.

Jinx charged. The crowd roared.

Rom did not will his demon to do anything. Spot acted on his own, doubling in size, all muscle and armour. He pawed at the sand and snorted, pointing his horn at his opponent. Then he ran, propelled by cheetah hind legs, a blur of blue, and crashed into his father's demon with such force that Jinx split in half against the cave wall.

The fight was over. The crowd was stunned into silence.

Diamond Teeth stood and clapped slowly.

"Well done, well done," he boomed into the arena. "Easily the best match I've seen in all my years in the caves. But it wouldn't be a finale without a bit more show." He snapped his fingers, and dozens of guard demons descended into the arena.

36

THE SKY DANCE

As the meks rose from the dust cloud below, climbing slowly up wires attached to grappling hooks, the sky villagers were spurred into action. They distributed anything that could be used as a weapon to anyone capable of holding it. Unable to cut the hooks, they began throwing their heavier supplies overboard – barrels of rice, buckets of oil – anything to knock the meks back to the earth or at least to slow their ascent. But the meks continued climbing.

The clouds parted, revealing a vast flock of birds circling in the sky. Mei's first thought was that they were there to revel in the destruction of the Sky Village from their lofty height, but just as the first mek was about to topple over the lip of a basket, the birds dived. Three birds peeled an approaching mek from the wire and sent it plummeting to earth.

"We're saved," Ai-ling cried out. "The birds have returned."

But Ai-ling was wrong. The birds fell like a heavy blanket on the Sky Village. Mei could feel their rage as they shredded balloon fabric with their claws and beaks.

Sumi grabbed Mei's arm.

"Hurry. Follow me!" She rushed Mei across the ropes to Morning Man's balloon.

Morning Man was standing next to an intricately carved wooden box. Birds shrieked behind him, rising and falling as they attacked neighbouring baskets, but Morning Man remained still, his expression grave. "Mei," he said quietly, "you've made your choice, and you know what you must do."

Mei nodded. She would have to perform the Sky Dance now, with the meks attacking from below and the birds from above.

As the chaos exploded around them, Morning Man spoke. "We can hold off the birds for a while, but when the rest of those meks reach the village, we'll be caught in the middle of a battle that none of us will survive. Our only hope is for you to reach out to the birds before it's too late."

Mei had no choice.

Morning Man opened the chest in front of him, revealing a costume of silk and feathers, woven in the colours of the Sky Village. "Your mother made this costume," he said. "The material is something from her experiments. She used it sometimes to enhance her powers when she needed to communicate with the birds."

Mei reached for the costume, but Morning Man stopped her. "Remember your training, Dragonfly. Remember balance. Your powers are stronger than you know, and this costume will only enhance them. If you lose balance, you'll be lost, and so will we."

"There's no more time for lessons," Mei said, reaching for the costume again.

Morning Man frowned, but this time he relented. "I'll go pass word along to the drumline," he said. Before he climbed out of the basket, he paused. "The opposite of balance is chaos, Dragonfly."

The sleeves of the robe extended several feet past Mei's hands. Underneath, she wore a silk dress. A feathered headdress completed the costume. By the time she arrived in the centre of the village, where a net of ropes spread out like a field, most of the village was crowding around to gawk. Archers shot at the birds, trying to keep them at bay, and others continued hurling pots and barrels at the meks. A few smaller balloons had collapsed, and others listed towards earth. Helpless inhabitants watched as the birds tore into their homes and the meks climbed towards them.

Mei stood on the perimeter of a large net of ropes. The headdress felt weightless on her head. The silk robe flowed in the wind, the long sleeves flapping like flags. Mei tried to calm herself. The birds were everywhere. What would keep them from attacking her?

The villagers watched her with rapt attention. They knew her dance was the only chance of stopping the attack and saving the village. Mei tried to ignore the crowd, but she could feel all eyes on her. It was crazy, but she was more afraid of looking foolish in front of them than falling to her death.

For all his distractions and grumpiness, Morning Man had been a good teacher; Mei had learnt many of the skills she needed for this ritual. But she lacked the most important thing, which even the youngest sky villagers had: a confidence as deep as blood and bone that they belonged in the sky. Mei felt like an impostor.

But she also had something no sky villager had. It gave her strengths she was only beginning to understand. The kaimira gene – the mix of human, beast and mek elements that allowed her to become more than simple Mei Long from Luo Ye Village. She wondered whether it would be enough.

Mei knew she had to look down. She had to let the fear flood over her now, so it wouldn't ambush her later. She had to remember her mother, her father and Breaker. She had to acknowledge her love of the Sky Village and her wish to escape it. She had to accept the range of her emotions in all of their complexity to find balance in her mind and in her body. But that was not all. Mei had to call on the beast and mek aspects inside her as well, no matter how much they terrified her.

She looked down. Far below, through the web of ropes and balloons, through drifting tufts of cloud, she saw the mek army climbing towards the village. Above her were the birds, circling while they gathered themselves for a second assault. She breathed in deeply, and again. Her heart beat a rapid rhythm, but it was steady. She could breathe normally, and her legs held steady. She took her first step, then the next, and continued until she had joined Morning Man in the centre of the ropes.

He turned away from her as she approached and raised his hands to the air. "Witness young Dragonfly's Sky Dance," he shouted. "Should she survive, and should she win back the friendship of the birds, she will heal this wound, and we may yet be saved."

There was applause from the villagers who had crowded close enough to see. As they watched Mei, they glanced anxiously at the sky, their makeshift weapons at the ready. A second wave of meks had begun to climb. It wouldn't be long before they reached the balloons.

Three elders playing ancient instruments began the song. It was a tune her father used to play on his one-string instrument. He called it "The Dragonfly Song". Mei smiled, thinking of the silly lyrics she and her father had come up with together:

> *Little dragonfly, zip zap zop.*
> *Why does she fly instead of hop?*
> *She's got long hair and teeth like thorns.*
> *She's got bright eyes and the deadliest horns.*
> *Little dragonfly, buzz buzz buzz.*
> *Why does she fly? Because, because.*

Mei was alone in the centre. She thought about her family, and her home, and what she must do to save them. She saw her parents as they had once been, playing this tune on their instruments and laughing. And then they appeared as she had last seen them, her mother sleeping, her father growing smaller as Mei rose into the sky.

Mei let the sadness and wonder and terror of the past weeks well up inside her. She opened her mind to the birds, who circled frantically above, preparing for slaughter, blocking the sunlight and casting shadows like falling leaves upon the surrounding balloons.

She began to dance, starting with a few moves her mother had taught her. Mei felt the movements and allowed her instincts to take over until her steps were sure and smooth. Equations flowed through her mind, attaching themselves to wordless feelings, and she moved without trying to understand what she was doing.

She thought of her parents and the sunsets they'd shared back home as the bright orange sky became a blanket of moon and stars wrapping its arms around them – the same sky she could never truly call home. She thought of the secrets she had shared with Breaker, who was a stranger and yet so much like herself. Through intangible bits of writing, they'd found a deeper understanding. She thought about her confusion and embarrassment and hope about her powers, her fear of facing the meks, and her terror of the beasts. She tried to express all of this in her dance. Each movement was a flash of meaning. Her long sleeves wrote madly on the wind, the fabric of the costume animated by Mei's thoughts, while her body stayed steady and smooth.

She wrote the characters for *I'll miss you, Morning Man,* surprising herself with the tenderness she felt for the stubborn old man. Then she switched to the dance-writing she had created alone in her mother's garden. The sky villagers would not be able to understand her meaning as her sleeves traced words into the air, but it helped Mei to tell them her thoughts, fears and feelings. She told them how much she wanted to belong here, and that once she left, she'd never be able to look up into the sky without a painful longing. She told them how she had felt that first morning, waking up to the sight of the Sky Village at sunrise. She told them how afraid she was of what she knew she had to do. And finally, she told them how alone she felt, even as she was surrounded by people who wanted badly for her to be part of their lives. She reached out to the birds above, to the meks approaching on the ropes, to the villagers, and to all living creatures on the ground below, and opened herself to them.

When she stopped, there was silence. She rose from her bow and stood still and tall. Morning Man seemed to have forgotten his role, mouth hanging open as he stared. Sumi had tears in her eyes, as did many others. The birds descended, but there was nothing vengeful in their movements now. They did not screech or dive, but rather circled towards the village, as serene as falling feathers. The meks had paused in their ascent, equally transfixed by the Sky Dance, and hung motionless on the wires, the lights behind their eyes pulsing rapidly. By the time a round of applause surrounded Mei like a hug, the meks had resumed their ascent. Mei knew that she had passed the ritual. But she also knew that it no longer mattered. What she must do now would be too terrible to forgive.

37

THE RESCUE

Spot was surrounded. Diamond Teeth's guard demons circled, their liquid-metal muscles shimmering in the torch-light. It was just as Ramirez had predicted, and Rom saw that now the old man had his chance. He would use one of his devices to sever the guards' connection to the Demon Wheel. The residents of the Grotto would be free to escape, and he and Rom would fetch Riley and destroy the Demon Wheel.

But then Rom saw Ramirez being dragged off by two thugs and Diamond Teeth crushing the device under his foot.

There was no back-up plan.

The guard demons pounced. Rom used every bit of power in Spot's legs to jump high into the air. The guards slammed into one another as the demon dived on them, horn first.

What followed was a blur of metal and teeth. Rom's body felt the pulsing ache of every blow, but he channelled the pain back into the fight. He was controlling Spot effortlessly now, his demon leaping, snapping and pouncing with violent grace.

Guards attacked from every direction. Spot held them off, but he was outnumbered twelve to one. There was no time to eliminate one without leaving Spot vulnerable to all the others. Spot fought as well as he could, but Rom could feel his fatigue. He couldn't win this one.

Then another demon formed to Spot's right. This was no guard. It was Shakes. To the left, Aiko's demon, Muddy, materialized, then the twins' two-headed demon, Boomer. Rom glanced up at the stands through Spot's eyes and saw the gang, helmets on, eyes closed. They had joined the fight, but on which side? If they joined the guard demons, Spot wouldn't last a minute. Rom's body screamed with pain, and Spot was losing power fast.

A guard demon leaped straight for Spot. Rom would have just enough power to hold it off, but nothing more.

Shakes charged. He knocked the guard to the ground, picked it up, and flung it across the arena. Rom's heart leaped. He didn't know whether they had forgiven him, but with their help, he might just survive.

Spot, Muddy, Boomer and Shakes stood in turning-wheel formation, their backs to one another, facing all four directions. Through Spot's peripheral vision, Rom noticed one of the heads on the twins' demon had vanished. Moments later, he heard Leo's voice in the Pit.

"Aiko wanted me to tell you: Diamond Teeth will add more guard demons to finish us off. That means there won't be as many guards in the Grotto. When they attack, go get your sister and Myra."

Rom nodded, struggling to hear Leo's words while maintaining control of Spot.

"Promise you'll get Myra. Promise."

"I promise," Rom stammered, not even sure whether his mouth would work. It must have, because a few moments later, the second head reappeared on the twins' demon, just as the next wave of guard demons streamed into the arena.

Diamond Teeth bellowed, "Now those odds I like much better." He laughed, and the crowd hooted and cackled along with him. "But it's been a long show, and it's well past time for dinner. Let's finish it."

He clapped his hands, and the guards attacked. Rom withdrew his mind from Spot, and the demon vanished as Rom ran from the Pit.

He didn't summon Spot again until he was just outside the Grotto. In the fight against his father, Rom had connected with the demon as never before. Now, he would have to ask Spot to fight for himself.

"I need you to do this for me," Rom urged the demon, appearing now in his true state, smaller and without armour. "For Riley."

Spot nodded, eyeing the two guard demons. They were at least four times his size. He looked back at Rom as if to tell him how insane an idea this was.

"I know it's crazy, Spot. But it's our only chance."

Spot lowered his head, clawed the ground with one foot, and charged. Despite his bulky front end, his cheetah hindquarters gave him speed. He speared one guard with his horn, and in a single, graceful whip of his neck, flung it into the air, knocking the other guard over and pinning it down.

Rom and Spot slipped through the gate while the second guard struggled to free itself.

Rom saw the Grotto through his own eyes for the first time. The place was even more horrifying than before. Rom's senses were not as keen as Spot's, but it was easier now to compare it with the places he'd been aboveground. Even in the poorest dwellings in Las Vegas, there had been sunlight and fresh air. Rom saw shacks collapsing into stagnant pools of fetid water. He saw piles of food, leftovers from the Avenue so slick with rot that even the starving Grotto beast-brains wouldn't touch them. The smell made his stomach heave. Rom pinched his nose and breathed through his mouth so he wouldn't gag.

Spot shoved Rom into a nearby shadow, nearly knocking

him down. Two guard demons walked past, several metres in front of them. Rom held his breath as the guards moved on.

Five demons guarded the entrance to Riley's hut. There were no places to hide, no way to sneak up on them. Rom and Spot walked towards them slowly. Rom wanted to draw them away from the hut, to make sure the fight was nowhere near his sister.

The guards advanced to meet them. Rom and Spot stopped and waited.

"Are you ready, Spot?" Rom asked, looking down at his demon. Spot glanced up at him, then snorted and pawed the floor with his foot. He lowered his head to the ground, ready to charge. Rom couldn't help but grin, touched by the demon's show of courage.

"Let's give them something to remember us by," Rom said as they charged. Rom knew he wouldn't last long in the fight – Spot and the guards were far more powerful than any human, but he couldn't let Spot fight this battle alone. Rom rammed a guard with his head and shoulders, and somehow managed to knock the creature onto its side. He climbed on top of it, his hands scrambling to peel back the chest armour and snatch the triggit. The demon snapped its metallic teeth an inch from Rom's arm, then swung a tentacle into Rom's gut, throwing him back a few metres and knocking the breath out of him. Before Rom could move, the demon was on top of him, black eyes gleaming, three-fingered tentacles holding him down.

But Rom had managed to loosen the chest armour, and it was hanging free on the demon's chest. He reached through the armour and grasped the triggit. The demon snapped at his head, but he dodged, and the creature's teeth lodged in his shoulder. He felt a piercing pain as he yanked the triggit from the chest cavity. The demon trembled for a moment, then collapsed.

Spot was having an easier time with the other four, darting between their legs, jabbing with his horn. He had disabled two of the guards and was taunting the other two. Rom saw his chance.

Riley had heard the commotion and was watching the fight through the door of the hut. When she saw Rom she ran out to meet him, smiling wide and wiping fresh tears from her eyes. They hugged, and then Rom nudged her back. "We don't have much time, Riley."

She glanced over at Spot, who was finishing off the last of the guards. "Your pet got bigger," she said.

"Come on," Rom said. "Let's get out of here."

Just then, Ramirez poked his head out of the hut. Rom noticed a large gash across the side of his face and several bruises. Riley motioned for him to come.

"He's been trying to bust us out of here since they brought

327

him in," Riley said. "He kept fighting the guards. And losing."

"Rom," Ramirez said, panting as he hobbled towards them. "I know you want to get out of here, but we've got to destroy the Demon Wheel. I can't do it without your help."

"The only thing I care about," said Rom, "is getting my sister out of this hole. If you're smart, you'll come with us."

"I can't, Rom. I helped create this technology. I can't let it be used this way."

Ramirez was beaten and bloody, but his eyes were resolute.

"Fine," Rom said. "Get Riley out of here before the guards rematerialize. Spot and I will take care of the Demon Wheel."

"I'm not leaving you, Rom!" Riley said.

Rom looked to Ramirez.

Ramirez didn't argue. He grabbed Riley and rushed for the front gate, leaving Rom and Spot standing in the open.

Rom looked at Spot. He wasn't sure he was going to do anything about the wheel, but he had promised to rescue Myra, or what was left of her. He owed her and the gang that much.

There were at least a dozen demons guarding the wheel. Spot looked up at Rom again. They needed a plan. It wouldn't be long before the fight in the arena ended and those guards were sent back to the Grotto.

"It's just the two of us," Rom said to Spot. "Which gives me an idea." Rom thought again about feeling divided, about outside forces pulling him several ways at once. As Rom concentrated, Spot crumbled into pieces, each piece forming a tiny version of the demon. This time, however, Rom tried to connect with all of them at once. He needed every single one. But they ran in all directions, too slippery for Rom's mind to reach.

He tried a different approach. Instead of trying to control the tiny Spots by force, he fed them a request. *Please,* he thought. *Distract the guards. I'm asking you.*

Suddenly Rom could feel them all in his mind. Like a hundred tiny windows, they revealed the scene to him from all angles.

The throng of Spots attacked the guards. They were too tiny to do much damage, but they were also hard to catch. They bit at the guards' limbs, leaped onto their backs, stabbed at their heads. Rom concealed himself among the half-brains who pushed the Demon Wheel forward like the walking dead. Then he saw Myra. Her clothes were dirty and torn, as if she hadn't changed since the fight. He approached from behind and put his hands on her shoulder. She didn't react.

"Myra," Rom whispered. He took her shoulders more firmly and turned her around.

Her face was grey, her pupils dilated. Rom gently removed the helmet from her head. She collapsed into his arms, panting, barely conscious. Rom carried her a few metres and leant her against a large stone.

He knew they had to go. Riley was out of the Grotto, and the demon guards were still distracted by the tiny Spots. He could carry Myra and leave. But then he looked again at the hundreds of others pushing the wheel, trapped inside a nightmare of Diamond Teeth's creation. He couldn't just leave them this way.

He looked at the helmet he'd taken from Myra. It was attached to the wheel's centre by a long wire. He placed it on his head, and a sharp pain pierced his temples, blinding him for a moment. He fumbled for the wheel and began to push.

Then his vision returned, but he couldn't make sense of it. He saw dozens of scenes at once, in windows scattered across his vision. The images swirled in on one another, looming larger and smaller. The pain in his temples sharpened, and he cried out, but he couldn't hear his own voice. He had no sensation in his hands as they pushed the wheel, or in his feet as they stumbled along. He tried to stop, but he could not. He had lost control of his body.

Rom slowly realized he was seeing the fight in the arena, but from the perspective of the guard demons. The fight was still raging. He saw Shakes, hairy fists blazing, and Boomer, flinging guards across the arena with her thunderous back kick. Muddy swung his spiked tail, ready to strike a charging opponent. The crowd was in a frenzy, cheering and brawling in the stands. It no longer seemed to matter who was winning – the battle had taken on a life of its own.

When Rom had controlled Spot, he had felt a bond and a certain warmth, even in the midst of battle. Now, powering these guard demons, Rom felt nothing. He tried to seize control of one of them, but something blocked him. All control diverted to Diamond Teeth. Rom tried again, but the harder he pushed, the colder he felt. He started to see the gang's demons as enemies, threatening to destroy the stability of the caves, threatening their brave benefactor, Diamond Teeth. He tried to shout, but his mouth wouldn't open.

This is wrong. It's the wheel making me think like this. I need to be stronger.

He couldn't feel his limbs. He had no idea where he stopped or started, which molecules clung together to create the entity called Rom, or Breaker. He scanned the windows and found his own image in one of them, through the eyes of a nearby guard demon. Then he saw himself from another perspective through the eyes of another guard, and then another, until he was viewing himself through dozens of eyes. By fitting together these images like pieces of a puzzle, he was able to find himself again.

He couldn't feel his body, but he focused his thoughts on moving his arm. He saw that it was working. Using the same demon's view to manoeuvre, he grabbed the Tree Book from his bag and opened it. There was no way to see what was written on the page, but he knew that Dragonfly was there, and he needed her help. He held the open book to his chest with one arm as he pushed the wheel with the other, hoping for something, anything, to give him strength.

He felt a dark power coming through the Tree Book, spreading across his body like poison. It was Animus, multiplying into countless voices. All of them demanded to be freed. Dragonfly was doing something – something dangerous. He could feel her thoughts in his mind.

His jumble of thoughts formed into a single question. *Dragonfly, what are you doing?*

38

A HUNDRED THOUSAND EYES

The meks climbed into the baskets, slashing sky villagers with their bladed arms, and dropping their wounded bodies to the earth.

Mei saw Morning Man, Jun and others rushing to help. Using cooking knives and bamboo sticks, they knocked the meks from the baskets and waited for the next wave to arrive. Mei took refuge in the nearest basket and opened the Tree Book. She saw the spiralling symbols, and the voice of Animus rumbled in her head.

You know what you must do. Set me free.

Mei shivered. *Breaker,* she whispered, *I need your help.* Breaker didn't respond, but she could sense his presence, and she hugged the open book, drawing energy from its power and from the knowledge that Breaker was with her.

She closed her eyes and summoned the worst image she could think of – her mother in a mek cage. She took a deep breath and manipulated that image in her mind, so that it was a mother bird inside the cage. She drew on her feelings of hatred and loss, using them to strengthen the vision. She took another breath and then pushed that image into the minds of the surrounding birds.

The meks were everywhere now, communicating in cold tones as they sliced through the wicker, canvas and rope that held the Sky Village together. Baskets and the people in them dropped to the ground, the screams of the falling trailing off into silence.

Mei held on, urging the birds into action. The image of the caged mother bird blazed in her mind.

Animus had said it. She knew what she had to do. "Destroy the meks," she whispered.

The birds dived. They were mad with fury, with no thought for their own lives or any sky villagers unlucky enough to get in the way. The formations of the meks could not withstand the chaos, and many fell. But it was not enough.

As Mei hugged the Tree Book more tightly, she felt its power surging through her like electricity.

Her robe flowed in the wind on all sides, the colours glowing bright. She raised her arms so fast her long sleeves shot out like daggers. Meks tumbled from the baskets. She willed her sleeves into the shape of swords and spun around, slashing at meks, narrowly avoiding the birds. She thought of Feifei's brilliant wings, and suddenly her robe burst into hundreds of butterflies. Underneath, her silk dress took on the colours of the butterflies, its colours shifting as they swarmed out to engage the meks, slivers of coloured lightning blasting from their wings.

Mei expanded her thoughts as far as she could reach, beyond the desert territory. She drew on the power inside the Tree Book. She was invincible.

Dragonfly, what are you doing? It was Breaker. She could hear his voice in her mind. He sounded weak, and scared.

Can you feel it, Breaker? So much power. I can use it to find my mother.

I can feel it, Dragonfly. But I don't think it wants balance. I don't think it's on our side.

Our side? What side is that? The only thing that matters is that I can use it. I can see everything – through the eyes of thousands of birds.

Dragonfly, we don't know what Animus really is—

Help me, Breaker. Help me break these meks. It's what you do, isn't it?

There must be a reason it's locked up.

Help me, Breaker, or get out of my head!

I'll help, but—

You can use it, too. To destroy Diamond Teeth!

Oblivious to the battle raging around her, Mei looked for her mother through the eyes of the birds. She hugged the book, which had grown hot against her stomach, and drew on the power inside it. She expanded her awareness, searching for more birds she could control. She needed their wings, and their eyes. Soon she could see the entire continent, and beyond, through a hundred thousand windows in the sky.

Urgency. Trapped mother bird. Danger. Mei forced these images and emotions on the birds, telling them, in the language of images and patterns shared by humans, beasts and meks, to find her mother. She isolated the hatred deep inside the birds. The hatred that drove them to destroy their enemies.

Mei knew now that this hatred and her own powers came from the same source – the intelligence inside the Tree Book, the voice that called itself Animus. She saw the code in her mind, a swirling cloud of symbols, and she drew on it, harnessing it to drive the birds into action. "Find her." Even as she said it, she felt Animus's influence on her growing stronger, pushing around the edges of her mind.

Do you feel that, Dragonfly? It was Breaker. *It wants chaos—*

Wait. I see them! Through the eyes of a lone lyrebird, running through a clearing, Mei caught a glimpse of the mek army that had captured her mother and destroyed her village. They were pausing for fuel and repairs in the middle of beast territory, surrounding their camp with a wall of flame for protection.

Mei remembered how small she had felt when the book had shown her these terrible machines. It seemed so ridiculous now. Even in their large numbers, with their metal skin and weapons, Mei knew they could be destroyed.

She urged the lyrebird into the air. Its wing muscles were weak and unaccustomed to flying. *Just my luck,* Mei thought, but she pushed harder, and it flapped, struggling to gain altitude. She was so closely connected to the bird, she felt as if she were fighting with her own body. Through the bird's eyes, Mei saw her father, sitting cross-legged in a cramped cage, sawing fruitlessly at a metal bar with a sharp stone.

Father! I've got to help him. She urged the lyrebird closer, and it perched on one of the bars. Her father looked up, surprised.

Mei wanted so badly to say something that she nearly lost her connection to the bird. She held on tight and tried to keep her human feelings at bay. She had to *be* the bird for just a while longer, long enough to give her father a message. She urged the bird to sing.

The lyrebird opened its mouth and screeched.

Her father looked startled. Mei had to try again. She focused her awareness on the bird's body – its stubby wings, its long, elegant tail, its pulsing heart, and finally its vocal chords. This bird was equipped to mimic almost any sound it heard.

Mei planted a sound inside the bird's mind, one she knew her father would recognize. The lyrebird flipped its long tail

feathers over its head and sang. It mimicked, with astonishing accuracy, the sound of her father playing "The Dragonfly Song" on his one-string instrument, including the high note he always missed.

Kai stared at the bird, his eyes wide.

Mei made the bird bow, and her father extended his hand to pet it. "Mei?" he said, his voice wavering.

They were interrupted when a mek marched between two rows of cages and towards them, dragging an unconscious deer. Mei made the bird scurry just out of sight. The mek paused and inserted a thin finger into a lock. After a series of tones, the cage door popped open. The mek tossed the beast inside and pulled the door closed.

This was her chance! But how could she make the machine do what she wanted? She willed the lyrebird to run straight at the mek. She felt fear swelling inside of it, ready to burst, but she pushed it onward. The mek stood ready.

As the bird clawed at the mek's legs, Mei shifted her focus and tried to sense what the mek was thinking. The bird's fear faded from her mind, and she felt suddenly cold. She sensed the even rows of cages, the roles of the other meks, the next task in her queue.

The lyrebird continued to attack, pulling at the mek's wires. Through the machine's eyes, Mei saw the bird as nothing but an interruption of its daily tasks, and as a package of equations – the velocity of its dive, the pressure exerted by its talons, the force required to break its neck and continue with the next task.

Mei found it alarmingly easy to add a new task into the mek's list of duties. Ignoring the bird, it moved towards the cage holding Mei's father. Kai moved as far back into the cage as possible. The mek inserted its key-finger into the lock, and the door opened.

Mei's father lunged forward at the mek's legs, knocking it onto its back. Mei sensed the mek switching into defence mode. *Stop*, she ordered. The mek stopped moving as her father twisted its head off.

Mei once again sensed the presence of thousands of beasts surrounding the camp, terrified of the fire. She focused on the birds circling high and was once again seeing through their many eyes. Her father was free. Now she needed to find her mother.

Paying no heed to the mek guards or the fog of smoke, Mei circled low, looking. Her friends, her extended family, her teachers – each was in a separate cage. Some slept, while others sat coughing, red eyed and ashen faced.

In the last row of cages, she saw her mother, unconscious, pale, and very thin. It was so much worse than the terrible image she'd conjured and forced into the minds of the birds.

Is she alive? Breaker asked.

I don't know! Mei was too furious to cry, too angry to think.

Mei opened her mind to the beasts surrounding the mek camp, using her remaining power to ignite their hatred for the meks, inciting them to blind, murderous fury. *Leave no mek alive.*

39

THE HALF-BRAINS

The Demon Wheel was draining Rom's will. He had wanted to save Myra, to use those abilities that made everyone want a piece of him to somehow stop the Demon Wheel. But the technology was too powerful for him. Diamond Teeth's control was too great.

Then Rom felt it: Animus, the whirlwind of symbols, battering at the walls of his mind. Its power burnt him, until his only choice was to let it in.

The power seared through him like a lightning bolt. He dug in against it, trying to maintain balance, but it was like a vortex inside him, spiralling out of control, pulling him in. His heart skipped a beat, then slammed alive. He saw through the eyes of all of the demons in the caves. Their thoughts ran like streams into Diamond Teeth's. Rom smelled with their heightened senses and felt the rush of their combined powers. The sensations flooded his mind and made it impossible to focus. His only thought was to use the power to kill Diamond Teeth before his mind was lost.

Rom struggled to focus. He traced the thoughts of a single demon guard until he found the link with Diamond Teeth where all the guards received their orders. Rom could sense Diamond Teeth's presence, and he was sure the gangster felt his.

Rom pushed his mind against Diamond Teeth's, struggling for control of the link.

Diamond Teeth didn't waver.

Rom let the power of Animus surge through him, finally giving in to the temptation to let it flow unchecked. He crashed into Diamond Teeth's mind like a stone plunging through water.

Images flashed and exploded, a brush fire of memories. Rom saw burning cities and human crowds stampeding in terror. He saw towering meks collapsing like felled trees and smelled the acrid stench of slain beasts rotting in sunshine thick with falling ashes. These were memories of the Trinary Wars, of pain and death and chaos.

Rom felt the gangster's appetite for power, his need to control everything so that he would never suffer as he once had.

Rom's grip on the link weakened.

A voice boomed through his mind. *You don't know what you're doing, kid. You're letting something loose you can't control.*

It was Diamond Teeth. He was pushing back, struggling to regain the link to the guard demons.

Rom fought back. *You make others suffer, so you won't have to.*

Diamond Teeth held strong. *You could have been the king of the caves. You could have had anything you wanted.*

King of the living dead? No thanks.

Rom pushed harder and felt his power surging. He saw Diamond Teeth through the eyes of those he had enslaved – his father could have been one – the perspectives multiplying exponentially through a thousand scorched minds until Rom felt like all of the hatred of the half-brains and beggars was his own. *You exploit people by giving them hope...*

Diamond Teeth's voice was a whisper. *You don't know what you're doing!*

For the first time, I know exactly what I'm doing.

As Rom pushed with all his strength, he felt the gangster's presence slipping from the Demon Wheel. Diamond Teeth was no longer in control.

Rom was in charge. He shut down the demons guarding the Grotto. They stopped their patrols, sank to their knees, and dissolved. Rom shifted his attention to the arena, where the gang's demons were on the verge of being defeated. Boomer lay crumpled on the ground, and Shakes and Muddy were cornered and fading.

Rom ordered the guard demons back. Shakes cocked his head in confusion until Rom made one of the demons perform an elaborate bow.

Shakes grinned and clapped his hands.

Rom sent the guard demons after Diamond Teeth and his human thugs – and any of the gamblers who decided to get in the way. Rom took his time, enjoying the sight of the beefy gangster shouting and trying to get out of the way.

Rom ordered four of the guard demons to surround Diamond Teeth, pinning him to the cave floor.

Animus's voice thundered inside Rom's head: *Unleash the power. Destroy them.*

Rom directed his thoughts to Dragonfly. *I beat Diamond Teeth. I'm going to put him in a cage.*

There was no answer.

Dragonfly, I'm not so sure about killing him. Animus just wants chaos and destruction.

He could feel Dragonfly's presence, and finally her response came. *We have to use the power while we have the chance.*

It would be so easy to order one of the demons to crush Diamond Teeth's skull. The gangster shouted, red faced, as he tried to free himself.

But as the conversation continued, the tone of Dragonfly's thoughts frightened Rom. Why wasn't she afraid of what they were unleashing? How could she be so sure that they were doing the right thing, while he was full of doubt? Maybe letting go and giving in to it was their only choice. Maybe doubt was useless at a time like this. Everything was against them, and this was their only source of real power, their only chance to gain an advantage. Still, Animus felt evil. But could it be any worse than Diamond Teeth? Or the meks that Dragonfly was facing?

It was all so confusing. But one thing was certain. Dragonfly was his friend, and he had to help her, regardless of the consequences. Regardless of right and wrong.

A faint handprint spanned the cover of the Tree Book, pulsing in rhythm with Rom's aching head.

I'm going to regret this, he thought as he placed his hand on the cover. He felt the presence of Animus flowing out of his Tree Book. But where was it going?

He opened the book and saw the Sky Village. Dragonfly stood on the ropes, holding her own Tree Book, a cloud of symbols flowing from it. What had they done? What had they unleashed?

Rom had survived too much to lose his mind now, and he didn't want Dragonfly to lose hers either. He forced Diamond Teeth and his thugs into one of the giant cages that hung over the Avenue. He needed to pull back, to get back into his own body and to stop Dragonfly before it was too late.

He tried withdrawing from the demons' minds, but his body and mind worked against him. *You're blowing it, Breaker,* he told himself. *You'll wind up pushing this wheel for ever.*

Rather than pulling back, he tried going in deeper, focusing on the cold, cruel minds of the guard demons. Buried deep within them was the presence of the desperate humans pushing the wheel, giving them power. Rom pushed into these minds, reaching through their link with the guards. He needed their help as much as they needed his.

He'd never experienced such emotional bedlam. The humans pushing the Demon Wheel were screaming silently, imprisoned inside their own minds. Rom knew he had to release them, but how could he do it on his own? And once their minds were free, what would prevent them from going mad?

Rom felt a soft touch on his arm and caught the scent of wild berries. It was Myra. He couldn't see her face, but her breathing was steady. She didn't speak. She grasped his hand and walked stiffly alongside him as he pushed the wheel. Her hand was shaking, her palm slick with sweat. Something inside her was still human, still Myra. This was exactly what he needed. Hope.

As the feeling swelled inside Rom, he passed it to the others – the mek-heads, the beast-brains, those half-dead humans pushing the Demon Wheel.

He felt them coming alive, their blindness lifting. The dim Grotto light was enough to hurt their eyes after the endless dark of the wheel. Memories flooded their minds. One man looked around frantically, trying to remember how to speak.

Where's my son? his mind cried out. A teenage girl collapsed, sobbing, ripping at her hair with trembling fists. An old couple embraced, their thoughts racing to remember how many years they'd been pushing the wheel.

Myra squeezed his hand tighter, and the feeling of hope grew stronger. Those who were the furthest gone, whose human thoughts were buried deep inside, stirred and became aware. Those who had gone mek were stuck in a loop, with a human voice screaming from deep inside. Those who had gone beast were a jumble of needs – escape, attack, cower. Rom thought of his father and wondered if this was what it was like inside the man's head.

There was one thing the prisoners of the wheel had in common. For the first time, they were in control of the demon guards. And they were angry.

40

UNLEASHED

Mei's robes flowed, her long sleeves dancing in the wind, as beasts burst through the flames and attacked the machine settlement. A group of meks tried to form a line as two massive lions the size of wagons, manes flaming, charged them. Smoldering boars punctured metallic skin with their tusks and tossed the lifeless machines aside. Meks and beasts destroyed one another in blind fury. Mei had started something too powerful for her alone to stop.

Through the smoke, Mei saw people from her village freeing others from cages. She glimpsed her father carrying her unconscious mother, dodging the fights erupting around him.

Mei wanted to command the beasts to protect her parents, but they were lost in their need to destroy meks. She could no longer reach them.

Mei's attention came back to her own body, to the birds clouding the sun above the Sky Village. She could still control them, and she ordered the birds to redouble their attack on the meks. They did, without mercy, fear or restraint.

The power inside the Tree Book pushed against Mei's mind. *Let me out,* it said. *I'll destroy them all for you. I will be your vengeance.* A faint handprint formed on the cover of the book, covering the etched tree like a pulsing ghost.

Breaker interrupted. *I beat Diamond Teeth. I'm going to put him in a cage.* He sounded so far away. *Dragonfly, I'm not so sure about killing him. Animus just wants chaos and destruction.*

We have to use the power while we have the chance. Look what they did to Mother. Put your hand on the cover.

Dragonfly, I think it just wants to make things worse.

How could they be any worse? Help me, Breaker. My parents are still in trouble!

I'm going to regret this.

What does regret matter, Mei thought, *when we have this sort of power?*

And with that thought, Mei pressed her hand into the handprint. She felt the power of Animus swelling, growing stronger. The book grew hot, but Mei held tight as it began to shake. She was so cold, but not even the searing heat from the book could warm her. Her thoughts turned dark. She felt angry and empty, as if she would never be happy again. And Animus, trapped so long, rushed like a bitter wind out of the Tree Book and into the world.

41
INTO THE LIGHT

The Demon Wheel ground to a halt as the Grotto dwellers gathered around it. They stood trembling. Then, all at once, they rushed for the wheel, removing loved ones and friends, tearing off helmets and offering comfort. Mica and Leo were there, guiding Tick away. Myra pulled Rom from the wheel just as the mob attacked with everything they had – shovels, boots, fists – and tore it to splinters.

Rom took a moment to summon Spot, who appeared, looking disoriented. Someone from the crowd shouted, and everyone rushed for the front gate. Rom, barely able to walk or see, let Spot and Myra guide him.

As he walked through the gate into the large cavern, Riley came bounding towards him. "Are you OK?" she shouted.

Ramirez limped behind her, a look of concern carved into his face.

Rom could only shake his head. He didn't have the strength to speak. He wanted to say something about Dragonfly and the monster they had unleashed, but he couldn't find the words. He just wanted to get out of the caves. He had to see Riley in the sun. That's the only way he'd feel sure that she was safe. The procession moved through the caves and on to the Avenue. Diamond Teeth's thugs glared at Rom and shouted insults from their cages as he passed, but Diamond Teeth grinned as he watched Rom's face.

Aiko and the twins taunted the former boss, bragging about having put him in his place. Rom wanted to say something clever. He wanted to feel like he'd won. But the grin on Diamond Teeth's face made him uneasy. Had they really defeated him? Or was this all part of some larger scheme?

The silent gamblers made a respectful channel, allowing Rom to pass. Aiko, Robertson and the twins joined the procession, walking next to Myra, Tick and Riley.

They would not feel secure until they felt the sun on their faces. They trudged forward behind Rom until they came to the main entrance to the caves, beneath a building in the Triangle. They all streamed through, up and out into the bright, hot streets of Las Vegas. No one was thinking, for now at least, about the beasts roaming there.

ANIMUS

Mei held out the Tree Book as a cloud of spiralling symbols billowed forth from its pages and drifted across the sky. The cloud's colour changed to match its background as it passed over villagers, birds and meks. Birds plummeted from the sky. Meks went silent and dark. Humans collapsed where they stood. The cloud changed shape and grew more solid with each victim. To Mei's horror, shadowy images of the unlucky sky villagers it had consumed, as well as birds and meks, emerged like cancerous growths from its forming body. Tiny symbols raced over its translucent skin. Two dull red eyes glowed from its misshapen head. Animus landed on the net of ropes where Mei had performed her dance.

Dragonfly? We have to stop it! Breaker said. *We should never have let it out!*

Mei knew he was right. She also knew it was too late.

The creature, now twice as big as a balloon basket and growing fast, hulked towards Mei. It had legs and arms now, all stuck in the wrong places. Unable to walk properly, it slithered across the ropes, pulling its massive weight with three thin, meklike hands.

Mei heard the creature's voice inside her head. It was the voice from the Tree Book. *I am free. I have form. I must feed.*

"Get out of my head!" Mei shouted. She could feel the thing poisoning her thoughts, turning them darker. She'd felt such unimaginable hatred for the meks, and now she wanted to feel nothing. She took a step towards the monster. The meks and beasts were pests. The land walkers, her own people, seemed like insects that should be stamped out. Mei felt hatred for all intelligent creatures, and a desire to drive them to annihilate one another. She took another step.

Don't do it! It was Breaker, hearing her thoughts.

Mei didn't respond. She continued to walk, entranced by the creature's pulsing eyes.

Then Breaker began to sing, his voice raspy.

Little dragonfly, zip zap zop.
Why does she fly instead of hop?

Mei paused. An image of her parents flashed through her mind.

She's got long hair ... just like her mom.
She's got courage and a friend named Rom.

Mei stopped. A wave of feeling washed over her. Breaker had forgotten the lyrics and was making up his own. Then the scene came back into focus, and she saw that she'd been standing on a rope, mere feet from the hideous creature. Too terrified to scream, Mei swallowed, and she tried to join Breaker in the last two lines, her voice shaking.

Little dragonfly, buzz buzz buzz.
Why does she fly? Because, because.

Mei turned and leaped into the nearest basket. She took out her yak-bone knife and sawed at the ropes. The monster slithered towards her. She cut the last rope just in time, and it fell.

The creature broke into several pieces on the hard earth below. Mei was horrified to see the sections crawling towards one another and reforming. The monster then cut a path through the mass of meks and beasts before striking off to the west.

43
NEW BEGINNING

Rom sank to his knees, luxuriating in the burn of the Las Vegas sun on his face. His father stood in the distance, shielding his eyes from the glare. He suddenly whirled around like something was attacking him, then sprinted down an alley and out of sight.

Myra stood next to Rom, silent and expressionless as the others gathered around.

"These half-brains are going to get themselves killed," Robertson said. "Someone will have to take charge."

"Let 'em take care of themselves," Aiko said. "We've got transporting to get back to."

Mica said, "We have to take care of Myra."

"We have to find a way to make her better," Leo added.

"Why does she fly? Because, because," croaked Rom before he shut the Tree Book.

The gang turned around.

It took every bit of energy for Rom to raise his head and open his eyes. "Riley?"

His sister crouched closer, an uncharacteristic look of concern on her face. "What is it?"

He fished the black wire out of his pocket and handed it to her. "I was holding on to this for you."

Riley paused, and Rom could see that her mind was racing back, through everything that had happened, back to those moments in the Alamino Casino, when she and Rom were just two buzzers on an errand.

"Finish your puppet," he said. "Be sure you give Mom beautiful hair. She had really beautiful hair, just like you." He sighed, then fell to the ground.

44

CUTTING THE ROPE

Mei knew she had to go after the creature she and Breaker had released.

"I'm not helpless," she said to the unconscious Feifei. "Or innocent. Not after what I've done."

There were only two ropes attaching her to the rest of the Sky Village. She sawed at the first until it snapped. Her balloon jerked downward, and she glanced around at the people she was leaving behind. Many were still unconscious, others stared open-mouthed at Mei, and still others sawed at the meks' grappling hooks so the Sky Village could break free.

There was still time to change her mind. She could help with repairs, then find Sumi and Ai-ling and make sure they were safe. Whatever she had let loose, she could let the ground dwellers deal with it.

But as much as she wanted to belong here, her mother needed her. Her parents were free now, but they were far from safe. And she was no longer sure whether the kaimira gene was helpful or destructive – but she had to find out.

Mei sawed the other rope until her balloon ripped free. She manoeuvred it down, closer to the sea, then turned up the heat and steered it in the opposite direction. As the Sky Village grew smaller, she gazed at Old Hug. It looked like a pair of strong arms reaching out to call her back as she drifted away. She wished she could see Sumi once more, and Ai-ling, and even Morning Man. But there was no time.

She had no supplies, no map, no food, and no one to help her. But she was on her way to find her mother.

AFTERWORD

It was two days since Mei had left the Sky Village. She was hungry, thirsty and cold. With nothing to do but watch the controls, look out for angry birds or meks, and get lost in her tortured thoughts, she distracted herself with the Tree Book. It seemed again like the gentle storybook she had grown up with. The sinister voice inside was gone. She read about other Guardians and their lives, but could find no mention of the entity she and Breaker had released.

But one thing Mei did know – she had a responsibility to find the creature, and stop it if she could.

A pigeon flapped by on its way to the Sky Village. Mei called out to it. The pigeon paused, then swooped towards her. She ran a finger along its back and removed the note.

> A monster has recently attacked several villages in the area. It consumes souls. It leaves its victims – humans, beasts and meks alike – in deep sleep. No one knows its nature, whether mek or beast, or some combination. The locals call it the Terrible Everything.

Mei scribbled a note to Ai-ling and gave it back to the bird. "Go on to the Sky Village," she said, and the bird flapped away.

"The Terrible Everything," Mei said. She thought of the horrible, amorphous cloud that had spewed from the Tree Book, and the nightmarish shape it had taken. Yes, that was what it was.

She wanted to try writing the name in her book, to see if it might trigger the release of some useful information – such as how to destroy it. She opened the book and was surprised to see writing on the page. It was not her own, nor Breaker's clumsy scrawl. It was a careful penmanship, steady with a bit of flourish.

Dear Diary,

Rom's been out cold for two days. His weird pet vanished yesterday. Into thin air. While I was petting him. Which is bad, because the beasts have been sniffing around the camp. I mean the real beasts, not the beast-brain humans in the camp who are always getting into fights with the mek-heads. Anyway, the beasts are starting to look at us like dinner; they just haven't decided which one of us is the first course. They seem wary, but who knows for how long. We're building some walls (the mek-heads are good for that). The transporters are trying to run the place, especially after Ramirez sneaked off. They're the only ones with demons, because of those helmets. But I don't think it's healthy. The more time they spend inside those demons, the weirder they get.

I guess that's all for now. I'm about to do another puppet show for the half-brains. They're not very demanding.

Yours truly,

Riley

Mei smiled as she wrote a response.

Dear Riley,

You might find this hard to believe, but this is Dragonfly. My real name is Mei. I believe your father read you some of my stories when you were younger, just as my mother read me stories about your brother. Don't ask me how the Tree Books are able to do this, or why. I'm still trying to figure that out.

The only thing I'm sure about is that your brother is one of the bravest people I know. And that he cares about you more than he cares about anything, including his own life. You have to take care of him. You must. He has to get better. And when

*he wakes up, tell him that Dragonfly is OK. Tell him there's
something I have to do, and I'm going to need his help, because
I'm not brave enough to do it by myself.*

    Sincerely,

    Dragonfly

By the time she closed the book, the sun had shifted, and
the wind had settled down. Then she saw a bright red speck
in the distance, slowly growing larger. She held her hand over
her eyes to get a better look.

When it got close enough, she could see what it
was – a basket attached to a small balloon. It was pulled by an
entire flock of birds, including the pigeon she'd seen just a few
hours earlier. There was a small oriole painted on the side of
the balloon. It was a gift from Ai-ling and Sumi.

The birds brought the balloon close enough for Mei to
grab the basket. Inside there were supplies – dried tofu,
enough rice for several days, several bottles of water and, best
of all, the tapestry blanket that told the history of the Sky
Village.

As Mei ate, bundled in the warm blanket, she surveyed
the sky and landscape below. She was headed in the right
direction, with no sign of trouble on the horizon. This might
be her only chance to sleep.

Just then, she felt Feifei struggling inside her pouch. She

opened it, and Feifei crawled out and onto Mei's hand. Her colours were dulled, and she moved slowly, but she was alive.

Mei snuggled up in the blanket, and Feifei snuggled next to her. The blanket smelled like crisp air and warm feathers. Mei would sleep for just a bit. The sunrise would bring a new day.

ARTEFACTS

Once a year, on Looking Back Day, work in the Sky Village ceases. Villagers decorate paper lanterns to represent people and things left behind and string them across Old Hug. And everyone gathers to listen to the elders' stories, starting with the tale of how the Sky Village came to be, in the beginning days of the very first Trinary War.

HOW THE SKY VILLAGE CAME TO BE

All sky villagers should know the story of how we first came to be in the clouds, lest we forget how lucky we are, and how important our ways are to our survival.

Before the Trinary Wars turned the world upside down, during the time when humans, beasts and meks lived and worked side by side, there was a hot-air balloon business called Famous Transport in the canal-crossed city of Suzhou, China. The family who owned it were the ancestors of the one and only Mei Long.

Back then, the world seemed to be growing smaller and moving faster by the day, and Famous Transport offered residents and tourists a slower-paced way to experience Chinese landscapes. It was also one of the only forms of transportation that didn't have to follow customs laws, so it attracted its share of rogues looking to transport illegal materials or escape the law.

In the days shortly before the Trinary Wars spread to China, Mei's great-grandfather Shu, a teenager at the time, returned from a mysterious journey to the West.

"Father," Shu said, "recall the fleet now."

"Impossible," his father said.

"Father," Shu said, "I've seen what's coming. It will spread across the earth like a plague. We must go as high as we can, above the clouds."

"Nonsense," his mother said. "I've heard nothing about a plague. Now go wash yourself. You look as though you've been in battle."

That's when the reports started to come in. In Europe and the Middle East, meks built to serve humans turned on their masters; zoo animals escaped their cages and rampaged down city streets. Herds of cows, yaks and other grazers demolished mek factories. Armies were amassing – meks of all shapes and sizes on one side, beasts of all species on the other. Humans, caught in the middle and no longer in control, had also begun to lose their minds to a plague.

Shu's parents were stubborn, but they finally realized the danger of staying on the ground. They recalled the fleet and brought in family members from all over China on express trains. They claimed they were throwing a family reunion in the sky, but the fear in Shu's eyes told another tale, and some had heard reports of their own. Anyone left on the ground was likely to meet a horrible death.

"Father," Shu said, "we must save as many as we can."

"You may think me callous, but we can't save everyone. Family is most important."

"If we leave our possessions, we can save twice as many."

Shu's father gave him a stern look. "Without our possessions, son, what are we? We'd be no better than the beasts. How would we survive? Your grandparents were poor farmers. We didn't have snacks, or shoes. We had to chew on bamboo stalks, and tie strips of tree bark around our feet—"

Shu stopped listening. He had heard it all before, how his father worked his way up from poverty. None of this mattered now. The world was about to end.

So, the night before the launch, Shu travelled around Suzhou, offering a free sunrise balloon trip to everyone he met.

When he returned to Famous Transport just before dawn, there was a huge crowd waiting, old folks and young, Chinese locals and foreign tourists. None seemed to know about the conflict heading their way. They just wanted a free balloon ride.

When Shu and his family were finally ready to launch,

several hours late and with five hundred people instead of the intended fifty, they left most of their possessions behind. They brought materials for making new balloons, great quantities of fuel, windmovers for flying against the currents, and as much food as they could carry. None of the balloons had ever been so overloaded, and it looked as if they might not fly. But fly they did.

During the following weeks, as they drifted above the carnage, they rescued as many humans as they dared, built new balloons as quickly as they could, and linked them all together with ropes. Shu's parents were paralysed by what they saw on the ground and were lost without their possessions. Like everyone else, they turned to young Shu to lead.

As the war raged on and supplies dwindled, Shu realized that his Sky Village, as they started to call it, was in a perfect position to trade information, which above all else was the commodity that had made humans masters of the world. Seeking out tribes of the surviving land walkers, they traded news with them in exchange for food and fuel.

The sky villagers watched and recorded the details of the battles below. Though meks had been created to serve humans rather than fight, their metal skin and mastery of electrical power helped them to dominate at first. But without humans to do repairs, they fell victim to an array of malfunctions, and then they fell prey to the beasts, who had become expert at finding the meks' weaknesses. It looked as if the beasts might conquer the world.

But the wars ended with no clear victor, and an uneasy truce was struck. Humans, beasts and meks retreated to the territories they had claimed, the plague of Animus still inside them. Hostilities ran deep, and skirmishes along borders were common. But the madness had begun to fade, and it was time to start over, to rebuild human societies without the help of beasts or meks.

When Shu died, his son took over as leader, and even with things calmer on the ground, the sky villagers chose to stay in the clouds. The sky had become their home, and the security of life on the ground was still uncertain. And when Shu's son died, Mei's mother was too young to lead, so her guardian, a Cloudwatcher named Old Su, took her place.

Old Su established this day of looking back. It is the way of our people never to regret, never to lose ourselves in what we've left behind. But we are human, and the past runs hot in our veins. So today we gather to remember. Old Su always said that we've survived only because our elders found a way to escape the tragedy that befell the lands below. Remember her words, and always remember our village's legacy.

NOTEBOOK OF
ERNESTO BECERRA RAMIREZ

Day 12

We finally discovered the function of the triangular
devices. They are unlike any science I've read about.
Upon my suggestion that they could be thought
activated, Gavin held one tightly and concentrated.
A shimmer appeared before him, a wisp of
something vaguely animal shaped, but distorted and
grotesque. Like a demon conjured from thin air.

It seemed to be made of swirling microscopic
elements, as if it were trying to bridge the gap
between concept and form.

But it was undoubtedly real. We all saw it. And I
won't rest until I see it again, and understand what
it's made of and, more important, its purpose.

Day 35

Gavin succeeded in fully conjuring the demon (as we've begun calling it). A truly magnificent and terrible creature. It tore him in half within a minute and immediately dematerialized.

Question: Is it best to cancel the tests? We've come so far, but at the risk of human lives? The cost may be too high.

Gavin's death was a tragedy, but one that yielded a valuable piece of data: if the conjurer dies, so does the demon.

The demon had a grotesque appearance, with features of more than one beast, as well as mek elements. We've all been trying to replicate the results, but so far nothing.

Question: If one of us succeeds, will we see the same demon, or another?

Day 60

After a few unfortunate accidents, we finally got another volunteer, Park. I informed her of the dangers, and even tried to talk her out of it, but she insisted.

I've designed a helmet that should help focus the conjurer's thoughts and provide controls to manipulate the demons. We also built a barricade for ourselves in case things go badly.

Park's demon was less grotesque and had more obvious mek elements than the others. We know now that a demon's form is not connected to the triangular device used to summon it (they seem interchangeable) but rather to the conjurer's mind.

Park was able to control the creature for several minutes, but then she began having convulsions and passed out. The demon dematerialized.

I'll check on Park this evening. If there is no serious damage, we may continue the test tomorrow.

Day 75

Today was our biggest success to date. Zed, a deaf-mute we brought along for muscle, was able to use the helmet. He maintained control for nearly twenty minutes and made the demon attack the clay beast figure that we fashioned for the test.

He came away from the test unharmed. In his report, he claimed that he was able to feed commands to the demon through images, impulses and emotions.

During the test, he'd given his demon a name, Flanker, and he claims the bond helped him control it. The entire thing was astonishing.

Note: must revise parameters for testing conjuring aptitude.

В— ширина слива равна...
Н— напор равна 30,00 — 27,8 = 2,2 м
hн— глубина в нижнем бьефе равна 29,5 — 12 = 17,5 м
Рн — высота порога со стороны Нижнибьефа 27,5 — 12,0 = 15,8 м
hn — высота подтопления равна 29,5 — 27,8 = 1,7 м
Z — разница в уровне бьенов и Нижним бьефе
300 — 29,5 = 0,5 м

Day 92

Living conditions:

It will be necessary to rig up electric lighting in the labs, but it shouldn't be used in common areas or sleeping quarters. We must always be reminded that we are trapped belowground, and that our mission is not to get comfortable here, but to get out.

Sleeping quarters should be simple and bare, like the rooms of ancient monks.

Food should be simple and nutritious. The caves should be devoid of frivolous entertainments.

Simple bedroll. We don't want these beds to be too comfortable. Soft beds produce soft thought!

Cold dirt floors remind people they're living underground!

Day 100

Fight rules:

Start every fight with a ritual.
A solemn chant to remind us of our purpose:
Why do we fight? To conquer the beasts! By
controlling the demons, we will conquer the beasts!

No talking during fights. Talking leads to
cheering and may obfuscate our purpose.

Fights will be judged on a point system and stopped
before serious injury.

If fights become too competitive, they will
stop immediately and be replaced with ......
(Solo performances? Demon ballets?
Reconsider in the future.)

Demon controllers will dress in sombre clothing
and avoid ornamentation.

~~Crowd sizes will be limited.~~ Only scientists will
be allowed to observe fights.

Children will never be allowed to participate in
the demon fights.

Day 110

To my dismay, the idea of demon fighting appeals to a certain type of individual: young, brash, arrogant and generally unpleasant. But the real problem is that they are overconfident and seem to have no interest in achieving the sort of balance that will allow them to sustain control.

I shout about the risks until my voice fails, but there seems to be an addictive element to controlling demons. I'm on the verge of suspending the fights.

Day 142

It is absurd that I should be concerned with issues of fashion, but it has become clear that we must have some sartorial regulations. We face a deluge of individuality, competitors hoping to seize undeserved attention through outlandish costumes and hairstyles, further distracting them, and the audience, from our purpose. I would like to dress these young aggressors in burlap sacks, but should probably show some restraint.

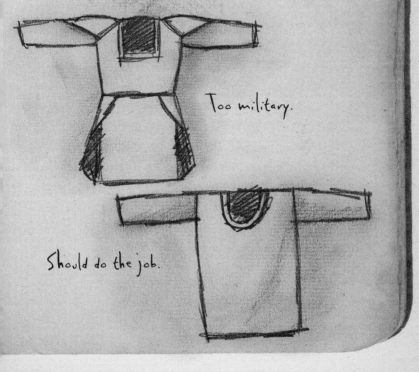

Too military.

Should do the job.

Day 175

A young transporter named Jack Saint-Pierre
arrived a few days ago. Despite our efforts to
block all routes from intruders, he somehow
found us. He had a message for me from
someone named Julius. A man with resources,
offering to help our work.

How does this Julius know about our work? I
tried to get some answers out of Jack, but he
doesn't know anything. Typical transporter.

None of that matters now. The only thing
that matters is Jack. He someow broke into
the demon-testing cavern and opened the safe
containing the triangular devices. Just as we
were about to subdue him, he figured out how
the devices worked. He summoned a giant wolf
with gleaming tentacles. The demon was beautiful,
not at all like the grotesques conjured by the
others. Jack sent the creature leaping through
the air, controlling it with unimaginable fluency.

He did all of this without a helmet.

Since then, Jack's been referring to himself as
a DEMONSMITH. Joking, as always, but the term
seems to have stuck.

If I can convince him to stay, I can study his
link with the demon. He may be the key.

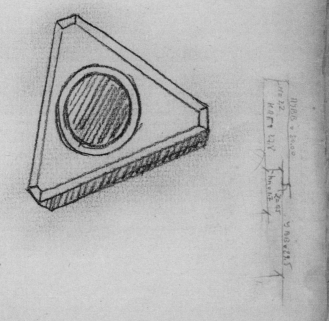

Day 215

What I know about Julius thus far:

* Gregarious. A real talker. Since he arrived, he's been attempting modesty, but he doesn't wear it well.

* Knows too much, but he won't talk about his background. I suspect he's been around this technology before. He calls the triangular devices TRIGGITS.

* Teeth and jaw made of solid diamond. One of his men called him Diamond Teeth. Julius patted the man's shoulder, smiled, and then nearly broke the man's neck.

* His team has won three demon fights in a row. They mock the rituals in private, but nothing stays private long in the caves.

* He brought enough food for us to survive another year, and enough weapons to enable us to make short runs to the surface. He trades in favours, and his power is growing fast. I have to find a way to check his power.

Day 302

I've stopped pretending I'm in charge. I'm forced to run decisions by Diamond Teeth, and he does whatever he likes. The fights are deteriorating into madness. And now he's begun construction of a wheel to generate power. Everyone loves the idea, but I've seen the designs. He's up to something.

First of all, how is it going to move? We have no wind power, and the water is nothing but a trickle. Does he plan to push it himself?

Day 371

After three weeks of wandering around from hovel to hovel in this beast-infested shell of a city, I've found something vaguely approximating livable accommodations. A group of half-feral children was living here, but I bought them off with nuggets from the caves.

It's a bank. An ideal place to start over. For several reasons:

1. It's close to the tunnel I built, my secret back door into the caves. With some effort, I can extend the tunnel to the bank.

2. It is a fortress, built to withstand robbery and fire. Which means it will also withstand attacks by beasts as well as burglary attempts by bothersome buzzers.

3. The roof will provide a guarded place for me to collect water, grow a few vegetables, and enjoy the breeze and sunlight I've lived without for too long.

4. I just need some time alone to think. I'm sure I can find a way to take back the caves and return them to their true purpose.

Dragonfly's Unexpected Adventure

Dragonfly was bored.

Her parents were safe at home – her mother cutting wood instead of performing dangerous experiments in her lab, and her father wrestling weeds in the garden instead of chasing meks at the border.

Dragonfly relaxed, free for the moment from the worry that overcame her when her parents followed their dangerous pursuits. It was a normal day, and she intended to leave it that way. Today she would just stay close to home and enjoy the security and the easy breeze that flowed through the nearby mountain pass.

But she was bored.

She practised dancing in the garden, just out of sight of her father. Her mother had taught her these moves, so graceful and strange, in secret. But today her limbs felt heavy and slow, and she couldn't concentrate.

So she went to the woodpile, where her mother was chopping wood for the evening fire. Dragonfly used the small axe and chopped the wood pieces into splinters, and her mother told the story of the wild boar in the temple, but the repetitious *thunk* of her mother's axe made Dragonfly yawn. So she put her splinters into the bucket, collected her favourite books from a nearby stump, and wandered off to find something more interesting to do.

As she came to her favourite tree, she saw that sunlight filtered through it in such a way that it looked as though the ground were covered by leaves made of shadow. Dragonfly leant against a mossy root and spread the books around her, open to her favourite pages.

The book of beasts, called *Szechuan Wildlife Park*, was opened at the page that showed a girl reaching out from inside a rolling machine and touching a yak's head. She opened *Weapons of Order and Chaos* at the page with the largest drawing of a katana sword. Other books lay scattered about, one with a poem about the moon, and another depicting a map of China from before the Trinary Wars. Surrounded by these books, she felt she was in the middle of the long, rich story of humans, who used to be stronger than beasts and meks.

Dragonfly looked up, searching for shapes of beasts and meks in the clouds, and watching for a glimpse of the Sky Village, due to pass by today, high overhead.

Still, she was restless. Her legs itched to run through the long grass outside the village. And she was thirsty for a drink from the waterfall near the pass, because it was so much colder than the well water.

Suddenly Feifei landed on Dragonfly's nose. The little creature wasn't supposed to be outside during the light. What if somebody saw her? Dragonfly tried to scoop Feifei up, but the hybrid flitted off, away from the garden, away from the house.

"Come back!" Dragonfly leaped up and began to run.

Feifei was fast. She darted from one tree to the next, stopping each time to peek back. Soon they were both outside the village.

"Stop playing games," Dragonfly shouted. Then she looked around to make sure nothing scary had heard her. Luo Ye Village was very near mek territory, and meks had been known to stray this far.

Feifei flew from behind a tree towards Dragonfly, then darted between her feet and out of sight.

Dragonfly summoned her loudest whisper. "Feifei!"

Which way to go? She closed her eyes and spun around in circles, faster and faster, and then stopped.

When she opened her eyes, the view was shaky, and she had to hold her arms out to keep balance. Then the dizziness faded, and she was facing the mountain pass.

The pass, where the wind farms were. Mek territory.

(story continued at www.kaimiracode.com)

Breaker and the Water Lair

Breaker woke before dawn.

There was no more water, and his little sister was getting weaker. Their father had been gone since the end of the cold season. Now it was the middle of the hot, dry time, and Breaker knew that rain would not come in time to save them.

He had to find a water source, or something he could trade for water. He strapped his biggest canteen to his leg. It would hold enough for two days – if he got lucky.

In the Triangle, he saw two teenage buzzers coming out of an abandoned casino.

"Know where I can find any water?" he asked.

"If we did, we'd be drinking it," one said.

"Why don't you go ask the Jackals," the other said. "They always seem to have water."

The Jackals were a tribe of kids outside the city who acted like beasts. They were said to shout a lot and wear bones in their hair. Breaker had never seen them, but the stories terrified him.

"The Jackals smell like beasts," Breaker said. He wasn't going to let these older buzzers think he was afraid.

"Good luck," they shouted, laughing, and continued on their way.

Breaker skipped the casino and headed for the outskirts of the city. Buzzers never ventured this far unless things were truly desperate. It was even more dangerous here than in the city. Beasts liked shade, and the houses provided it.

The first house was hardly worth searching. The stench was overwhelming, and beasts had chewed and clawed everything. He made his way through the kitchen area, looking for remtech devices he could convert to other uses, but the cabinets were empty.

The second house was also nearly empty, but Breaker smashed in a wall upstairs and found a few pieces of copper wire. It wasn't enough to buy water, but it was a start.

In the third house, sunlight streamed from the broken windows as Breaker dug through piles of wood and scrap. He found nothing valuable, but he pocketed a few small strips of colourful cloth, which he could use to make something for his little sister's dolls. Riley was probably already half awake and calling out for their father, he thought.

A hot gust of wind blew in through a hole in the back of the house and brought with it the smell of wet fur.

Beasts.

Breaker crept towards the back of the house and looked outside.

A pair of lions, both damp, moved towards the house. Where had they got wet?

Breaker snuck through the front of the house, circled around, and waited until the lions were inside before he followed the tracks they'd just left.

The tracks led out into the desert and disappeared in the dry, hot sand. Breaker looked around for a sign of water, or other beasts, but saw only dots in the distance. He started to run.

It wasn't often that he found himself running towards beasts. But he and his little sister needed water. And this was his best chance.

As he got closer, he could make out the shapes of the beasts. Three wolves and a scrawny monkey, all dry, moved deeper into the desert.

The sun was at the highest point, and his thirst nagged at him, but the prospect of finding water kept him moving forward.

One by one, the beasts disappeared.

Was the sun making him see things?

He went to the spot where he was sure he had last seen the beasts, but there was nothing.

He'd have to explore. But which way should he go? He walked forward a few steps, then stopped. There was another pack of beasts heading his way. There was no cover, and Breaker had no choice but to scramble as far away as he could and keep low to the ground. His head was down when he ran into a hard surface.

He jumped back and stared at his own confused face. He'd run into a mirror.

A mirrored dome the size of a house covered the sand. On the opposite side was an entrance into the dome. Breaker knew there were beasts inside, but he also knew there might be water.

Inside the dome a steep staircase descended below-ground. Breaker heard splashing sounds and snorts. After a short time, he came to a ledge overlooking a large, narrow underground cavern, supported by columns adorned with elaborate carvings and mirrors. Slivers of light filtered in from the dome above and danced from mirror to mirror and across a floor.

Breaker peered across the cavern, but it was hard to see clearly. From the noises, he knew there must be dozens of beasts inside. He scrambled down from the ledge to get a better look, then leaped down the last few steps. He landed with a splash. He was standing in water up to his knees.

Breaker looked around. The entire cavern floor was covered with water, and packed with beasts.

(story continued at www.kaimiracode.com)

Cloudwatching Notes from San Lu Trading Village, Archived
Presented by San Lu News Gatherer, Little Tang

美丽的坤惠和丑子赵欧结婚了。真希望他俩生的孩子个个长得像坤惠。

今天村里来了一邦猎兽人。他们面相凶巴巴的，但他们带来的那些骨和角制的小玩意儿还蛮受大家欢迎。

老鹰的关节又疼了，意味着暴风雨的来临。
暴风雨将从东面袭来，漫天村最好向西北方向撤退。

一个魔客机器人独自窜进了三路村。这家伙一路放火，烧了两座房子后，被咱们的夜喵击毙。

三路村的集市终于开张了。四面八方的小贩们抱着货物涌向村中心来赶集。据说武技士也在其中，但只是谣传，不可轻信。

我今天在当地遇到一个女佣佣兵。她以一袋枣干为谢，要我向大家转达她的原话："我是乔青，十年前离开漫天村去了我姐姐的部落。我俩都参加了西安与巨兽的战斗。我明知漫天村"不做回头客"的村规，还是求你们允许我回来，回到蓝天白云里。"

刚收到消息，后山脚村正经历灾荒。该村四面不是大山就是巨兽的领地。饥饿已经迫使他们冒险去猎兽充饥。村委在商议是援助他们两桶萝卜还是一撮盐。但现在谈援助已经太迟。山脚村人恐怕末日临头了。

今晨一只发着烧的麋鹿跌跌撞撞进了营地。向玩笑没过脑昏了头的野兽闻到迅的肉摊上偷食，迅连发数枪才击中它。现在迅正用它的角挂面条吃。

咱们傻头傻脑的信差是在三热坊被一个满口黄牙嚼食虫多的家伙给骗了。那家伙伪装不知怎么玩儿疯狂魔客儿游戏，赢走了数信差身上所有的金干。受害者已向村委投诉。村委却似乎无心干预此事。

今天有个小贩来求我们帮他穿过魔客的境内。他不久前和一个西伯立亚驯兽师谈生意，时假扮成女人而得到了犹惠。目前驯兽师的部落在四处搜捕他。若漫天村帮他一把，他会以棉衣种子作为报答。

收到消息说咱们与魔客的争议领土——"为时不晚"，已经被对方攻占。当地幸存者正在为亲人收尸并向四方求助。村委正在商议是援助他们一位医生，一个葬葬师，还是两桶萝卜。

今天坤恩和×鸥宣布了他们儿子出生的消息。小家伙叫赵吉，三公斤重，看上去就象个有着胖脸腮的土豆。当然，他的爸妈视其如宝。

最近好象没有什么消息可报。庄稼照样长着，婴儿们照样哭着，孩子们照样到处闯祸，老人们照样唠叨个不停。三路村的日子，还是老样子。

Weapons of Order and Chaos

by Hiro Miyazaki

INTRODUCTION

I started this survey of weapons when I was a small boy. The world was big and slow then, but growing smaller and faster by the day. The few machines that existed were not much smarter than stones, and beasts were content to carry our burdens and feed our families.

It was a time of bombs and guns, but I was fascinated with the simpler weapons of my grandfather's age. He was a true samurai, in a time when samurai were already an anachronism. I began my study of weapons in his weapons room. The most respectful of my siblings, I was the only one allowed inside that sacred place. I sat silently, sketching weapons of order, the elegant armour, and warriors from a more honest time. They fought in reverential silence on the pages of my notebook.

As a young man, I walked the razor's edge between the simple nobility of my grandfather and the sickening indulgence of my businessman father. I wanted only the graceful slope of a katana, but I was forced to learn the business of warfare. We developed machines for factories; as the machines grew more intelligent, the employees grew increasingly stupid and lazy. At the time of my split with my father, they were little more than dumb animals standing at a trough of mechanized efficiency.

As our weapons grew more sophisticated, their wielders killed more men from further away. This was a cowardly path. Killing a man from such a distance removes the humanity from the act and reduces it to little more than pushing buttons on a factory floor. These weapons of chaos were used without wisdom or discipline, by those who did not deserve their power.

When you kill a man with a sword, there can be no pretence. You see the life drain from him. You hear him call out his final prayers. The knowledge of what you have done is like fire in your veins. Thus, a true warrior kills only when its necessity screams with a thousand voices.

When I made the choice to oppose my father, I had no interest in becoming a leader, nor hope of changing humanity's path. I wanted only to escape a dehumanizing place and find a way to feel alive, and whole.

But necessity conscripted me, and I became its servant and its soldier. I was forced to use my father's soulless science, and his cold, characterless weapons, to save my countrymen from losing themselves. I used machines to fight the looming mechanical threat. I used science to slow the disintegration of our ways. I once again walked the razor's edge.

All those who join me walk the same impossible line, trapped between past and future, with no place among the spectres who populate the present. We, the scientist-samurai, will become powerful beyond imagination, because we bring discipline to the power of science. We will save Japan from the misguided will of its leaders and people. The price we pay is that we will slowly amputate our own souls.

I am an old man now. I've lived much longer than a man should live. I've seen humanity use science to chase its dreams and nightmares. This book tells a story of that chase, from the noble weapons of a simpler time to the monstrosities of today.

In some ways, I am still that small boy in my grandfather's weapons room. But instead of creating warriors on the pages of my notebook, I train real warriors and pass to them my own discipline and focus. We fight not with beautiful swords made of pen strokes, but with weapons that show no respect for our enemy. Though my grandfather would not approve, his wisdom lives in everything I do and everything I teach.

Perhaps our science will ruin us, and we'll be forced to return to a simpler way. But if we can find our way back to simpler times without destruction, that is the path we must choose.

Zephyr's Journal
Recovered Excerpts

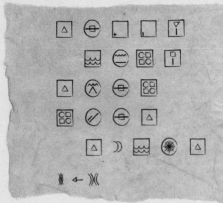

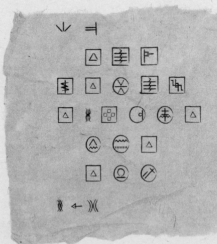

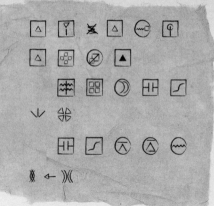

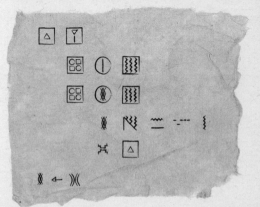

Crack the code at www.kaimiracode.com

GLOSSARY

Animus: the biotech virus resulting from the corruption of the Kaimira Code

battle circle: the circle of battle in the Demon Caves, where demons conjured by demonsmiths fight each other

beast: term commonly used for animals of all species. Beasts are larger and stronger than animals of past generations.

Boomer: demon conjured by Mica and Leo; appears with heads of two hares and a protective turtle shell on its back

buzzers: loosely affiliated group of tech scavengers in beast-controlled Las Vegas

Cloudwatcher: in the Sky Village, the person who gathers news brought by birds and reports relevant information to the Sky Council

demon: term referring to hybrid creatures "conjured" through kaimira technology that possess human, beast and mek elements

Demon Caves: the series of interconnected caves beneath Las Vegas

Demonsmith: one who conjures and controls demons

Demon Wheel: the power source of the Demon Caves and the guard demons, fuelled by former demonsmiths who have experienced meltdowns and by bankrupt gamblers

flowing map: a smartmap that shows a real-time, three-dimensional representation of terrain

the Grotto: squalid section of the Demon Caves where the Demon Wheel is located

guard demons: hybrid demons controlled by Diamond Teeth

Hiro: leader of the Scimurai who uses technology on his quest to destroy all meks

Jinx: Jack's demon; appears with wolfish features and metallic tentacles

Kaimira Code: a system of symbols used to access and control kaimira science

kaimira gene: a biotech gene containing elements of human, beast and mek that gives powers to those who possess it

land walkers: the term used by sky villagers to refer to those who live on the ground

Lightning Catcher: in the Sky Village, volunteer who uses a special kite to "catch" lightning during a storm, diverting it away from the balloons and storing it for the village's use

Lizard Girl: a character in the Tree Book stories, member of a travelling circus

Master Watcher: one of two watchmen in the Sky Village, stationed in High Watch

meks: a species of artificially intelligent machines sharing a single operating system

meltdown: in demonsmithing, the harmful shutdown of a demon-smith's consciousness due to an overwhelming surge from the demon connection

Muddy: Aiko's demon; appears with muscular, spike-covered body, metallic, horned head and spiked tail

newtech: technology created since the start of the Trinary Wars

Old Hug: the large, arched platform that serves as the central gathering place for the sky villagers

power cell: a small, battery-like cell that powers certain newtech and remtech devices

remtech: technology from before the Trinary Wars

Scimurai: a tribe of scientist-samurai led by Hiro who favour the old ways and adhere to a strict code of behaviour

Shakes: Robertson's demon; appears with four legs and the upper body of a monkey

the Sky Council: the governing body of the Sky Village

the Sky Dance: a Sky Village ritual meant to appease the birds

Spot: Rom's demon, a rhino-cheetah hybrid

the Terrible Everything: a biotech demon powered by Animus, which absorbs the consciousness of humans, beasts and meks, and then uses the victims' DNA to pattern its own growth

transporters: a tribe of messengers based near Las Vegas

Tree Book: a rare, powerful and interactive book that can be used only by those with the kaimira gene

triggit: triangular device that, coupled with a demonsmith helmet, allows for the conjuring of demons

the Trinary Wars: series of wars in which humans, beasts and meks fought one another

West Wind: legendary scientist who tried to use science to save the world, but nearly destroyed it

windmover: a device used in the Sky Village to propel the balloons

Zephyr: the real name of the legendary scientist known as West Wind